Contents

D1127976

OLIVER & HENRY

OLIVER & HENRY

MICHAEL HARTWIG

Herring Cove Press

Cover Photo By Author
Piazza Navona

I

Chapter One

"Let me see your picture," Anna inquired of Oliver as he carefully folded the passport into a pocket of his backpack.

"Ma, you've already seen it a dozen times," Oliver said in retort.

"And I'll probably ask to see it another dozen before you leave."

Reluctantly, Oliver opened the fresh passport and flashed the photo of himself to her.

"And me?" Rita interjected, "Can I see it, too?"

"Mom, not you, too?"

Rita nodded and grinned widely at the photo waved in front of her. Oliver was handsome – piercing blue eyes, wavy blonde hair, and dark Mediterranean complexion. She took a sip of wine from the glass on the coffee table where his clothes were laid out, ready to go into the suitcase. She glanced over at Anna, raising her eyebrows in alarm.

"And do you have the fanny pack we got for you to secure your money, credit cards, and other valuables. Remember, pick pockets are notorious in Rome," Anna added.

"I know, you've told me a hundred times how clever they are. I'll be careful," he insisted.

"When do we need to leave for the airport?" Rita asked.

"The flight doesn't leave until 9:45, so we can have dinner and still have plenty of time to get there and go through security," Oliver explained. He folded some shirts into the base of the suitcase, lined the grooves with socks, and rolled several pairs of shorts on top of them.

"Are you sure you're okay meeting your biological father on your own?" Rita inquired, seeking assurance from Oliver.

"Yes. I think it will be best. I don't want to put you both through any unpleasantness."

"But we don't even know who he is or what kind of person he is," Anna added with concern. "You still haven't found out what he does?"

"That's right. I've looked. He isn't on social media. All I found was an administrative position at Fordham University several years ago. I think he must be in higher education. Maybe he works at one of the American campuses in Rome."

"And you're sure he's okay meeting you?" Rita inquired.

"He did the DNA test. He's obviously curious and discovered a way to circumvent the rules of the private adoption."

"We're still not comfortable with it, but you're old enough to make your own decisions, and we will be here for you if you need us," Anna said with warmth, holding Rita's hand. They looked affectionately at their boy fussing with his suitcase.

"I just hope you don't try to press him to give you your biological mother's name and contact. It was clear in the adoption papers that she didn't want her identity revealed. Please respect that of her," Rita added to Anna's concern.

"I won't try to get that information. But, if he gives it to me, what can I do?"

"You can respect her wishes and not reach out to her," Rita said emphatically.

Oliver looked into the suitcase, avoiding eye contact with his mothers. He knew they were uneasy about his seeking out his biological parents, but he was resolved to carry through with the plan.

"Now, let's have some dinner," Anna said as she got up from the table and went into the kitchen to pull the chicken out of the oven. Oliver finished placing the clothes in the suitcase and checked to see if it would close.

"Looks like it all fits!" he said gleefully.

"Save room for gifts you're going to bring back. A leather purse from Florence would be nice!" Rita said with a smile.

From the kitchen Anna shouted, "I vote for pottery."

"That's too heavy and bulky. How about some napkins or scarves?" Oliver retorted.

"Pottery and leather – you heard us," Anna said emphatically.

Oliver put his arm around Rita and, as Anna came into the room and placed the platter on the table, she joined the hug. They took their places at the small oak table set in an alcove of their apartment. Steam rose from the chicken as Anna began to carve the breast. Oliver spooned some roast potatoes onto his plate, passed the platter to Rita and then reached for the green beans. Anna had offered to make pasta as a send-off, but Oliver insisted on their traditional family menu of roast chicken.

"Although we wish the circumstances were different, we're so proud of you going off to Europe all by yourself," Rita said.

"I'm twenty. This is hardly that daunting," he said as he put a piece of chicken into his mouth.

"But it's your first trip overseas," Anna argued. "It's a big deal to go all that way on your own."

"Weren't you about the same age when you went to Madrid during college?"

Anna and Rita looked at each other, leaned across the table and kissed. "And look what happened to us!" Rita said jokingly.

Rita and Anna had met during their semester abroad, both just coming out and exploring gender and sexuality in a place far away from their conservative parents. Rita was from Boston and Anna from Chicago. Anna transferred to Boston University when they returned and, after graduation, they both got their MBA's and began careers in management at two pharmaceutical companies in Cambridge.

Rita's parents were first generation Italians, her grandparents having come from the Abruzzi region of Italy. She was a short, thin, and mercurial – prone to wild extremes of emotions. She had curly dark hair and deep set penetrating brown eyes. She was the more affectionate and tactile of the two. Anna was from an Irish family in Chicago. She had typical mid-western features – blonde hair, luminous skin, and a beautifully shaped figure. She was considered a lipstick lesbian and confounded most people who never suspected she was married to a woman, much less to an Italian one.

Their jobs afforded a stylish condo on the top of Beacon Hill in Boston with sweeping views of the Charles River and Cambridge. They had devoted much of their time to launching their careers but, after a couple of years of marriage, decided they wanted a child. They considered IVF but felt that if they could adopt, it made more sense to give an unwanted child a good home. A unique opportunity arose to adopt a newborn who they named Oliver. To their surprise, their own parents had been quick to embrace their daughters' marriage and even more excited to learn they would be grandparents.

The terms of the adoption included strict rules about confidentiality, all parties remaining anonymous. Oliver loved his mothers and called them Ma and Mom. He attended private schools where many of his classmates had gay parents. He was smart, affable, and handsome. Rita and Anna were always amazed at how he seemed to embody their own physical features. He had darker olive complexion, much like Rita's, but blonde hair and blue eyes like Anna. In high school he was a star lacrosse athlete and popular with both the boys and the girls.

Over the years, he became increasingly curious about his birth parents. He wondered who they were, what had led them to give him up for adoption, what characteristics he had inherited genetically, and what aspects of his personality he had developed growing up with Rita and Anna.

When he was eighteen, he began to search for his biological parents. He found nothing until he took an ancestry DNA test. A link popped up on his profile suggesting a father. He researched the link and, through process of elimination settled on a certain Henry Montpierre. He contacted him and found out that he had been curious himself and wanted to find out what had happened to his son – thus his own DNA test. All Oliver had been able to ascertain was that Henry lived in Rome and worked in higher education.

Initially Rita and Anna were distressed that Oliver longed so deeply to meet his biological parents. It felt like a betrayal to the relationship they had forged over the years. It was only in third grade that enough questions were raised by his classmates that they felt they had to tell him he was adopted. Oliver took the information well, telling them he considered them his real parents. So, when he told them he wanted to meet Henry, it stung. Nevertheless, they supported his quest and trusted that when he returned, they would still be his moms!

"Remind us of your itinerary again," Anna inquired.

"I'm flying tonight to Zurich where I catch a flight to Rome in the morning."

"Do you have enough euros?" Rita inquired nervously.

"I'm going to get some at the ATM at the airport. Besides, I have my debit card and credit cards."

"I still can't believe you're doing this on your own," Anna said with concern.

"Ma, I'm going to be fine!"

"I know dear, but we still worry. So, when do you meet Henry?" Anna inquired.

"We emailed the other day. He suggested that we meet on Thursday, for lunch."

"And when do you get to Rome?" Rita asked.

"On Tuesday."

"What are you going to do in the meantime?" Rita pressed further.

"It's frickin Rome! I'm going to sightsee. I want to see the Forum and the Colosseum."

"That's so exciting. Remember when we went there?" Anna said, looking affectionately toward Rita.

Rita nodded, looked off in the distance and said, "Remember going to see the Pope in St. Peter's Square? That was so exciting. Are you going to see the Pope?"

"I don't know."

"Can you bring us back rosaries blessed by the Pope?" Anna asked.

"Neither of you go to church anymore. Why would you want a rosary?"

"Yes, I guess it is a bit hypocritical of us. Even if the church is misogynistic, homophobic, and corrupt, there is still something comforting in getting something from the Pope," Rita continued.

"I'll see what I can do," Oliver said, winking at them both.

Oliver was raised Catholic, but when the Church opposed gay marriage and was caught up in the sex abuse scandals, Rita and Anna said they had had enough. They joined a local Episcopal congregation where the female priest created an inclusive and welcoming environment for all. As an adolescent, Oliver was indifferent to religion and didn't understand what all the fuss was about. However, he was curious and, when his moms and their friends gathered for dinner, he would listen in on their conversations, noting the various positions they articulated on cultural politics and theology.

"Oliver, are you sure your phone will work in Rome? We want to be able to keep in touch," Anna said with concern.

"And when you two were in Madrid, were there cell phones?"

"No, but we want you to send pictures and keep us posted," Anna continued.

"Yes. It will function just like here, and I will send pictures and updates."

Rita sighed with relief and said, "And the hotel in Rome?"

"The Santa Chiara. Henry recommended it."

"Is it a good place? We don't want you to be in an unsafe area," Anna continued nervously.

"It's right in the center. It's a four-star hotel. I think it will be fine."

Rita relaxed her shoulders and reached for Anna's hand, "We're so proud of you. We're worried, but we're proud. You're so grown up and brave to do this on your own."

Oliver smiled. Deep down he was nervous but didn't want to show it. He had never left the country except to go to Canada and, while he could put on a brave face, he had spent hours in the past few days double checking information about the flights, taxis, money, phones, and other contingencies. He knew Spanish and figured it would help in Italy, but he was nervous about the language barrier. Added to the idea of traveling abroad, he was about to meet his biological father. He had always dreamed of the day but now was anxious that it wouldn't live up to his expectations – that Henry might be cold, distant, or a sociopath. He assumed he was married and perhaps had other children. He wondered how that would make him feel.

Oliver excused himself and went to the bathroom to clean up. He felt his pulse race as he realized his departure was imminent. He used his fingers to place some errant locks of hair back into place, spread some cream on his face, brushed his teeth, and went back into the living room to check his suitcase and backpack and wallet.

"All set?" Anna asked as she came into the room, car keys jingling in her hand.

Oliver looked at his moms. They could see the anxiousness in his face. They both reached for him, gave him a warm hug, and said, "Let's go."

The drive to the airport was a short fifteen minutes. Oliver sat in the back of the car and gazed at the skyline of Boston all lit up, emotionally gazing at the familiar landmarks before he embarked on his overseas flight. They parked at the central garage and walked across the skyway to the terminal where a short line formed in front of the Swiss Air check-in. Oliver rolled his suitcase to the counter, handed his passport to the agent, and said, "I'm Oliver Monte-Fitzpatrick."

"And your final destination?" the agent inquired, looking intently at him.

"Rome."

"First time?" she inquired with a warm smile.

"Why, does it look it?" Oliver said part in jest and part in alarm.

"No. Sorry. I was just making conversation," she said, typing his name into the computer.

Oliver was attractive, and he continued to be amazed at how friendly young women were to him. He could walk into a party or a bar and feel the heads turn. He had dated occasionally in high school, but no one ever felt right.

Growing up in a gay family, Oliver had been exposed to countless discussions about gender, sexual orientation, and theories about the fluidity of gender roles and gender identities. His moms had made sure he had male role models – namely straight male friends from work, coaches, and teachers. When Oliver would go out with friends in high school and later in college, they would ask carefully, 'is there anyone special you're going with,' or when they referred to his friends' dates, 'who is Jennifer's partner or who is Fred's date?' never, 'who is Jennifer's boyfriend or Fred's girlfriend.' He appreciated the gender neutrality they used.

Over the years, Oliver felt pressure to be authentic, to forge his own identity. Many people suspected that kids of gay parents would be gay or gay leaning. But just as kids of straight parents ended up gay, kids of gay parents were statistically more likely to be straight. Oliver didn't want to default to either – the gay or straight son of lesbian parents. Thus, he felt deeply conflicted and ambivalent about his sexuality.

Oliver smiled at the agent and then said, "Yes, this is my first time in Rome, and I am very excited and a bit nervous."

The agent now relaxed and beamed. "You'll love it. Make sure you try their gelato and be careful of pickpockets."

"Did my moms pay you to say that?" he asked as he glanced back over his shoulder.

The agent looked over at Rita and Anna and said, "No, but be careful!" She handed him his boarding pass and put a tag on his suitcase. He slung his backpack over his shoulder and walked over to his moms and said, "Well, I guess I'm all set to go," glancing at his boarding pass and passport.

Both Rita and Anna began to tear up, a few streaks of mascara forming under their eyes.

"Oh – you'll be fine. You've always wanted to be empty nesters. Now's your opportunity."

They laughed and rubbed the tears off their cheeks. They each kissed him on his cheek, gave him a warm hug, and then pushed him off to the security lines where he passed into the other part of the terminal and to the departure gate for his flight.

At the gate, Oliver began to hyperventilate, thinking about the long flight and the prospects of being untethered so far from home. He opened his phone and scrolled to pictures of his moms and him at the beach on the Cape, memories of soaking in the warm sun, sharing home-made sandwiches, and listening to the lively conversations of his mothers' friends gathered with them. He took several deep breaths and began to relax.

The agent announced the boarding of his flight and he lined up with other passengers in front of the gate. Slowly they filed onto the ramp and Oliver squeezed past passengers stuffing suitcases into overhead bins before he found his seat, slid the backpack under the seat in front of him, and settled into his seat next to the window.

As the plane filled, Oliver realized no one was going to be sitting next to him. He laid his iPad on the seat beside him and began to make himself comfortable, strategically positioning his pillow and blanket in ways that would help him sleep overnight.

As the plane took off, he pressed his face against the window and watched as the city of Boston passed underneath. He sighed. It felt as if his former self was receding as they banked out over the ocean. He wondered what was to come. He closed his eyes and let the gentle rocking of the plane lull him to sleep.

2

Chapter Two

Oliver landed the next morning in Zurich and made the quick connection for his flight to Rome. He took a seat next to a matronly woman who only spoke Italian. "*Buon giorno*," she said. Oliver nodded, feeling the inadequacies of his language skills. She flipped through a tabloid magazine with photos of celebrities in summer attire and clandestine liaisons on yachts caught by paparazzi. She wore a classic wool skirt, a white cotton blouse, and a turquoise scarf. Her nails were painted blue, and a faint smell of rose and vanilla emanated from her.

Oliver observed the other passengers file into the plane, a new world encircling him – people with olive complexion, dark hair, more angular facial features, all more animated, gesturing with their hands as they sought to make their way down the aisle and find their seats. The playful sounds of Italian permeated the cabin. Oliver closed his eyes to listen, letting the full impact of the foreign environment sink deeply within him. It was both strange and comforting, an odd sense of returning to a familiar culture even while being different from his own.

The plane took off and quickly began to cross some of the highest peaks of the Alps, still covered in snow in early June. He glanced out the window and watched as the dramatic landscape passed below. The mountains eventually gave way to deep verdant hills of Italy, farmland dotted with villas and tree-lined roads connecting small villages.

Soon the plane banked over the Mediterranean and began its descent into the Rome airport stretched out just beyond the yellow sand dunes of Ostia. As they landed and parked at the gate, passengers erupted into a chaotic contest to disembark, something Oliver eventually came to appreciate as a cultural idiosyncrasy of the Italians who resisted the orderliness and patience of northern Europe. The woman next to him showed unexpected agility, making her way through the jumble of people, waving to him as she advanced down the aisle, "*Buon viaggio, caro,*" she said with glee.

Oliver managed a timid, "*Grazie,*" and began to collect his backpack from the overhead bin.

Oliver made his way through passport control and then to the luggage area where his blue bag was already circling. He grabbed it and headed out into the main terminal area where he quickly found an ATM machine, retrieved some euros from his account, and walked outside to find a taxi.

It felt good to breath fresh air. The sun was warm, filtered through tall stately palm trees planted in a garden in front of the terminal. The sidewalk was an unruly scene of passengers trying to make sense of the taxi system and abusive free-lance drivers trying to pick them up. Oliver pressed pass the fray and entered the queue for taxis. He made his way to the front of the line and jumped into a car as the driver pulled up.

"Where are you going?" the young driver inquired, flicking a cigarette onto the pavement, and pressing the reset button on the fare machine. The car was clean and smelled of air freshener.

Oliver responded, "To the hotel Santa Chiara, *per favore*."

"*Subito*," the driver said. He sped off, circled the ramps of the airport, and hit the highway. Oliver looked at the dashboard and calculated he was driving 85 miles per hour. The highway passed several modern office parks interspersed with farmland. After 15 minutes, the driver took an exit and ended up on a crowded urban boulevard lined with drab five-story apartment buildings, covered in rusty balconies, laundry hanging on lines, and graffiti covering soot-darkened walls. He had imagined a more sophisticated and historic city. The jet lag and less-than-beautiful surroundings made him feel sad. He pulled out his phone and turned it on. He then texted his moms, "Got here safely. On way to hotel in a taxi."

They were undoubtedly asleep, but he imagined Rita had left her phone on the bedside table. After a moment, the message indicated it had been read.

The taxi made a sharp set of turns and then crossed through a wall that stretched off into the distance. In broken English, the driver said, "The walls of Rome."

Oliver nodded, arching his neck back to look at the red brick fortification, a ribbon of trees and grass separating dilapidated suburban neighborhoods from the more historic and gentrified center. The driver took a few quick turns and passed by a large column in a square, a huge church, and graceful apartment buildings. The streets were crowded with cars jostling with each other, paying no attention to lane markers, signals, or pedestrians who carefully inched their way through the stream of traffic. Oliver clutched the door handle and held his backpack tightly as the car lurched left and right, speeding down a hill.

Oliver looked out the front window and noticed, to his surprise, the contours of the Colosseum appearing in the distance. He was dumbfounded by its dimensions – a massive structure looming in the morning haze. As they got closer, he wondered if he shouldn't have planned a more ceremonial first encounter, not a casual drive by. How could all these people indifferently circle the structure as if it were just another building and not one of the most incredible architectural wonders of all time – a 1st century stadium, as large as any built today, still standing intact? He peered out the window as the taxi passed under the shadows of the high arches, his heart racing with excitement.

The taxi passed several other ancient monuments and then entered a large square dominated by a monument almost as impressive as the Colosseum, the Victor Emmanuel shrine, dedicated to the man who had unified Italy. The driver circled the square, made several sharp turns onto a small road which seemed more like a pedestrian area, and then came to an abrupt halt.

"Your hotel is there." The driver pointed to a small door archway tucked in the corner of a couple of shops and a small square. Oliver paid his fare, pulled the suitcase out of the trunk, and walked through the front door of the hotel. The lobby was warm and intimate, decorated in classic mid-19th century furniture with sitting areas looking out onto a courtyard. Oliver approached the long wooden counter set in front of a wall of antique keys where a young man dressed in a dark blue suit welcomed him.

"I'm Oliver Monte-Fitzpatrick."

"Yes, Mr. Monte-Fitzpatrick." The young man typed his name into the computer and then looked up and smiled, "We have you here for seven nights, correct?"

"Yes. I believe in a single room."

"Someone upgraded your room to a double. Looks like a Rita Monte-Fitzpatrick."

"Ahh," Oliver said. "That would be my mother." He smiled at the affection his mothers always showed him, even when he was following a path they weren't too keen on.

Oliver guessed the receptionist was about thirty. He was tall and athletic. His jacket was tight fitting, showcasing his muscular torso. He had short black hair and dark stubble around his mouth and chin. He had a warm smile and seemed eager to be welcoming.

"Is this your first stay with us?"

"Yes. It's my first time in Italy."

"Ah," the receptionist sighed, giving Oliver an even more radiant smile. "I hope it won't be your last. Can I see your passport?"

"Is there a problem?" Oliver inquired.

"No, we have to register our guests with the local authorities, that's all." The receptionist looked at Oliver's passport, smiled, jotted down the number and expiration date, and then handed it back to Oliver, looking intensely into his eyes. "Here's your key. You can take the elevator at the end of the hall to the fourth floor."

"*Grazie.*"

"Let us know if we can do anything for you while you are here."

Oliver said *grazie* again and headed down the hall. He squeezed into the small elevator and took it to the fourth floor. His room was down a hallway that zig-zagged haphazardly. He opened the door and the room beamed with bright light streaming from, what Oliver imagined, was a balcony.

He placed his bag on the stand and walked to the floor-to-ceiling glass doors, pulled back the sheer curtains, and opened the door to a broad balcony that looked out over the red tile roofs of nearby structures. Looming just beyond them was the massive dome of the Pantheon. "Oh my God," he said to himself. "That's the Pantheon just outside my window."

He took a picture with his phone and then texted it to Rita and Anna. "Look at my room with a view! Thank you!"

Rita was just getting up, sipping her first cup of coffee, and reading newspapers online. She texted back, "Glad you got there safely – and enjoy your hotel! Looks like it's very nice."

"Are you kidding?" he texted back. "It's amazing."

He began to unpack his suitcase, hanging slacks and shirts on hangers and placing socks, underwear, and shorts in the armoire drawers. He unpacked his toiletries and decided it was time to wash the smell of the airplane off with a nice warm shower.

After the shower, he felt groggy and decided to take a short nap to overcome jet lag. At about 2:30, he heard a ping on his phone. It was a text from Henry. "I hope you arrived safely. Are you still free on Thursday for lunch?"

Oliver texted back, "Yes. That would be nice."

"Let's meet at the Ristorante Archimede – a nice place just down the street from your hotel. 1 PM on Thursday?" Henry texted.

"Perfect," Oliver texted back.

He got out of bed, threw on some shorts and a pullover, slipped on a pair of sneakers, zipped some euros and a credit card into one of the pockets of his shorts, and grabbed a small guidebook he had picked up before he left Boston. He headed out the door into the mid-afternoon light of Rome.

The June air was warm and pleasant and smelled of stone, earth, and roasted coffee. He turned left out of the hotel and followed a small street toward the front of the Pantheon. He had read up on it and remembered that it was built in the early part of the 2nd century by Emperor Hadrian. The dome was a single cast cement structure that, until modern times, was the largest dome in the world. Engineers still marveled that the Romans had poured the entire dome at one time to prevent it from cracking. The temple was dedicated to all the gods during a time when Rome had reached its zenith of power. Some argued that it was Rome's embrace of religious plurality that encouraged those it conquered to buy into the Roman ideal, to participate in the Pax Romana, a civilization of prosperity, peace, and stability. It was ethnic diversity that made Rome so formidable.

He walked in the front doors of the immense structure and instantly felt transported. The writer of the guidebook had explained that the dimensions formed a perfect sphere – that the height and diameter were equal – each 142 feet – creating the sensation of expansion when one walked inside. It was one of the first religious structures designed to create a spiritual experience just by entering the building. One felt as if one were part of the universe. The "oculus," or opening in the top, allowed light to beam inside and suggested a kind of divine reality that illuminated all things and unified all forces.

Bramante, at the beginning of the Roman Renaissance, originally envisioned a dome for the new St. Peter's that would be like the Pantheon's. Later, as the Renaissance was giving way to the Reformation and Counter Reformation, Michelangelo envisioned a dome whose height was significantly greater than the diameter, an elevated dome. Scholars suggested that from the time of Bramante at the beginning of the 1500s to that of Michelangelo during the latter part of the same century, the mood of Rome had changed. The discovery of whole new continents in the Americas and new astronomical models of a sun-centered or perhaps even non-centered universe had destabilized Rome's sense of being the center of the world – the *Caput Mundi*. The Reformation in northern Europe, the democratization of knowledge through the printing press, and the threat of the Ottoman Turks in the East had made Rome feel as if its claim to truth and authority was in jeopardy. Michelangelo's massive dome soaring in the heavens above St. Peter's tomb was intended to re-center the universe, to make Rome the hub again, and to remind pilgrims as they entered the building to submit to the authority of God and to the authority of God's representative, the Pope. Oliver couldn't help but think that Hadrian must have felt a certain confidence and largesse during his time and that the popes in the 16th century had been more anxious and felt the need to reassert control and authority.

After admiring the arched ceiling, Oliver walked toward the tomb of Raphael, the Renaissance artist who first began to encourage the preservation of ancient structures rather than mining them for raw materials to build St. Peter's and other projects. An inscription on the tomb read, "Here lies that famous Raphael by whom Nature feared to be conquered while he lived, and when he was dying, feared herself to die." It was fitting that he was buried here in the structure that represented the best of Rome, its humanism, its ingenuity, and a spirituality that was enlarging.

Oliver strolled around the inside of the Pantheon, breathing deeply as he felt the energy of the place. His mothers taught him early in life to trust his intuition, to describe what he felt in certain places and at certain moments – to, in essence, take the pulse of things. They helped him appreciate how things radiated a kind of energetic presence and how to distinguish between energy that was positive and helpful and energy that might be more toxic. He felt light and expansive here. It was a good omen for his journey.

He walked back out into the square lined with cafes where people were chatting, sipping coffee, and soaking in the sun. The small square was lined with 15th and 16th century structures, many stained in traditional yellow and orange ochre pigment. The late afternoon light bounced off the various angles of the buildings casting a golden glow across the cobblestone pavement. There were no less than six small lanes that fed into the square, and Oliver was curious to explore each one, plunging deeply into the densely packed historic center of Rome.

He took one leading away from the Pantheon, a small lane that zig zagged between structures. The aroma of coffee filled the street, people pouring in and out of the famous Café Tazza d'Oro, one the guidebook claimed to be the best in Rome. Oliver went inside, squeezing through the throng of people lined up at the counter to gulp down shots of dark frothy espresso. He paid the cashier, pressed his way toward the bar, gave his receipt to the barista and, in moments, his coffee was ready. Oliver liked espresso and frequented cafes in Boston, but he had never tasted or seen anything like this. The frothy *schiuma* – foam - was thick and golden brown, the coffee syrupy, and the flavors a mix of toasted earth, spice, and chocolate.

Getting back out the door was a challenge. A river of people was attempting to enter the doorway, and the space was already packed. In Boston people would have been in a panic, but here people continued to smile, almost as if they enjoyed being pressed body to body. Oliver turned sideways and began to inch his way toward the door, his buttocks rubbing against those standing at the bar and his face inches from those in front of him.

He headed back onto the street and continued walking away from the Pantheon. The lane was lined with boutique shops selling ties, leather, pottery, and clothing. He began to think about souvenirs for his moms and lingered at the windows here and there. The small road emptied into another square, this one dominated by several Renaissance-era palaces and a large column – perhaps five stories tall. He opened the guidebook and learned that it was the column of Marcus Aurelius. The column was the Roman equivalent of an animated film, a series of panels encircling the pillar, recounting the exploits of the emperor. At one time the column was polychromatic, but now it was a luminous yellow-white marble with perfectly preserved carvings. Oliver walked up to the base and gazed at the fine artwork, work that had survived nearly 2000 years of pollution, weather, and wars.

Oliver pivoted in place, looking at a kaleidoscope of buildings, traffic, and shops surrounding him. The walkways were crowded with people passing quickly back and forth. He couldn't believe he was in Europe for the first time, a dream he had since high school and one he had deferred in favor of his academic career in finance. He had only left Boston twenty-four hours ago and was already immersed in an entirely different world filled with assorted smells, sounds, colors, and looks.

Oliver had imagined Rome to be an adult Disney World – a city filled with ancient and religious monuments with tourists lined up to enter various sites. Instead, he found a bustling metropolis filled with people going to work – bankers, lawyers, teachers, shopkeepers, and students – a stream of people making a living and going about their lives, indifferent to the tourists who flocked to the eternal city. He wondered who his biological father was, what kind of work he did, where he lived, and what parts of the city he frequented. As he thought of him, his stomach twisted in knots, a sense of apprehension about the kind of person he was going to meet and how the encounter might shape his future, his destiny, his sense of self. He took a deep breath and pushed forward, resolute in facing his past and imagining his future.

Oliver wandered across a busy boulevard and through another series of small lanes, mere spaces left between ancient apartment buildings with slivers of blue sky barely visible above the overhangs of roofs and balconies. Small restaurants lined the streets each with a few tables set precariously on the uneven cobblestone pavement. Oliver glanced at a few menus, thinking already of dinner.

He rounded a corner, and to his surprise, the Trevi Fountain appeared. In the middle of the dense urban landscape, architects had carved out a large space into which water from an ancient Roman aqueduct poured through statues of Tritons and the god Oceanus positioned in a large niche. The blue cascading water created a refreshing sensation despite the throngs of people gathered at the edge to cast coins for good luck and taking selfies with their phones.

Oliver paused for a moment in the background and then continued on his way, taking an inclined road to the right.

He meandered through the maze of small streets, taking in the smells, sounds, and bustle of the city. He opened a map in his phone and found directions to return to the hotel. He went inside, washed up, and then headed downstairs to the front desk. The young handsome receptionist was still there and smiled broadly when he saw Oliver approach.

"Excuse me, but would you have any suggestions for dinner?"

The receptionist paused in thought, took a careful look at Oliver, and began, "It depends on what you're looking for. There are pizzerias, there are casual places for pasta and salad, and then there are more formal restaurants where you can get a variety of main courses as well as pasta."

"I'm interested in a nice plate of pasta," Oliver noted.

"Well, my recommendation," he paused again, looking intensely at Oliver, "would be Di Rienzo's – in the square in front of the Pantheon. It's a little expensive but, if this is your first time in Rome, you should sit in a picturesque place and feel the history and life around you. If you need something more economical, I can make recommendations, but I think you would enjoy it."

"How expensive is it?" Oliver asked a little concerned.

"Pasta is about 15 euros, salad about 10, and wine – if you stick with the house wine – maybe 8 or 10 euros for a half-liter."

"You're kidding," Oliver said in response.

"No. If that's too much, I can recommend something else," the receptionist said in alarm.

"No, in Boston that would be an inexpensive place. It sounds perfect. Do I need a reservation?"

"No, but I will call them and have them give you a good table – right on the square."

Oliver nodded gratefully at the receptionist who winked at him.

The receptionist continued, "If you go out the door and turn to the left it will be the main restaurant on the left of the square as you face away from the Pantheon. I'll call them. They will be waiting for you."

Oliver said, "*Grazie*," and then headed out the door.

The sun was lower on the horizon with deeper hues of orange and crimson reflecting off the plaster fronts of the buildings. People were taking their after-work strolls, leisurely making their way home, visiting with friends, and savoring the pleasant weather. Many had cones of gelato in hand, others were arm in arm, their free hands gesturing some point or story about the day. Oliver made his way to Di Rienzo's. He approached the maître d' and said, "I'm Oliver Monte-Fitzpatrick. The Hotel Santa Chiara said they were going to call for a reservation."

"Yes, we have your table here waiting." The maître d' pointed to the edge of the restaurant's section of tables, a small two-person table covered in starched white cloth and decorated with a small vase of flowers and bottles of wine and mineral water. "Is this okay with you?"

"Perfect," Oliver replied, taking his seat. He grinned as he looked out over the square and glanced at the imposing façade of the Pantheon. It was magical. The early evening sun filtered through the surrounding buildings. Wispy rose-colored clouds drifted across the sky. A small fountain in the center of the square splashed soothingly, and the square filled with whimsical notes coming from an accordion being played in front of a nearby café.

The waiter brought a menu and asked what he wanted to drink. Oliver's moms had taught him to drink wine at meals, a tradition carried over from Rita's Italian family. Oliver ordered a half-liter of the house red and a bottle of mineral water. He glanced over at the table next to him and noticed a heaping salad of arugula, slivers of parmesan cheese, and small cherry tomatoes. He felt his mouth salivate at the thought of fresh salad. A gentle breeze blew the aroma of fresh cooked tomatoes under his nose. He could feel his appetite rising.

He chose the arugula salad and a plate of amatriciana – a typical Roman dish of tomatoes, pancetta, onions, and cheese. The freshness of the ingredients was apparent as the flavors exploded in his mouth. The red wine was light but flavorful and complemented the spicy pasta.

The sun set, and the streetlights came on, casting a glow of warm light over the square. The sky became a deep blue indigo, and the contours of the Pantheon were softer, cast in an iridescent pink hue. Oliver ordered an espresso and some profiteroles for dessert and relaxed in his chair.

"He thought of his moms back in Boston and gave them a quick call on his phone. Rita answered, "Oliver, are you okay?"

"Yes, mom, I just wanted to hear your voices and say hello. Everything is perfect. I just finished a nice plate of pasta in a charming square. I wish you were here to enjoy this with me."

"We do, too. But it is good you are there on your own. This is a big step for you – to go to Europe, to be away from home, and to meet your biological father. It will bring clarity to you."

"Mom, you're always so encouraging and supportive."

"That's what moms are for! We love you."

"I know. And I love you, too."

He hung up and began to think of his upcoming meeting with Henry. After speaking with Rita, he began to have second thoughts. 'Maybe I shouldn't do this. Rita and Anna are my parents – my only parents. I have biological parents, but they aren't really who I am,' he thought to himself.

'But I'm curious. Who was my biological father? Why did he give me up, and what characteristics did I inherit from him? How might meeting him help me make sense of my life?' he continued to ponder.

Everyone always said Oliver looked like his mothers – the Italian features of Rita and the Irish ones from Anna. He was thoughtful and serious – much like Anna – but prone to agitation and emotional outbursts like Rita. Was personality rooted in our genes or were we shaped more by our environment, by those who nurtured us?

One of Oliver's classmates at college, Martha, had gone to a woman who hypnotized her so that she could connect with past lives. Martha discovered that her fear of flying came from a plane crash in her last life and her intolerance for heat from a fatal fire on a farm in France. She discovered that her boyfriend was one she had when she died in the fire, a relationship that was deep but never able to be lived out. She had been struggling with fear that her life would be cut short or that the relationship with her boyfriend would end unexpectedly and, after the hypnosis, was now able to relax, trust her current life and relationship, and look forward.

Oliver wondered if personality was shaped by more than genes and environment, perhaps by the accumulation of one's past lives. What relationships and experiences were enfolded into one's soul in such a way that the current life represented an opportunity to continue certain lessons, resolve old conflicts, heal wounds, and gain new insights. If that was the case, who was he and what were the lessons or things he needed to confront in his life?

He pondered the circumstances of his life – the fact that he had two mothers who had adopted him, that he had grown up in a world where the diversity of gender and sexual orientation were celebrated, not shamed. What did that possibly have to do with past lives or experiences? He didn't have a father. Was that significant? Was he tempting fate by trying to find a father or was there a lesson in that, too?

The idea of fate stumped him. Is everything in life preordained? Are we actors in a play where the script has already been written or are we the authors, those who compose the story with the choices and decisions we make? Was his decision to come to Rome already part of the story handed to him or was he rewriting the story?

He began to think of the responsibility implied in his authoring his own life. If he was to be the author of his life, what kind of life did he want and what kinds of decisions did he need to make? Would he then have to take responsibility for his happiness or unhappiness, no longer able to shift blame onto someone else or onto other circumstances.

His head was swimming with thoughts, and he decided it best not to go too deep at that hour and with that much wine in him. He looked forward to tomorrow, a day he had dedicated to exploring the Forum and Colosseum. He asked for the check, paid his bill, and took the short stroll to his hotel where, after slipping in under the covers, he fell into a deep sleep.

3

Chapter Three

Two days later, Oliver woke with great anticipation. He had spent the previous day exploring the ruins of ancient Rome, strolling along the Via Sacra in the Forum, climbing the Palatine Hill to get a glimpse of the Circus Maximus, and poking around the earliest excavations of an area of huts from the time of Romulus and Remus. The Palatine had been the most surprising of the sites he visited. It was one of the seven hills of Rome that included the ruins of vast palaces encircling an ancient temple of Apollo and the house of Romulus, underscoring the divine origins of Rome – Romulus being conceived by the god Mars and Rhea Silva, one of the vestal virgins.

The forum had been the adult Disney World he anticipated, a larger-than-life archaeological park with soaring monuments dating back at least two thousand years. Oliver had a vivid imagination and was able to fully immerse himself in the setting, imagining throngs of people - the rich, the senators, the slaves – all going about their business in the political center of the Empire. He imagined the roars coming from the nearby Colosseum and the vendors outside selling grilled meats, fruit, and cheese as spectators chatted with one another between events.

The day had been long, and he felt soreness in his back and lower legs from walking on the old Roman roads, still intact but uneven from centuries of wear and tear. He slipped on some shorts and shirt and headed to the breakfast room where he ordered a steaming cup of cappuccino and loaded his plate with chocolate croissants and cold cuts. Most of the guests were businessmen, reading newspapers or chatting with colleagues about new deals they were about to make. He grabbed one of the Italian papers and pretended to read it, scanning in search of words that were like the Spanish he knew.

After breakfast, he returned to his room, took a shower, and began to contemplate what clothes to wear to meet his biological father. He selected a pair of dark jeans, a cotton dress shirt, and a pair of casual shoes. He looked at his watch and realized he had several hours before lunch. He was restless and needed to do something. He pulled out the guidebook and began to scroll down a list of mustsees in Rome and decided to explore the Castle Sant'Angelo. He thought about heading to St. Peter's, nearby, but had already made plans to visit the Vatican Museums on Friday, so he decided to wait.

The walk to Castel Sant'Angelo was pleasant, a path through some of the more historic neighborhoods of medieval Rome. The roads were no more than spaces between old apartment buildings meandering haphazardly through dense neighborhoods. New regulations had made most of the central historical district a pedestrian zone, so the walk was pleasant and quiet, even meditative. People walked casually down the middle of the pavement occasionally stopping to chat with neighbors.

On several intersections, medallions of the Virgin Mary stood guard, a few dried flowers wedged between the paintings and the plaster walls. He passed several small grocers where crates of oranges, pears, apples, and lettuce were staged artfully in the doorways. Small workshops were filled with woodcarvers, metal workers, and repairmen bent over their projects. Here and there people stood crammed into small cafes where they sipped coffee or ate a simple sandwich as they took breaks from their work.

At some point Oliver had no idea where he was heading, all sense of direction lost in the maze of passageways. He pulled out his phone, typed in his destination, and a route lit up the screen. He took a few more turns and ended up on a small road that led directly onto the Ponte Sant'Angelo, an old Roman bridge built by Hadrian in the 2nd century to link the city with his mausoleum on the other side of the river. He walked up a small hill onto the bridge and saw the towering castle on the other side and St. Peter's dome in the distance.

The castle was built on the ruins of Hadrian's family's tomb, a large tumulus or round earthen structure in the center of which were placed the remains of the imperial family. Originally it had been topped with grass and cypress trees and a monumental statue. As Rome fell prey to invading armies, the tomb was converted into a fortress, surrounded by moats, walls, and topped with residences where rulers could retreat to safety. Its location on the Tiber River prevented armies from a river assault, and its proximity to the Vatican made it strategic for protecting Christian Rome's prized relic, the tomb and bones of St. Peter.

Oliver purchased his ticket and began walking up the interior circular cobblestone ramp that was built to accommodate horses and carriages bringing supplies and people to the upper residences where, he learned, the Popes had hidden the Vatican's treasury and had created a dungeon for prisoners. The view from the upper terraces of the castle were spectacular – panoramic views of St. Peters on one side and unobstructed views of the city of Rome on the other.

Oliver finished his visit, retraced his steps, and then crossed over the Ponte Sant'Angelo back into the historic district of Rome. He glanced at his watch and realized lunch with Henry was just 30 minutes away. As he walked toward the restaurant, he felt his legs grow weak, and his pulse race. It felt as if he were about to take a final exam, one for which he had not studied.

He entered a small square and noticed the sign for Ristorante Archimede. There was a large awning set up over a section of tables outside and a tan brick façade leading to a more formal interior. He realized, as he approached, that he and Henry hadn't described each other, nor had they identified how and where to meet. He noticed a single man sitting at a table drinking some wine. He introduced himself to the maître d' who then pointed to the man at the edge of the awning covered tables.

The man glanced over, stood up, and walked toward Oliver.

He was approximately fifty years old. He was tall, lean, and casually dressed – in khaki pants, a summer short-sleeve pullover, and light brown leather shoes. He smiled and extended his hand, "You must be Oliver. It's a pleasure."

Oliver held his hand strongly, looked intensely at him, and said, "The pleasure is all mine. Thanks for agreeing to meet."

"Come, sit down," Henry indicated to the chair just opposite him. "Can I offer you some wine, water, coffee?"

"Wine's good, thanks."

Henry had a full head of hair that was only showing a little grey at the edges. He had angular jaws and a large sensual nose. He had a closely trimmed dark beard, full dark red lips, and dimples when he smiled. He was tan. His skin was smooth, but he had pronounced creases emanating from his dark brown eyes. They were alluring, hidden behind wispy lashes and full dark brows.

His arms were muscular, pressing firmly against the elastic arms of his shirt. Dark hair ran down his arms and over the top of his hands that were resting calmly on the white tablecloth, his long sensual fingers taping nervously on a spoon.

Oliver felt self-conscious, Henry looking intensely at him and saying nothing. Finally, Henry began, "I can't believe this is happening. I thought it about it so often and never imagined I would be able to track you down."

Oliver nodded and said timidly, "Me, too."

Henry poured some wine into Oliver's glass and raised his own to toast him, "To our meeting."

"To our meeting," Oliver repeated and took a sip.

"I feel we have so much to talk about. It's hard to know where to begin," Henry said.

The waiter came to the table with a small pad of paper prepared to take their order, "*Cosa volete, monsignore?*" he asked.

Oliver glanced at Henry, picking up enough Italian to know that the waiter had just called Henry – monsignor – a title for priests.

Henry caught Oliver's inquisitive glance, hesitated, and then asked, "What would you like to eat. The *antipasti* are good here – as are their veal dishes and pasta."

"Why don't you order for us? I'll trust your recommendation – just nothing like tripe or squid."

"I hate those, too," Henry said, grinning.

Henry ordered a mixed plate of *antipasti*, a plate of tomato and basil spaghetti, and veal scallopini. He then turned to Oliver who, before Henry could open his mouth said, "Monsignor?"

Henry cleared his throat, "Yes, I'm afraid they know me here, and they know I am a priest." He paused and took a deep breath and said, "Whew, I'm glad that's finally out."

"So, you are a priest?" Oliver said half question half declaration, giving Henry a scrutinizing look.

"It's a long story as you can imagine."

"I'm all ears," Oliver said.

"I work at the Congregation for Education here in Rome."

"Ah ha," Oliver began. "I figured you were in higher education, the only trace on the internet being your position at Fordham a number of years ago."

"What else did you discover?"

"Nothing. You're pretty much off the grid."

"That's good to hear. It's intentional."

"Why?"

Henry rubbed his hands nervously and then tentatively began, "Well it all goes back to your birth."

Oliver nodded for him to continue.

"I was a young priest and had an affair with a woman in the parish. It wasn't of long duration, but we weren't careful, and she got pregnant."

"Was she married?"

"No, thank God, but she was well-known in the close-knit community in the suburbs of Boston. She went away discretely to have the child – you – and we both agreed to give you up for adoption. I wasn't willing to leave the priesthood, and we couldn't maintain an affair undetected."

"Wow!" is all Oliver could say in response to the stunning information already disclosed in less than five minutes. The waiter returned to the table with a platter of antipasti, and Henry began to place salami, prosciutto, and grilled marinated vegetables on Oliver's plate.

"So, you must have left the parish, right?"

"Yes. The relationship put my own vocation in question, so I asked the bishop if I could do some administrative work. The job at Fordham came up, and I took it."

"What did you do there?"

"I was one of the academic deans. It was a great job, and I realized I was more suited for administrative work than pastoral."

"But you're still a priest, right?"

"Yes. I got involved in the policies of Catholic higher education and was eventually invited to take a position here in Rome at the Congregation."

"You must be talented."

"I'm not sure about that, but it is a good fit."

Henry and Oliver finished the antipasti. The waiter removed their plates and returned a few minutes later with their plates of spaghetti. Oliver found himself shaking from nervous adrenaline and took a couple of long sips of wine before he dug into the pasta.

"We should talk about you," Henry continued. "What do you do, where do you live, what are your parents like?"

"I don't know where to begin. I guess at the beginning. My moms adopted me as an infant."

"Your moms?" Henry inquired as his forehead creased.

"Yes, I have two moms – Anna and Rita."

Henry shuffled in his chair and set his fork down on the plate. "Your moms – they're lesbians?"

"Yes. Why?"

"But that's not possible."

"Why not," Oliver inquired.

"We placed you with Catholic Charities. They would never have set up an adoption with gay parents."

"Why not?"

"It's against Church teaching."

"Well for some reason they did. Maybe it was because in Massachusetts you couldn't discriminate and still get state funding. I think there was a time when Catholic Charities complied with that requirement."

Henry rubbed his forehead in consternation and looked off in the distance as if searching for more information. Then he continued, "Well – go on – tell me more about your life."

"I grew up in Boston. I had a great education and am currently studying finance at Suffolk University on Beacon Hill."

"So, you want to be a financial advisor or something?"

"Exactly. That's what I hope."

"Bravo. That's a good profession."

"What interests do you have – hobbies or sports?"

"I played lacrosse in school and have dabbled in art and painting from time to time. I like to swim. We usually take a vacation on the Cape in the summer."

"Ah yes, Cape Cod. I imagine you go to Provincetown," Henry inquired condescendingly.

"Yes, I love the place."

Henry didn't look pleased. They finished the pasta. Henry poured more wine into their glasses and leaned forward on the table. "And are you Catholic?"

"We were. I was raised Catholic."

"But?" Henry asked, pressing for more information.

"Well, between the Catholic Church fighting against gay marriage and the sex abuse scandals in Boston, my moms decided to convert to the Episcopal Church."

"So, you go to the Episcopal Church?"

"Yes, although we don't go that often. My moms are probably more spiritual than religious."

Henry leaned back in his chair, "Ah, I see."

Oliver leaned forward and quietly asked, "And my mother – my biological mother – what can you tell me about her?"

Henry's face went blanch. Oliver surmised it was a difficult topic.

"I don't know. We haven't been in touch."

"Never?"

"Nope. After the adoption, I wanted to sever our ties – start a new life, be more responsible, truer to my vows."

"What about her?"

"She wanted me to leave the priesthood. She wanted us to be a couple, to start a family. It was hard for her to give you up."

Oliver's eyes began to tear up, thinking of his biological mother having to give her child over to a stranger and being shut out from the man she loved. It must have been terrifying, he thought to himself.

"Where is she now? What does she do?"

"I have no idea. She asked to remain anonymous after the adoption, and everyone has respected that. I've looked her up on the internet, but there's no information."

Oliver looked sad. "What can you tell me about her?"

"She was a beautiful woman, inside and out. She had blonde hair, silky smooth skin, and a beautiful body. I was smitten the first time I saw her. She had an outgoing personality and made people feel loved and affirmed around her. She was a social worker by profession, and that seemed to be a good match. I can see us in you, the combination of my French-Canadian heritage with her English and Irish background. I bet you are outgoing and thoughtful."

"People say that."

"And principled."

"Yes, that too. But my moms are like that, too. Anna is someone who makes everyone feel at home, loved, accepted, welcomed. Rita is more mercurial and emotional. She expresses the mood of the moment – invites people to get things off their chests – and then moves on, offering people something to eat and drink accompanied by hugs."

Henry chuckled reluctantly. "The old nature versus nurture dilemma, right?"

Oliver nodded.

Their main courses were served, and Henry became more pensive. He began to cut his veal and began to speak without looking up, "I still can't believe Catholic Charities placed you with a lesbian couple. That's so irresponsible."

"What do you mean irresponsible?"

"Every child needs a father and a mother, not two moms. It's abusive."

Oliver stiffened. He had heard these arguments before and always had good comebacks. "First of all, I can't imagine having more loving parents. My moms have sacrificed for me, provided me with incredible opportunities, and have loved me generously. They always made sure I had male role models but, even so, my identity as a man was never in question. The question I have is not how irresponsible Catholic Charities was in placing me with them but how irresponsible you were in conceiving me. I presume you didn't think it was moral to use condoms."

Henry put his knife and fork down on the plate and glared at Oliver. "Don't lecture me."

"I'm not. You're the one bringing into question my family."

"Well, it's not a good example for you. They've led you astray from your faith and taken you to degenerate places like Provincetown."

"If you want to talk about degenerate, why don't we begin with the abusive priests in the parishes. Where is the real danger – with my mothers who bring me to a welcoming and inclusive denomination and to a town that celebrates diversity and inclusivity – or with the predator priests who undoubtedly would have spotted me, an adopted sensitive child."

Henry's face turned red. "There's a small percentage of priests who are problems, and it's because of all the gay priests who create a permissive environment."

"Pedophilia and homosexuality are two entirely different things. It's dishonest to collapse them into one category. It's not the gay priests who are the problem, it is the shaming of sexuality that creates the conditions for abuse."

Henry looked over at Oliver and realized he had a formidable opponent and that he wasn't getting anywhere. "Let's change the subject. I don't want this to be contentious."

"Well, I think it has become so already – but I agree – let's see if we can find some common ground."

Henry's face relaxed a bit. He took a sip of wine and took up his knife and fork and continued to eat his veal. Oliver followed suit.

"So, besides work, what do you do for fun here in Rome?" Oliver continued.

"I like history and art. It's a great place for that."

Oliver nodded, realizing he had the same interests. "Do you have a favorite period of history or a favorite artist?"

"I tend to like ancient history, particularly the period when early Christianity arose. It must have been a fascinating time when old traditions began to give way to new ones."

"Yes," Oliver said, nodding.

"And, as for artists, I think Raphael is my favorite. Have you seen the Raphael rooms in the Vatican museums?"

"No, this is my first trip to Rome, and I've only been here 48 hours."

"Well, you'll have to be my guest at the museum. How long are you here?"

"I am leaving Saturday for Florence to meet friends."

"What are you doing Friday?"

"No plans at the moment?"

"We'll make plans, then. And you – your favorite historical epoch and artist?"

"Like you, I love ancient Roman history. As for artists, I'm more drawn to someone like Caravaggio. He has the talent of Raphael but captures the ordinariness of life – it's not idealized – it's dirty and real. And, of course, he is a master of light and darkness."

"Ah yes, Caravaggio. You know he was rumored to be homosexual?"

Oliver took Henry's statement to be a backhanded stab, dig, and insult, but he decided not to play into his hand. "And he had a favorite woman of the street he painted into his images – so was he bisexual?"

"I don't know about that," Henry pretended, looking evasively down at his plate.

Oliver knew he had caught Henry and could stay one step ahead of him, but he decided that he wanted his first encounter with his biological father to be more civil than not, so he let it go.

"Shifting subjects," Henry inquired, "what do you think of the food here?"

"You mean here – at the restaurant – or here in Rome?"

"Both."

"The food here is amazing – delicious. Since I arrived, I can't believe how fresh everything is. It's so flavorful – simple but rich at the same time."

"What have you seen so far?"

"The Pantheon, Castle Sant'Angelo, the Forum, the Colosseum – and lots of small historic streets."

"The city is like a history book."

"I love it."

Henry could see the wonder and curiosity in his son's eyes and, for a brief moment, felt proud of him. "You seem like you have done well for yourself."

"I have tried. Studying finance is a challenge, but I think it will be a great career."

"Will you stay in Boston?"

"At the moment, yes. There are lots of good financial companies there – and lots of wealth – so there are good employment opportunities."

"Do you have a girlfriend?" Henry realized he should be more gender neutral in his question, but he decided Oliver was on his turf and he had the right to presume a heterosexual relationship.

Oliver looked startled by the question. No one in his family or circle of friends would ever presume to know the gender of someone's romantic interests. He decided to make a point, "There's no one special in my life at the moment."

Henry looked dissatisfied by the answer. "So, do you date?"

"From time to time."

"Women?" Henry decided to be more direct.

"Yes, women."

Henry sighed in relief. Oliver noticed and elaborated, "Let me set the record straight. Just as straight couples have gay children, gay couples have straight children. Sexual orientation is not the product of one's upbringing. It is something that one discovers – perhaps something genetic or gestational – but certainly not the product of how one is raised."

"Point made," Henry admitted. "But aren't children of gay couples more confused about their gender and sexuality?"

"Where did you hear that," Oliver inquired pointedly. "All of the studies suggest that children raised in same-sex families are no more statistically inclined to be gay nor are they statistically more confused about their gender or sexuality. There is well established data on this point."

"So, back to my question – you date girls, right?"

"Yes. But no one in particular at the moment."

"But look at you – you're handsome, well-educated, sophisticated – why hasn't someone swept you off your feet yet?"

"I don't know. I'm still young."

"Yes, I guess so."

"When I was your age, I was just going into the seminary."

"What led you to be a priest?" Oliver inquired.

"I guess I had always been religious as a kid. In college, I was upset by the lack of morals and religious sentiment amongst my classmates, and I decided I wanted to do something to change that – to make the church better so that it would be more relevant."

"But isn't that the problem today – that young people feel the church is out of touch with their issues – whether it is with questions about gender, sexuality, or the environment?"

"But they are confused. The church needs to do a better job of communicating truth. That's why I am so involved in higher education."

"What do you mean?" Oliver pressed further.

"Young people are being fed disinformation – that somehow they can choose their own gender, choose their own orientation."

"What do you mean?"

"Well gender theory for one."

"You mean transgender issues?"

"That and gender roles."

"Gender theory doesn't teach that people have a choice about gender," Oliver began. Transgender people are seeking to affirm the gender that they have always felt deep down on the inside. It is often in dissonance with the gender assigned to them at birth. In some cases, they have underlying chromosomal differences that were overlooked. Sometimes, it is a matter of their not feeling emotionally and psychologically the gender assigned to them at birth. They don't choose their gender, they affirm it."

"But think about the young kids who are encouraged to embrace a gender different from their sex."

"It's been shown that if this occurs earlier, it is less traumatic and less harmful later. Besides, there are careful protocols put in place to make sure a child is experiencing gender dissonance and not something more superficial. And as for sexual orientation, there's no question today that one chooses to be gay. It is discovered – often at great cost and risk given the prejudices of society.

"But in both instances, it is contrary to nature and therefore harmful to the individual," Henry remarked, his forehead creased.

"I don't get that. If you are homosexual, how is loving someone of the same gender not natural?"

"But studies show gay people aren't happy and can't form authentic relationships. This proves it is contrary to human nature."

"I do recall seeing reference to this in one of the Vatican documents – I believe something published in 1980s. It claims it was based on evidence from the human sciences."

"Exactly. I'm glad you're aware of it."

"But the evidence today from all of the human sciences – sociology, psychology, biology – is that gay couples achieve the same marks of authentic love and happiness as straight couples."

Henry didn't have a response. He remained quiet.

"Frankly," Oliver interjected, "I would like you to meet my mothers. If after meeting them you can say that their 24-year marriage is a sham, that it is just two women who are using each other for sexual pleasure, and that they are not really happy or really in love or really committed to each other – then I'll support your blasted document from the 8os."

Henry didn't have anything to say, but he was becoming increasingly agitated. "Well, I see you have been brainwashed by your moms and by the liberal academic establishment. That's too bad."

"I haven't been brainwashed. The information is substantiated by countless studies that have taken place over the past thirty to fifty years. It's intellectually dishonest to perpetuate unfounded theories."

Henry's face turned red and the veins on his neck puffed out as he blurted out, "I'm sorry we met. I'm sorry we ended on this note."

"Me, too. I had hoped to establish a more positive connection, one that would complement not contradict everything good about my life!"

Henry gestured to the waiter to bring their check. He paid the bill, shook Oliver's hand as they stood, and said, "I wish you the best."

Oliver nodded but remained silent, shocked that the meeting had ended so contentiously and abruptly.

Henry walked off. Oliver remained standing at the front of the restaurant until Henry was no longer in site. He pivoted and walked the short block back to his hotel. He walked past the handsome receptionist who winked at him and took the elevator to his room. He threw himself down on the bed and began to sob.

4

Chapter Four

Several hours later, Oliver woke, his pillowcase damp from tears. He looked at his watch. It was 5 PM. He felt devastated at the exchange with his biological father and felt everything had been a mistake. How could he have betrayed his real parents – his mothers – for a fleeting encounter with a biological parent who was a certifiable bigot and embodied the worst of the Church's dishonesty.

He wanted to vomit, to expel the bile within him, the venom that was his father. He felt dirty, ashamed, and unsettled. He wanted to call his moms and speak with them, but he was afraid he would say something that would upset them.

Henry had confirmed Oliver's worse impressions of the Catholic Church – of its intransigence and unwillingness to look honestly at new information that might challenge its positions. How could someone like Henry – someone in higher education – be so unbending? How do you ignore information and perpetuate untruths that clearly hurt people? How is that possible?

Oliver went into the bathroom, rinsed his face, brushed his hair, and changed his shirt. He decided to take a walk to the Piazza Navona to clear his head. As he left the front door of the hotel, his phone pinged.

A text from Henry popped up: "Oliver, I'm sorry about my behavior this afternoon. Can we meet?"

Oliver hesitated, not sure he wanted to see Henry again. In fact, all he wanted to do was yell at him. He said to himself, 'I don't have to respond right away. I can let him sit with the silence for a while.'

He decided to walk a bit. But as much as he tried, he couldn't ignore the message on his phone and finally typed in a response, "Sure. When? Where?"

Henry responded. "Thanks. There's a nice pizzeria not too far from your hotel – Da Polese. It's in the Piazza Sforza Cesarini on the way to the Vatican. Meet you there in an hour?"

"Ok." Oliver responded. He walked toward the Piazza Navona and took a half loop around Bernini's fountain of the Four Rivers, a magnificent sculpture that celebrated the various corners of the world in a place where people from around the world gathered to eat, drink, enjoy art, admire monuments, and simply savor the air and light of Rome. It was a beautiful evening, and he wished he could just get a table at one of the cafes and watch people as they strolled past. He wondered why he had decided to subject himself to Henry's negativity but was hopeful there might be a better conversation.

He made his way through several narrow medieval streets. It was darker, lights were coming on, and people were beginning to shutter their businesses for the evening. The air began to cool, and Oliver was glad he had brought a light sweatshirt. Aside from a few vespas he had to dodge, the walk was relaxing. The pace of life in Rome was slower. People stopped, chatted with neighbors, took their dogs for walks, and stepped into cozy coffee bars to have a drink before dinner. Oliver found the pizzeria Henry had suggested. There were tables spread across pebble stones and lights strung between the branches of a large oak tree. He scanned the tables and saw Henry seated at the edge.

Henry rose, smiled, extended his hand and said, "Thanks for agreeing to see me again. Sorry about earlier today."

Oliver nodded but said nothing, noticing that Henry had a different pallor. He was blanch and had small beads of sweat forming around his forehead.

"Have a seat," Henry said, pointing to the chair across from him.

The waiter came, took their drink orders, and returned to the kitchen. Henry leaned forward, wringing his hands, and said, "I have something I need to share with you."

Oliver looked alarmed but curious.

"After we parted today, I felt ashamed of myself."

Oliver's mouth dropped open, surprised at what looked like a confession about to unfold.

"As I walked home, I realized I had just met a handsome, smart, resourceful, and thoughtful person – someone who had been raised by loving parents and who had, himself, become a loving and sensitive young man. You are the son every parent would want, obviously raised by two women who have been in a life-long committed loving relationship."

Oliver relaxed a bit and smiled but was on alert at the dramatic change in demeanor of his father. The waiter brought their wine and asked what they wanted to order. Henry pointed out a few pizzas at adjoining tables and suggested a margherita and one with prosciutto and onion. They were large but thin crusted, and Henry explained they were easy to finish off. Henry and the waiter seemed to know each other well, referring to each other on a first-name basis. Paolo took their order and retreated into the kitchen.

Henry continued, "I asked myself how I could I have reacted the way I did? I concluded that I was angry, an anger that had been festering in me for some time. I think seeing you triggered painful memories."

"I don't get it," Oliver interjected. "What are you so angry about?"

"Maybe a number of things but, most importantly, the loss of the love I had for your biological mother." Henry looked down at the table with a sullen look. He nervously turned the fork several times and then set it down.

"Tell me what happened."

A few tears trickled down Henry's face, his eyes watering up.

"Go on," Oliver pressed.

"I grew up in a very unhappy family. Maybe I was jealous of you. My father was extremely critical of me. He made fun of my interest in art, history, and philosophy. He wanted me to play football and go hunting with him, but I preferred books and brushes. He called me a sissy."

Oliver couldn't believe what he was hearing. He nodded for Henry to continue.

"My father pushed me to date in high school, trying to set me up with who he thought were good matches. They were invariably the bad girls, the girls who were sexy, provocative, and ready to do anything with a guy. I was frightened by that and retreated into my moral religious world, judging them and my classmates harshly."

He paused and then continued, "To get him off my back, I eventually declared my interest in becoming a priest. I thought that would mollify him since he was a conservative Catholic. I think he suspected I was entering the priesthood to get away from him, but he supported it anyway."

"So, you went to the seminary. What happened?"

"I loved it. I loved the studies, the music, the art, and the aesthetics of the church. It was amazing."

"But – I sense there's a but here." Oliver said as the waiter brought their pizzas to the table and both began to cut into the thin crusts.

"Yes. I was surprised to find so many gays in the seminary. I was handsome and the focus of a lot of attention and speculation. It made me feel uncomfortable, and I became angry that the priesthood had been so infiltrated with homosexuals."

"Was it that rampant?" Oliver inquired.

"Well, I guess it wasn't as bad as I'm suggesting – although it was and still is bad. A lot of guys were just looking for a close friend – someone they could hang out with, travel with, and confide in. They may not have been gay, but they are what some called – homosocial – more comfortable with same-sex friendships. But that still made me uncomfortable. When I met your biological mother, it was the first time I met a woman who was gorgeous and who didn't seem flirtatious. She was an upstanding, generous, thoughtful, and caring person who happened to like me. It felt good to be pursued by a woman, not by all the sissies in the seminary."

Oliver rubbed his chin and tentatively asked, "And did this make you feel better about your father?"

Henry bristled. Oliver had touched a raw nerve. At first, he shook his head no but then looked up from his pizza, knife and fork in hand and said, "I suppose so."

He then continued, "When your mother became pregnant, it was a wake-up call for us both. We realized how deeply we had strayed into something and that we had to embrace it fully or walk away."

"So, I assume you decided to walk away."

Henry nodded. Oliver took a bite of his pizza and looked tenderly at Henry.

"Yes. I told her I couldn't leave the priesthood. She was devastated. We spent months sorting it out and finally concluded to give you up for adoption and go our separate ways."

"That must have been horrible," Oliver said with some ambiguity, feeling both compassion for his father and disdain for his earlier views.

"It was. It was the hardest thing I've ever done. And I'm sure for her it was heart wrenching."

"So, what happened to her?" Oliver inquired.

"We eventually lost touch. The last I heard, she was a social worker in Chicago."

"Did she have more kids?"

"I suspect she did, but she didn't mention it. She was angry at me for not leaving with her."

"And that's when you went to Fordham, right?"

"Yes," Henry said, looking off in the distance.

"And how did you end up in Rome?"

"I was recruited after I published some articles."

"On what?"

Henry hung his head as if embarrassed. He didn't look like he wanted to answer but slowly said, "On the right of the Church to monitor professors at Catholic colleges."

"You mean to censor them?" Oliver said pointedly.

Henry nodded timidly.

Oliver waited for Henry to elaborate, to express regret for his work, but he didn't. He realized his father was morally and politically against everything Oliver's family represented.

"So, I don't understand what you're sorry for, what you're apologizing for."

"Let's not get in an argument again. I feel bad enough for what transpired earlier today."

"But your work," Oliver began, "your work consists in fighting against families like mine."

"Not exactly," Henry continued defensively. "I just want to make sure professors are following sound Catholic theology."

"But that theology condemns me and my family."

"There are exceptions, like you and your moms. You obviously seem to have turned out well despite things."

"I would say in light of things, not despite them."

"That's where we disagree," Henry insisted.

Oliver nodded. He was frozen with a sense of ambivalence – a desire to avoid animosity with his father but an equal sense of indignation that his family was brought into question.

"Oliver, we need to get to know each other better. I need to understand you, and I hope you would understand me. Can I make a proposal?"

"Sure."

"You mentioned you would like to see the Raphael rooms in the Vatican. I'd like to take you for a private tour. What do you think?"

"That would be nice, but I don't want to take any more of your time."

"It's no bother. I want to do this. I would like to get to know you better. Can we meet tomorrow at 7:30 AM at the Porta Sant'Anna – the entrance to the Vatican near the Borgo Pio?"

"Sure, that would be nice."

"Then it's a plan. I'll see you then."

They finished their pizzas. Henry asked for the check, paid, and they shook hands, each returning respectively to their opposite ends of Rome – Henry walking toward the Vatican and Oliver toward the Pantheon and his hotel.

5

Chapter Five

The next morning, at 7:20 AM, Oliver walked up to the Porta Sant'Anna, a medieval gate through which most people entered the Vatican City State. He stood on the pavement just outside, staring at the Swiss Guards standing stoically in place, their blue and orange uniforms perfectly pressed and their hands holding traditional long pikes. He pulled out his phone to look busy, waiting for Henry to appear.

At 7:30, Henry appeared just inside the gate and presented documents to police officials behind a glass window in a small office. They examined the papers and then looked out onto the street. Henry pointed to Oliver, and the police official waved Oliver in.

"It's good to see you again. You clean up nicely," Henry said as he surveyed Oliver's dark slacks, dress shirt, and dark shoes.

Oliver scrutinized Henry dressed in a black suit and Roman collar. Despite being handsome, Henry looked older in his clerical clothes. All he could manage to say at the moment was, "Thanks for making this possible. I can't believe I am inside the Vatican City."

Henry led Oliver through a square, past a door with another set of guards, and into the foyer of the Vatican Museum where officials were getting ready for the official opening of the museum an hour later. Henry showed some documents to a guard who then escorted them up a flight of stairs into the museum proper.

Aside from a guard here and there, the galleries were empty. Bright sunlight beamed into the oversize windows casting diffused but bright light onto statues, paintings, and assorted artifacts. Henry began, "I don't know how much you know about the Vatican Museums. They were started during the Renaissance when statues and artifacts were brought from excavations in the city to be part of the collections of the Popes. Let me take you for a quick detour before we go to the Raphael rooms and the Sistine Chapel."

They made several turns and walked up a steep ceremonial staircase into a courtyard filled with statues. Henry led Oliver to a niche and began, "This is the famous Laocoon statue."

"Wow," Oliver said, standing mouth agape in front of the lifesize carving of a naked older man surrounded by two younger men, all three being squeezed and bitten by serpents. Their agony was apparent in the writhing of their bodies, something Oliver assumed required an incredible degree of skill to carve. "Who made this?"

"We aren't sure exactly – whether the artist was Greek or Roman - although there are some theories. One of the ancient Roman writers, Pliny, described it and mentioned that it was sitting in the imperial palace of Titus. In 1506, some workmen discovered it in some ruins in a vineyard, probably the remains of an imperial villa. At that time, the ruins were on the outskirts of the inhabited part of medieval Rome. Michelangelo and other notable artists raced to the site and supervised its extraction and repositioning to the Vatican Palace of Pope Julius II."

"Wasn't he the one who commissioned the Sistine Chapel ceiling?" Oliver inquired.

"Very good. Yes. He was. He was also the one who began construction of the new St. Peter's. He saw himself as a new Julius Caesar who would rebuild Rome."

"What's the story behind the old man and two younger men?"

"There are a number of theories depending on which ancient author you follow. In Virgil's story, he is a priest of Poseidon. He and his sons are being punished for having exposed the hidden danger in the Trojan horse. In Sophocles' story, he is the priest of Apollo who should have been celibate but married. Thus, his sons were killed to leave him alone."

Oliver couldn't help but note the irony of his standing next to his biological father gazing at the agony of a priest punished for his sexual misbehavior. He looked over at Henry who seemed unfazed by the point he had unwittingly made. Instead, he continued to recount the artistic merits of the piece and the history of its placement in the Belvedere pavilion.

Henry showed Oliver the Belvedere Apollo, considered one of the greatest works of classical sculpture. The grace and poise of Apollo was notable, the embodiment of Apollo's virtues of wisdom and self-control. They walked through another hallway lined with sculptures and stopped at the Belvedere Torso, an impressive fragment of a once larger piece. The lower torso and upper legs were muscular and taut with energy and had inspired many of Michelangelo's works.

"We better move along if we want to beat the crowds," Henry said as he led Oliver out of the Belvedere section of the museum and into a long corridor. Oliver estimated it was at least a quarter mile long, first lined with maps and later with tapestries. Later they entered a maze of small walkways connecting them to the Raphael rooms, originally part of the papal palace.

"Why do you like Raphael so much?" Oliver inquired of Henry.

"I don't know exactly. Perhaps his paintings are more representational, an attempt to capture exact proportions, detailed features, and faces. They evoke a kind of certainty, order, and balance. They were done at a time when Rome was imagining its rebirth, and I'm fascinated with that period."

They walked into one of the rooms and up to the painting popularly called "The School of Athens."

"This is considered to be Raphael's masterpiece."

Oliver was dumbstruck by the radiance of the piece, its vivid colors, and the handsome figures in the painting stretched out along the foreground.

Henry began to describe the piece. "The two main figures in the center are Plato and Aristotle, one with his hand pointed up and the other pointing down. Plato is considered the philosopher who underscores the preeminence of the world of Being – the world above. Aristotle emphasizes the importance of substance and form, thus the world of our senses, the world of the here and now. All of the other figures represent famous philosophers of history, but they are depictions of people Raphael knew during his life in Rome."

"The colors are amazing," Oliver noted.

"Yes, they were recently restored. They are brilliant."

"And the arched monument in the background?" Oliver inquired. "It looks like Maxentius's Basilica in the Forum with its soaring arches."

"Good observation, Oliver. It's actually a depiction of the beginning stages of the new St. Peter's, but the inspiration certainly came from Maxentius' structure. When St. Peter's was conceived, Julius wanted it to be nothing short of the grandeur of ancient Rome."

"And the figure in the front, sitting on the steps and writing?"

"It is intended to be Heraclitus, but many historians believe it is a portrait of Michelangelo. As you may know, Raphael and Michelangelo were working at the same time in the palace,

Michelangelo on the ceiling and Raphael in these rooms. There must have been intense competition."

"And, if I recall, Michelangelo wasn't noted for his painting, but Raphael was. It must have been a daring move on Julius's part to commission Michelangelo."

"And perhaps a slight to Raphael."

"Hmm," Oliver noted. "So, all of this was taking place during the early part of the 1500s, during the Renaissance?"

"Yes. And Raphael's work celebrates that, the culmination of years in which ancient manuscripts made their way into European schools from Muslim libraries and the zenith of their integration with Catholic theology by people like Thomas Aquinas and later by the Platonic Academy in Florence."

"A so-called Christian humanism," Oliver mused.

Henry nodded.

"So, there's nothing contrary to the idea that Catholic theology is compatible with philosophy, with reason?"

"No. In fact, Catholic theology must reflect the best of philosophy, of reason, of science."

Oliver looked at Henry and wondered if this was the time to press his point further. He paused and then proceeded, "That's why I don't understand why the Catholic Church has such a difficult time accepting new information about sexuality, particularly about sexual orientation. It is a matter of integrating science and reason, right?"

Henry stiffened and his face got red. Oliver sensed he was going to lash out. Henry took a breath and then began, "Let's not discuss that now. Your point has been made. Let's go see the Sistine Chapel."

They walked through a series of narrow corridors with arrows pointing to the chapel. Oliver imagined crowds of people, just behind them, lining up to enter the space. They walked through a small doorway and the room opened in front of them, a tall rectangular chapel covered in a kaleidoscope of colors and figures.

Oliver was speechless and emotional. He pivoted in place, not sure where to focus as every inch of the walls and ceiling was covered with art.

He instantly leaned his head back and began to gaze at Michelangelo's bright frescos above, the image of God creating Adam and the larger-than-life prophets and oracles holding up the faux architectural supports on the sides and corners.

His eye was quickly drawn to the deep blue of Michelangelo's Last Judgment on the far wall, a monumental work with incredible movement of bodies rising to heaven and descending into hell. The image of Jesus – inspired by Apollo and the Belvedere Torso - presided over the spectacle. Oliver thought that he would have been mesmerized by the ceiling, and he was. But the Last Judgment was more impressive, and he stood in place contemplating the various symbols and messages of the piece.

He noticed Henry had taken a seat along a side wall. At first, he imagined it was a strategic way to get a better view of things, leaning back against the wall to gaze upward. But Henry had his head resting in his hands, bending over slightly. Oliver walked over to him and asked, "Are you okay? You look a little flush."

"Yeah, I'm fine. It's just the early hour, the humidity, and the lack of coffee. I'll be fine. I just need to rest a little. Come sit here," he said as he patted his hand on the space next to him.

Oliver sat. Henry pointed out some key features of the ceiling, the side walls, and the Last Judgment. He seemed to regain strength, but Oliver was still worried.

Henry looked at his watch. It was 9. He said, "Oliver, I have another surprise for you."

Henry unzipped the shoulder bag he had been carrying and pulled out a jacket that had been carefully rolled. He shook it out and held it up to Oliver's chest. "Yes, I think we are roughly the same size. Here, try this on."

"What's this for?"

"Where we're going, you need to have a jacket."

Oliver pushed his arms into the sleeves of the jacket. It fit perfectly, almost as if it had been tailored for him.

"Follow me."

Oliver looked curiously at Henry who led him down a broad staircase and then into a marble foyer where another pair of Swiss Guards stood. Henry showed the civilian guard some papers, and he waved them both in.

"I guess I should prepare you. We're going to see the Pope."

"What?" Oliver said excitedly.

"There's a private audience with a group of educators arranged by my office. It is good for me to be there, and I have told the papal household that I'm bringing a new assistant."

"You're kidding!"

"No. It will be a small group, a dozen presidents from several Catholic universities in Central America. How's your Spanish?"

"Actually, it's not bad. That's what I studied in high school and college."

"Perfect. The Pope will be speaking in Spanish."

Henry walked them into a small audience room where the presidents were sitting quietly waiting for the arrival of the Pope. Henry shook their hands and spoke fluent Spanish with them. He showed Oliver a seat to the side, near one he would be using himself. They sat down and, a few moments later, a priest came in the door and announced the arrival of the Pope. Everyone stood.

The Pope came in, nodded to the guests, and took his chair. He was old and frail but seemed in command of the situation, sitting calmly and nobly in his white robes. He made some introductory remarks welcoming them, and then one of the presidents approached the podium to present some remarks on behalf of the group. Henry looked on from the side, and the Pope glanced over to him occasionally.

When the exchange of information was complete, the Pope stood and walked over to the guests. He shook each person's hand, asked them where they were from, and exchanged pleasantries with them. When the Pope had finished greeting the guests, he glanced over to Henry who nodded to him. The Pope approached Henry who said, "Thank you, your holiness, for the meeting today. I would like to introduce a special visitor from the United States – Oliver Monte-Fitzpatrick."

Oliver bowed to him. The Pope took his hand and shook it warmly. "Welcome to Rome," the Pope began. "I understand this is your first visit."

"Yes, your holiness. Thank you for making it so special."

"Father Montpierre has told me of your studies and your interest in history."

Oliver looked at Henry in disbelief and the returned to look at the Pope. The Pope then continued, "Pray for me and for the Church that it be a welcoming place for you and your family." The Pope then winked at him and handed him a rosary that he had blessed. He returned to his chair, said a final prayer, and left the room.

Henry greeted the guests again and made some mention of a farewell dinner the following day. He then turned to Oliver and asked, "So, what did you think?"

"We have a lot to unpack. What did you tell the Pope in advance?"

"I mentioned that I would have a special guest – a bright and thoughtful young man – who believed he didn't belong in the Church. That's all."

"And the rosary – how did he know my mothers wanted a rosary blessed by the Pope?"

"You mentioned it in passing the other day. I picked one up and had him bless it for you."

Oliver reached over to Henry and gave him a big hug. "Thank you so much," he continued, tears streaking down his cheeks.

Henry grabbed his arm and led him off, "Let's go, we have another appointment."

"I'm not sure if I can handle any more surprises like this."

They descended a wide ceremonial staircase, exited the papal palace just outside the basilica, and then entered a nondescript door that opened to a long corridor that led to the other side of the basilica. Henry walked inside a small office, introduced himself, and received two tickets from the attendant.

"We're going to see the excavations under St. Peter's. Our guide should be here in a few minutes."

"What excavations?"

"Ahh, you'll see. But a little preview. During World War II, when Pope Pius XII was preparing the tomb for Pope Pius XI in the crypt of St. Peter's, workmen discovered a cavernous hole under the floor. They lowered some cameras and lights and discovered a Roman mausoleum. It was always believed that St. Peter's was built over a cemetery where St. Peter had been buried, on the side of a Roman amphitheater. Pope Pius decided to give archaeologists a green light to do excavations. After years of digging, it was ascertained that the tomb of St. Peter was directly below the altar and that, most likely, his remains were there, too."

A young woman approached them and smiled warmly at Henry. "Father Montpierre, a pleasure as always. Thanks for requesting me."

"Angela, you're the best. I wouldn't ask for anyone else. I would like you to meet Oliver - Oliver Monte-Fitzpatrick, from the US."

"It's a pleasure. Welcome to Rome. What has Fr. Henry told you so far?"

"Not much, only that we are going to see the excavations of a Roman cemetery."

"Indeed – and much more."

They entered a foyer with a model of the old St. Peter's and then walked down a narrow staircase to a glass door that opened as they approached. They walked inside a dark area. Oliver's eyes adjusted. In front of him was a wall made of slender red brick. As he looked to the right and to the left, he saw a long narrow passage lined with what looked like one story buildings.

Angela explained that these were ancient Roman mausoleums owned by wealthy families. The cemetery overlooked a Roman stadium where various types of spectacles and games were held. According to legend, after Nero's fire in 64, St. Peter and other Christians were rounded up to be crucified in the arena as a punishment for setting the fire. They, of course, did not set the fire, but Nero needed scapegoats.

It was believed that St. Peter's body was taken from the arena and buried in a simple grave on the hillside. When the Emperor Constantine was seeking to consolidate power in the 300s, he built a monumental basilica over the tomb of St. Peter.

Oliver recalled the imperial palaces he had seen a couple of days before, palaces built on top of the Palatine Hill near the location of what was believed to be the location of Romulus's and Remus's huts, the founders of Rome. The emperors wanted to associate themselves with the foundations of Rome, the birth of the twins conceived by a mortal woman and the god Mars. It seemed to him that Constantine was doing the same. He built a monumental religious structure on the site of the tomb of Peter who exercised the authority of Jesus – who was himself not unlike the legend of Romulus and Remus – born of a mortal woman and God. Constantine saw the shift of paradigms coming and wanted to associate himself with the new base of power.

Angela took Oliver and Henry through the various mausoleums decorated with frescos and plaster reliefs. Religious symbolism was predominantly pagan but, in several structures, there were symbols associated with the emergent Christian religion. As they proceeded farther up the hill and toward the location of the main altar in St. Peter's above, the ceiling height lowered. Angela pointed out an area where a monument had been erected along a wall that had been built over the site of St. Peter's grave. In front of the monument, a small area had been cleared where early Christians met to honor St. Peter.

It was above this monument and grave that Constantine located the altar of the huge basilica he erected, a tangible reminder of the authority of the Popes, the successors of Peter. When Pius XII decided to excavate, he did so secretly for fear no tomb would be found. Not only was the tomb found, but other evidence pointed conclusively to its authenticity, its connection with the persecution under Nero, and subsequent modifications of the site.

Oliver appreciated the importance of the place where he stood, an unbroken chain of history dating from the first generation of Christians to the present. He felt humbled and pondered his place in that history.

After their tour, Henry still weak from his earlier spell in the Sistine Chapel proposed to walk him through the main nave of St. Peter's. They walked slowly through the cavernous space. Henry pointed out the mosaic artwork inside the soaring dome designed by Michelangelo. Oliver was spell bound by the immense size of the space, the lofty arched walls, the gold encrusted ceiling, and the beautiful canopy sculpted in bronze by Bernini that stood over the main altar. People milled about, admiring the space and the work of art gracing the niches and altars around the sides.

Oliver couldn't help but think about the original plan to erect a Pantheon-like dome over the main altar and how Michelangelo's dome – undoubtedly beautiful and inspiring – had a different effect on pilgrims. Yes, it was impressive – and perhaps that was the goal – a structure that was unsurpassed in grandeur and dimension. In the Pantheon, Oliver felt enlarged and transformed, as if he were part of the universe, a part of God. In St. Peter's, Oliver felt humbled by the greatness of the Church and sensed that the point of the building was to remind people where they could find God – not in themselves – but in the Church.

They passed the markers in the floor of the basilica, comparing St. Peter's with other major religious structures in the world – all slightly smaller, Henry noted. They stopped at Michelangelo's 'Pieta,' the graceful masterpiece of Mary holding her dead son on her lap, marble turned into smooth skin and diaphanous garments. They finally walked out onto the front platform of the church and looked out onto St. Peter's Square, a vast space created for the crowds to gather at major religious events under the gaze of the Twelve Apostles on the façade and numerous saints lining the portico.

Henry squinted in the bright sunlight and turned to Oliver, "Well what did you think?"

"I'm not sure words are adequate to describe all I've experienced. It is amazing, and I have so many questions."

"Would you like to go get a bite to eat? We can talk more."

"Sounds good. My back and legs are a little sore," Oliver moaned as he stretched his back and raised his arms over his head.

The sun was strong, and the vast square was filling with people taking their place in line to enter the church. Water splashed in the twin fountains set on either side of a soaring obelisk. As they walked across the cobblestone pavement, Henry explained that the obelisk had been on the center spine of Nero's stadium but moved to the center of the current square after the building of the new basilica in the 1500s. They walked under the shade of the covered side porches and through a picturesque gate supporting the Passetto, a raised walkway connecting the Papal Palace with Castel Sant'Angelo. They turned right into a charming neighborhood and found an historic trattoria just off the Borgo Pio. An older waiter welcomed them and showed them a table near an open window looking out onto the street.

"*Monsignore*, welcome. What can we get for you?" the waiter added as he placed menus on the table and turned the glasses upright.

"I'm going to have some soup and a salad. Oliver, what would you like?"

"I'll have the same, please."

"And some wine?" Henry inquired.

"Yeah, sure."

The waiter nodded and retreated to the kitchen, bringing back a carafe of wine. Henry poured them both a glass.

"Don't you need something in your stomach first?" Oliver inquired as Henry began to take a sip.

He nodded and tore off a piece of bread that was sitting in a basket on the table. He began to regain some color and warmth.

"Henry, thank you so much for everything you organized today. I'm grateful."

"You're welcome. In part, it's selfish. I want you to appreciate my world, the world of the Church."

"It's hard not to be impressed with all of the history and art. It's very inspiring."

Henry creased his forehead, leaned forward and began, "I would be incredibly sad if I knew you hated the Church. It would feel like you hated me."

"I couldn't hate you."

"Even after what I said the other day?"

"Well, I can disagree with you, and I can be upset, but I don't know if I could hate you."

Henry relaxed a bit. Then he continued, "What I have come to appreciate living in Rome is that we are stewards of history. We have a responsibility to pass down the best of our tradition to the next generation, to preserve its teachings and life."

Oliver nodded hesitantly. "It's impressive."

"But?" Henry said. "I detect a but."

"What does it mean to preserve the tradition?" Oliver asked thoughtfully.

"What do you mean?"

"Well, you talk about preserving a tradition. But, if Christianity is anything, it is the community that preserves the life and teaching of Jesus. How do you think Jesus would approach me, my mothers, my friends?"

Henry shrugged his shoulders as if at a loss for a response.

"I think he would say and do what the Pope did today. He would say – you belong, and your family belongs."

Henry noted, "Even Jesus welcomed sinners."

"But that's not what the Pope said, and that's not how Jesus would frame things."

"I disagree," Henry retorted. "In order to love someone, you have to tell them the truth, uphold the truth."

"What is the truth," Oliver said with irony. "Isn't that the problem here?"

"Let's not get into this again," Henry said. "I'm sorry. Let's just enjoy the afternoon, the food, and the fact that we've reconnected."

Oliver nodded, realizing he wasn't going to change Henry.

The waiter brought them their soup, a steaming bowl of vegetables, white beans, and pasta. Oliver dipped his large spoon into the white velvety liquid and savored the rich flavors that filled his mouth. He took a sip of wine and said, "So, Henry, how often do you get back to the States? Do you still have family there?"

"I make a trip once a year to see my mother who is in a nursing home. My father has passed. I don't have any siblings."

"What about cousins or extended family?"

"I've lost touch with them. We used to be close, but my father and his brother had a falling out and, well, we just never reconnected."

"And where's your mom?"

"In western Mass."

"That's a nice area of the state. Do you miss it?"

"Not really. I think Rome has become my home. I've been here 12 years."

"Do you live in a residence for priests?"

"Actually, I have an apartment nearby, something I bought a few years ago."

Oliver smiled and said, "I love the historic neighborhoods of Rome. It's strange. Rome is a large bustling city, but the small medieval streets make it feel like a lot of small neighborhoods. There's an intimacy to it that I hadn't expected."

"That's why I like it, too. I know my neighbors, the waiters at local restaurants, and the baristas at the local cafes."

"Do you get lonely? I mean not having a larger parish or community to be a part of?"

Henry hesitated. He looked furtively off in the distance and then back to his soup. He seemed to be searching for words and slowly said, "I have my colleagues at work and my friends."

Oliver realized he hadn't really answered the question. He detected a kind of sadness in Henry and decided not to press the issue further.

"What do you do for fun?" he asked further, not sure what a priest's life was like.

"I like history. I go to archaeological sites, read books, go to special exhibits. I think that's my hobby – history and reading."

"You seem like you're in good shape. Do you exercise."

"I used to. I was a runner, but I've begun to take things easier lately."

Oliver was conscious of other people looking their way. Although it was common to see priests on the street in Rome, it seemed that most didn't anticipate sitting so close to one in a casual restaurant. They seemed intrigued, and Oliver wondered what they thought as they saw the two of them talking.

They finished their soups, and the waiter brought them two nice mixed salads accompanied by a pair of glass containers containing olive oil and vinegar. Oliver watched Henry dress his salad and followed suit – doing his best to gauge the right combination of ingredients – including a dash of salt and a generous sprinkling of pepper.

The restaurant was now full. The space was filled with a cacophony of diverse languages as tourists from all over Europe took a break after visiting St. Peter's and the Vatican Museums. Oliver tried to listen and distinguish French from German from Italian from Spanish. There was only one couple speaking English, and they seemed to have been British.

"Was it hard to learn Italian?" Oliver asked Henry as he pierced some of the salad with his fork.

"Like you, I had studied Spanish. So, it came easily. I still struggle with some of the local expressions, the dialect that people speak on the street."

"You seem to do well from what I see."

"One learns restaurant language quickly! It's a matter of survival."

Oliver grinned as he took a piece of bread and dipped it in the oil at the bottom of his salad bowl. The porous loaf had a crusty exterior but a soft and buttery inside.

They finished their salads, and Oliver took the last sip of wine from his glass. Henry only lifted the glass to his lips, leaving a few sips in the bottom, longing to delay the ending of their lunch.

"Will I see you again before you leave?" Henry inquired solemnly.

"I'm off to Florence tomorrow with friends and then back for a couple of days. We can touch base when I'm back."

"Sounds good," Henry said with a smile.

Henry paid the bill. They stood, walked outside, and embraced. Henry pointed out the best direction for Oliver to return to his hotel and watched him vanish into the crowd of tourists strolling along the Borgo Pio as he turned the corner to return to his office.

6

Chapter Six

The next morning, Oliver stepped out of the taxi in front of the bustling Termini train station. He walked inside the massive terminal filled with travelers and glanced at the oversize electronic monitor listing arrivals and departures. He found his train number and track and made his way through security.

The platform for his train was bustling with activity, porters wheeling suitcases and people walking back and forth in search of the right car for their reserved seats. The cavernous space echoed loud announcements in Italian and English of trains arriving and departing for destinations in Italy and the rest of Europe. Oliver found his car, entered, and then found his seat, a large comfortable chair adjacent to the window. The interior was quiet and calm. People took their seats, plugged in charging cords to the USB ports, and settled in for their journeys.

A few minutes later, a soothing voice on the intercom announced their departure for Florence. Oliver leaned back and enjoyed the passing landscape as the train pulled swiftly out of Rome.

He was amazed at the train's smoothness and speed. The overhead monitor indicated 95 MPH as the train left the suburbs of Rome. Most people were well-dressed with little more than a briefcase or shoulder bag, undoubtedly making quick day trips to Florence or Milan for business. Oliver thought how interesting it was that an old country like Italy was at the forefront of high-speed train technology. He felt embarrassed for the US and its antiquated trains.

As he gazed out the window, he recalled the previous day at the Vatican with Henry. It had been momentous. He couldn't believe the size of the Vatican Museums or the scope of the art. The Raphael Rooms and the Sistine Chapel exceeded his wildest expectations. The excavations had been an eye opener, a way to connect two thousand years of history to a simple gravesite of a Galilean fishermen who was martyred. But it was the memory of the gentleness of the Pope's hand and his tender words of welcome that brought tears to Oliver's eyes. He wiped them with the back of his hand. For an adopted kid, belonging meant so much. Recalling that the Pope had embraced him so unconditionally gave him hope that the Church might someday live up to its ideals.

He continued to be baffled by Henry – a handsome and smart man who seemed haunted by his own skeletons. He seemed contrite at times and belligerent at others. He seemed to be fighting something. Oliver wasn't sure Henry was winning.

In just an hour and forty minutes, the train pulled into Florence's Santa Maria Novella station. He stepped out of the carriage and onto the platform, looking for his friends as he exited the station and into the bright morning sunlight.

Out of the bustle of noise and people he heard, "Oliver!" A burly tall young man approached and gave him a forceful hug. "I can't believe we're meeting up in Florence of all places," Oliver's friend said excitedly.

"George, how good to see you!" Oliver replied as he embraced his high school friend and smiled warmly.

"Oliver, this is Steve." George pointed toward a tall red-haired bearded athletic guy – someone one might see on a rugby field in Scotland. He was wearing a long-sleeve tee-shirt and a Yankees baseball cap. "Steve, Oliver."

Oliver removed his Red Sox cap, waved it in front of Steve and said, "Nice to meet you."

Steve chuckled.

"And this is Daniela, a new friend we met here at the Institute. She lives here, and her parents go back and forth between Milan and New York."

"It's a pleasure," Oliver said, extending his hands to her.

Oliver was immediately drawn to her. She had a caramel-like complexion, dark brown eyes, and thick dark brown hair pulled back behind her neck. She wore a sleeveless cotton shirt over black shorts and had on a pair of gold sandals. She had a warm smile.

"So, what would you like to see?" George asked as he placed his hand on Oliver's shoulder and guided him out of the station.

"Everything. What do you suggest?"

"There's too much to do in one day, but the highlights are probably Michelangelo's "David," the Uffizi gallery, and the cathedral. If we're going to do them all, we should get going."

Oliver hadn't seen George since their graduation. George had gone to Georgetown and was studying diplomacy. He was finishing a year in Europe when, by chance, he learned Oliver was coming to Rome.

"By the way, how did it go meeting your dad?"

Steve and Daniela both turned to Oliver in anticipation of his response. "It was challenging. He's a priest."

"A priest?" they all said in unison.

"Yep. A certified priest."

"That must have been strange," Steve said.

"To say the least."

"So . . .?" George pressed further. "The details."

"Well, apparently he had an affair, and he and my mother decided to give me up for adoption. Case closed."

"Oh, I'm sure that's not case closed," George added.

"We'll talk later," Oliver assured him.

Steve and Daniela walked in front of George and Oliver as they headed toward the cathedral. George interjected in a whisper, "So, what do you think?"

"Of Steve?"

George nodded.

"He's very handsome and seems friendly and warm."

George smiled. Steve glanced back at George and Oliver and winked at George.

"We're so happy," George interjected.

"And Daniela, what's her story?" Oliver inquired in a low voice.

"She's a lot of fun to be with. She knows everybody – a party waiting to happen. She's very cosmopolitan, given her parents' background and dual residency."

"What does she do?"

"She works at the Institute where we are studying."

"That's convenient."

"It would be if we were straight. Since we're not, she just enjoys the opportunity to hang out without an agenda."

Oliver took another look at her. The sunlight gleamed on her round shoulders. She pulled a pair of sunglasses out of her purse and put them on, giving her a certain allure.

They arrived quickly at the cathedral, a massive structure rising dramatically from the city center, the red tile ribs of Brunelleschi's dome arching into the blue Tuscan sky. George pointed out various features of the complex, the historic baptistry and doors, the tower, and the beautiful multicolored marble façade.

"The dome is, of course, the star of the city. The ability to cover such a large space without supports was an engineering feat. Brunelleschi set the bar high for other Renaissance projects following him," Daniela noted as they stood near the altar, their necks stretched upward.

Oliver felt the space inside Florence's cathedral to be more like the Pantheon than St. Peter's and wondered if the architects had envisioned that or if it was accidental. The dome and space it covered seemed to have utilized the same concept as that of the Pantheon – with the diameter and height being similar and creating that sensation of expansion within oneself.

He recalled in his mind the stories he had read of the cathedral – the fiery sermons of Savonarola who seemed so critical of the rising humanism of the city – and the assassination of Giuliano de' Medici and Lorenzo the Magnificent's near death in the so-called Pazzi conspiracy.

They left the cathedral and walked through the busy pedestrian zone of the historical center to the Uffizi gallery, the most important collection of Renaissance art in the world. They stood in a long line and finally began to snake their way through the small gallery rooms crammed with tourists. Oliver had always wanted to see Botticelli's "Birth of Venus" and the "Primvera" and wasn't disappointed when he stood in front of the graceful figures in diaphanous dress. He leaned toward George and whispered, "Do you come here often just to gaze at these masterpieces?"

"Not often enough. They are amazing, though, right?"

"I assume you've been to the Vatican Museums. How do you think these compare to Raphael's rooms?"

Steve had picked up on their quiet exchange and interjected, "I tend to prefer Raphael's colors to Botticelli's. And Raphael definitely has more of a homoerotic bend, if you know what I mean."

George nodded and Oliver turned back to Botticelli's "Primavera" to soak in all its features.

They finished wandering through the Uffizi and grabbed a light sandwich in the museum cafeteria before heading back across town to see the Accademia where Michelangelo's "David" was located. The line was thankfully short, and they entered through the hall of the captives, four large male pieces that Michelangelo had begun for Pope Julius II's tomb. They showcased Michelangelo's emerging talent and style, muscular bodies twisting under the weight of architectural pieces they were intended to hold up.

As they entered the hall where the David is displayed, Oliver exclaimed, "Oh My God," grabbing George's arms as he stood mouth agape in front of the soaring Biblical figure. They walked up to the 17-foot sculpture standing on top of a pedestal and set within a sky lit apse. The poise and grace of David suggested the confidence of the Florentines in the face of other more powerful city states and empires and embodied the humanistic idealism of the Renaissance, the perfect form and stature of the human figure.

Oliver discovered that Daniela had a special interest in Renaissance sculpture, and he followed her around the apse as she recounted the history of the block of marble sitting near the cathedral, the commission from the cathedral officials, and the history of the placement of the statue in the main square. Oliver couldn't believe Michelangelo was only 26 when he sculpted the piece. He couldn't help but compare it to the masterpieces of the Belvedere palace at the Vatican, the Laocoon and Apollo.

After finishing their visit, George and Daniela proposed they buy some fruit, cheese, and wine and hike up to the top of the Boboli Gardens to enjoy a snack and look out over the Tuscan countryside. They found a small grocer on the other side of the Arno and entered the gardens. George and Steve walked close together, leaving Daniela and Oliver to talk.

They continued their conversation about sculpture with Daniela suggesting other things to see in Rome. They found a spot high on the hillside overlooking the formal gardens and the countryside and sat on the green grass, opening the bottle of wine and pouring it into some plastic cups.

Daniela leaned back on her elbows, pressing her breasts firmly against the white cotton fabric of her shirt. She sipped her wine with a sensuous flair, tilting her head back and savoring the flavors as they trickled down her throat. Oliver was intrigued by her accent, British and Italian roots peppering her English with melodious tones. He inched up closer to her, reaching for some of the fruit she had peeled and set on a plate near the cheese. As he leaned over her arm, she glanced at him and raised her eyebrow playfully. As he began to return to his position, he paused over her shoulder and tugged playfully at the narrow strap of her shirt with his teeth.

Daniela rolled her shoulder as if to say, 'ahh,' and leaned toward him placing a piece of fruit on his tongue. She remained close to his face, and as he finished sucking the juicy piece of orange, he kissed her.

George glanced discretely toward them and smiled. Steve rested his hand on George's thigh and whispered in his ear, "Looks like they might be hitting it off."

"I'm glad," George whispered back. "He has always seemed reluctant to take any initiative. It's refreshing to see."

Oliver leaned on one of his elbows, facing Daniela and asked, "So how does someone like Michelangelo just appear in time and space?"

"I don't know what you mean?" she replied.

"Well, you have these great ancient sculptors - the ones who did the Laocoon and the Apollo, for example - and then nothing for centuries. Suddenly, Michelangelo appears. It happens during a time when Florence is reviving the Platonic Academy. At 26, with little training, he completes one of the greatest sculptures of all time. How does that happen?"

"He's a genius."

"But what do we mean when we call someone a genius? Where does the information come from that shapes their imagination and creativity? It's not taught or learned. It's something that comes from within."

Daniela nodded; her forehead creased in concentration. "What do you think?" she asked.

"I have always wondered if someone like Michelangelo is evidence of reincarnation. Was he born with lifetimes of experience inside him? Were others reincarnating at the same time – philosophers like Ficino and Pico della Mirandola? Were Lorenzo de' Medici and Pope Julius II politicians who came back at the same time, all of them a group of artists, philosophers, and politicians set to recreate a past age?"

"I've never thought of that, but it makes sense," Daniela said, as she gazed at Oliver's animated face.

Oliver looked off in the distance pensively.

"What's up?" she inquired further.

"Sorry. I was just thinking how ironic it is that I'm asking those questions while I'm meeting my biological father. If reincarnation is true, how does it work? Do we travel through DNA? Is our own DNA an inherited packet of information and experiences? Or do we travel in a more spiritual way, our souls coming into a particular matrix of people, events, and institutions, like Michelangelo in the Renaissance."

"What is the soul?" Daniela said, half sarcastically and half curious about what Oliver might say.

"Good question. We've been conditioned by our scientific age to deny that anything is spiritual. Everything has to be accounted for in a material way. But new research into the structure of the universe is pointing more and more to the notion that the universe is a big hologram."

Daniela looked perplexed. George and Steve looked over their shoulders, intrigued by the conversation.

"A hologram is essentially an interference pattern on a substrate. It is created by different angles of light that intersect – like a wave pattern. The image created can be reproduced or called forth from any piece of the substrate. In other words, if I break a piece of holographic film into mini pieces, each piece includes the entire original image."

"Go on," she said.

"As quantum physicists have shown, everything is both energy and matter. So, an event or person or thought is a wave pattern or energy that gets registered in some universal interference pattern. They even think that's how we store memories in our mind. It's always there, and it can be recalled or brought back into some kind of existence with the right light or energy or imagination."

"So, we are ripples in a universal hologram?"

"That's what some scientists and philosophers say and, curiously, that is what the ancient Vedic texts of the Hindus said," Oliver noted, looking nervously at George and Steve who seemed alarmed at the seriousness of the conversation.

"But going back to your original question, how does that happen?" Daniela inquired again.

"I don't know. I want to say it's in our DNA, that DNA is a form of energy that stores information holographically. But it seems that the reality of our lives is much more than just genetic proteins. It's got to be a constellation of things intersecting energetically, spiritually, interpersonally. I am more than my DNA. I am an event that occurs in interference or interaction with other people and places."

"Whew!" Daniela interjected. "That was a deep conversation.

Have some wine," she said half in jest, pouring a big glass for Oliver and herself and signaling that she was ready to take a break. They took a long sip and looked out over the landscape below them. "Sometimes it's enough to just savor the smell of grass, the feel of the earth, the movement of a gentle breeze, and the flavors of food," she said, breathing in deeply.

"I agree," Oliver said, sipping his wine and taking a small piece of cheese and placing it playfully in Daniela's mouth.

The four of them sat quietly, taking in the view. Daniela and Oliver held hands as they laid on their backs looking up at the majestic pine trees beside them. A little while later, George looked at his watch and said, "Hey Ollie, when's your train?"

"Oh my God. I almost forgot." Oliver glanced at his watch. "It's in an hour."

"Let's go. It will take us a while to walk to the station," George said.

Daniela looked sad. She stood up, holding Oliver's hand. They all began the slow walk back to the Pitti Palace and then across the Ponte Vecchio into town. At the train station, Oliver gave George and Steve hugs and kisses and then turned to Daniela.

"What a pleasant surprise! I enjoyed this afternoon." He kissed her, and she rubbed her hand along his back and down his buttocks.

Oliver extracted himself and then walked down the platform to his train. He boarded the carriage as the conductor whistled to announce the departure. The train pulled slowly out of the station, and he returned to Rome.

7

Chapter Seven

Oliver woke early, his head still spinning from the events of the previous days. He was surprised and a bit skeptical of Henry's about face, but he was willing to give him the benefit of the doubt as long as possible. How often does someone become self-aware in such a quick amount of time after decades of entrenched denial and dishonesty? A ray of hope rested with Henry's love of Renaissance art and the underlying humanism of the Church during that epoch. Maybe Henry had the academic and intellectual background to change. He just needed to feel safe with that change.

It's so easy, he thought, to make choices and decisions that put in motion a pattern or dynamic that is reinforced with time. Henry's reaction to his father's shame and psychological abuse produced a dissociation from himself, a deep and growing distance from his feelings, emotions, dreams, and imagination. Once the dissociation arose, he made compulsive decisions to preserve the distance from information that would challenge his altered state of being. Oliver was still amazed that their meeting had such a profound and rapid impact on Henry.

Oliver began to ask himself, 'What patterns am I setting in place? I don't want to wake up someday like Henry and realize my life has been dishonest. What am I afraid of? What drives my choices and decisions?'

He thought of Daniela and their day together in Florence. He thought of her dark hair, caramel skin, dark brown eyes, and light-heartedness. He thought of her moist lips and the sweet taste of her shoulders as he slid the top part of her shirt down and kissed her. She had been playful and flirtatious and, after the momentous days with Henry, it felt good to just relax, play, and be in the moment. At the station, as they parted, he held her tightly, had run his hands up and down her back, and felt her full firm breasts press up against his chest. But, as he climbed onto the train and began the trek back to Rome, he felt empty. The day had been fun, satisfying, and savory. But he imagined he would have felt something deeper, more endur-ing, a longing to reunite with her as soon as possible, and he didn't. Sure, it would be fun to see her again, and she had a lot of character-istics he liked in a romantic partner, but there was something miss-ing – an aching, a longing, a fire.

He got a text from George: "It was great to see you yesterday. What fun. We have to do it again. BTW – Daniela can't quit talking about you. You made quite an impression."

Oliver texted back: "Yes – lots of fun. Let's get together when you're back in the States this summer. Give Daniela my love."

Oliver felt pressure from his friends to pursue a romantic rela-tionship. They had set him up on several dates. They all seemed like good matches, and Oliver always had a good time. But no one ever clicked the way he thought someone should click when in love.

He wondered if he still felt some ambiguity about his sexuality. He was the poster child of lesbian parents. Should he be the successful, smart, handsome heterosexual – confounding theories that kids raised by same-sex parents will turn out gay? Or should he be the successful, smart, handsome homosexual – raised in a family where sexual orientation is not an issue – but potentially feeding into conservative theories that gay parents create gay kids? He feared both and, as he pondered that, he realized he wasn't that different from Henry – someone making choices and decisions out of fear.

'What's the solution?' he asked himself. 'How do I avoid the default expectations and do what is authentic to me?' How do I know what is me and what is the me others have projected me to be? Am I gay, straight, or bi – or am I afraid to be any of them – frozen in a sea of social categories and expectations? Could I ever get outside of those expectations and, if so, how?'

A text from Henry pinged his phone: "Oliver, I hope your trip to Florence was good. Do you have time for breakfast this morning? I have something I would like to discuss."

Oliver texted back: "Had a good time. Yes, would love to meet you. Why don't you come to my hotel? We'll have breakfast downstairs."

Henry: "Perfect – see you at 9?"

Oliver: "9 is perfect. *Ciao*."

Oliver quickly got up, took a shower, and pulled on some jeans, a light blue polo shirt, and some new sneakers he bought in Florence. He headed downstairs and saw Henry waiting in the lobby, checking messages on his phone.

"Ah, Oliver, you look nice!"

"Thanks. And you look casual. You're out of uniform."

"Although it's Sunday, for us who work in the curia, it's a day off. I look forward to a long walk later today."

"Let's go in. Would you like a cappuccino or espresso?"

"A double espresso would be great."

The server brought them their coffees, and both helped themselves to some pastries and cold cuts from the buffet. Henry looked tense and finished his coffee quickly. He began to rub his hands, something Oliver had grown to appreciate as a sign of anxiousness.

"I have something to share with you."

Oliver could only imagine what other secrets were hidden in his father's closet.

"When my father died, I inherited a great deal of money. I've invested it and, when I moved to Rome, I bought a small apartment. You're my only family, and I'd like to name you the beneficiary of my trust."

"You're kidding," Oliver blurted out, setting down his cup of coffee and looking directly into Henry's eyes.

"No. I've thought about it carefully for the last couple of days. I was always wondering what I would do with my estate as I got older, as I passed, and this makes perfect sense."

"But don't you take a vow of poverty or something like that?"

"Monks do, but diocesan priests don't. We can own property and have a right to dispose of it as we see fit."

"Interesting," Oliver remarked, rubbing his chin. "Unbelievable. That's too generous."

"It only seems fitting."

"But still. Couldn't you donate it to a good cause or something?"

"You're a good cause."

"Hmm," Oliver said, pondering what Henry had just said.

"And," Henry began hesitatingly, "I would like to ask a favor from you."

Oliver looked stoically at Henry, realizing perhaps there was a catch.

"Could we stay in touch? I'm not asking that we become a family or that I substitute for your mothers. It would just be nice to be in touch with you and see you from time to time."

Oliver looked down at the table, deep in thought. He was concerned about what his mothers might think about such an arrangement and didn't want to do anything to hurt them. "Let me give it some thought. I need to think about my moms and their comfort with this."

"I understand. In fact, I have come to expect that kind of thoughtfulness from you. You're remarkable. The naming of you beneficiary has no condition placed on it. We can shake hands today and never see each other again, and you will still inherit my estate. But I would hope this might be the beginning of some interaction in the future."

"I think that would be nice."

"I took the liberty of booking an off-hours appointment with my financial advisor. He works at a bank here in town but has agreed to meet us to draft paperwork and make this official."

"Sure. That's okay with me. What did you have in mind?"

"He has an apartment not far from here. He said we could come to his place and meet in his office there."

"I don't have any other plans at the moment."

"Perfect. Let me text him."

Oliver finished his breakfast and waited for Henry to finish arranging things with his advisor. Henry looked over and said, "He can meet us in an hour. Would that work for you?"

"Sure. Where does he live?"

"Nearby – just over the river in Trastevere."

"Do we walk?"

"Yes. It's a nice walk, and I can point out some historical sites to you."

"Perfect. Let me clean up a bit, and I'll meet you back down here in the lobby."

Oliver went to his room, freshened up, and then met Henry downstairs. They headed across town, passing the Campo dei Fiori, a fresh produce market. The medieval square was filled with mounds of vegetables, greens, fruit, and freshly butchered rabbits, lambs, and piglets hanging from hooks. The cobblestone pavement was darkened by discarded pieces of produce, and the air smelled ripe. They squeezed through the crowd, passing into a quieter piazza nearby.

They approached the Tiber River and walked over a narrow cobblestone footbridge, the Ponte Sisto, with a view of the Tiber Island just downstream. The swiftly running emerald water split around the island, cascading over rocks, and passing under an old Roman bridge that had collapsed centuries before. The island had been a healing sanctuary in ancient times, and in the medieval era, monks founded a hospital that was still treating patients.

On the other side of the river, they descended into a dense neighborhood of old apartment buildings in a zone of the city that had always been home to immigrants. Henry noted that artists had begun to transform old spaces into lofts, studios, and galleries. Oliver read between the lines and, as he saw a few gay flags hanging from balconies, realized the neighborhood had a significant gay population.

They followed a maze of small streets and passageways. Henry glanced down at his phone from time to time and then stopped, held it up and said, "This must be it – 37A. I'll ring the bell."

A male voice answered, "Sì – pronto?"

"Sono io – Enrico – siamo arrivati."

"Come up!"

The door buzzed open, and Henry and Oliver began to climb a narrow marble staircase to the third floor. Oliver looked up and saw a man leaning over the interior railing. When they arrived at the landing the young man extended his hand to Henry and said, "Benvenuto – welcome."

"Giancarlo, questo e' Oliver. Oliver, Giancarlo." Oliver and Giancarlo extended their hands to each other and, in unison said, "*Piacere.*"

Oliver had expected to meet an older person, a frail accountant wearing a loose-fitting yellowed suit, glasses, and perhaps a felt hat. Instead, Giancarlo couldn't have been older than thirty. He was athletic with muscular biceps and chest pressing against a tight-fitting pullover, upper legs and buttocks that filled his slim jeans, and broad shoulders. He was tall for an Italian and had dark tousled hair. He hadn't shaved so he had a dark stubble of a beard lining his jaw, chin, and circling his mouth.

"This is your financial advisor?" he inquired incredulously under his breath.

Henry nodded and smiled, realizing Oliver had expected someone older.

Giancarlo waved them into his apartment. It was more spacious than Oliver had anticipated from the walk up. The door opened to a parlor that stretched the length of the building, opening to a spacious terrace overlooking a green oasis with trees, flowers, and a splashing fountain below. The parlor was decorated with classic furniture - oak chests, large wooden upholstered chairs, and dark red and blue Persian carpets.

Giancarlo led them through the room and walked them out onto the deck where the late morning light filtered through mature trees onto the terra cotta pots filled with bright red geraniums.

"This is amazing," Oliver said surveying the green courtyard and looking back into the parlor.

"I'm very fortunate. This belonged to my grandparents at one time. Let me show you the rest of the place."

They walked past a dining room and a compact but fully appointed kitchen to a staircase inside the front door that led to an upper-level bedroom, bath, and study. "This had been another bedroom," Giancarlo remarked as he pointed into the study that included an antique Chinese desk and three bookcases, "but I've made it into an office where I can work remotely."

"Looks like you have a nice collection of books," Oliver noted as he walked toward the shelves to see what titles he could make out.

"Like Fr. Henry, I'm fascinated with Renaissance art and history. Most of these are manuscripts about Rome during that epoch."

Henry walked up next to Oliver and ran his fingers over the bindings. "Ah, I've actually been looking for this book," he said as he turned to Giancarlo holding a maroon bound book in his hands. "Where did you find it?"

"The usual – Franco's shop."

"Ah, yes. Franco. I wonder where he gets his merchandise. He always seems to have surprising things available."

Oliver noted the camaraderie between Henry and Giancarlo and wondered if there might not be more there than a professional client relationship. He gazed at his father again, wondering if he might discover more secrets that were just below the surface.

"Well, Giancarlo, we don't want to delay you more than necessary. As I mentioned, I would like to name Oliver the beneficiary of my trust."

"Yes, you mentioned that. It shouldn't be a complicated process. I have a copy of your original trust. I can draft the paperwork, and I can have you both sign the documents. I'll file them with the courts."

"That would be great. What kind of information would you need?" Henry continued.

"I need Oliver's date of birth, marital status, and contact information. It's not necessary, but some indication of the relationship between you two would be helpful, avoiding any complications later."

Henry looked at Oliver inquisitively. Giancarlo noticed their reticence and said, "Do you need a moment to confer?"

Henry nodded.

Giancarlo left the office, closed the door, and Henry began, "I had initially thought to identify you as my nephew or even godchild, but I'm nervous that if we are dishonest, someone could contest my estate in the future. But I can't admit that you are my son on a document like this. It is too risky."

"I understand. Why don't we just leave it blank. Giancarlo said it isn't required."

"I'm thinking the same. Maybe in the future we can amend it."

Oliver nodded but then inquired, "Does Giancarlo know about you and me?"

"I haven't said anything to him. Romans are used to all sorts of unusual relationships. If you lived in Rome, he would think something sordid. Since you live in the States, he's probably suspicious that you're a nephew or, maybe worse, an illegitimate son."

Oliver raised his eyebrows at the word illegitimate and then asked, "Then what's the problem?"

"As long as it's unnamed, no one can use it against me or you."

Oliver looked askance at Henry.

They walked out into the hallway, and Giancarlo came out from his room. "Let's leave the information about our relationship blank. Oliver prefers to keep it discreet."

"That's fine, Fr. Henry. As you are not married, there's no legal preferred beneficiary. You are free to name whomever."

"Perfect. When might you be able to draft the paperwork?"

"When are you headed back to the States, Oliver?"

"In a few days."

"I could do the paperwork today and bring it to your hotel to sign later this evening. Fr. Henry can sign later in the week with a notary."

Henry and Oliver both nodded. "I'm at the Hotel Santa Chiara. Should we set a time?"

"Is 6:30 good? You could do some sightseeing or whatever. We could sign the papers later."

"That's very kind of you," Henry noted. "I can pass by the bank during the week."

There was an awkward pause and silence as Oliver and Giancarlo waited for direction from Henry. He then said, "I've got some things I need to do today. Why don't I walk Oliver back to the hotel and leave you?" he said to Giancarlo.

He nodded and extended his hand to Oliver and looking intensely into his eyes said, "It was a pleasure to meet you. I'll see you later."

Oliver felt the intensity of Giancarlo's glance. It threw him off balance. He stumbled for words, "I ... well, I will be at the hotel ... yes, at 6:30."

Henry looked over at Oliver, noticing his unease. He looked at Giancarlo and detected the intensity of the moment. It alarmed him.

He and Oliver left abruptly and headed down the stairs and out onto the narrow cobblestone street. They returned to the hotel where Henry hugged his son goodbye and said, "I hope we can meet before you leave."

"I should hope so, too."

Henry walked away, and Oliver went to his room to get his guidebook to explore more of Rome.

At 6:30 he went to the lobby of the hotel to wait for Giancarlo. A few minutes later, he appeared in the doorway. He spotted Oliver and waved with a smile.

It was a warm evening. Giancarlo was wearing shorts, a long-sleeve linen shirt with the arms rolled back and the top buttons loose. He had on a pair of grey leather sneakers. Oliver found himself glancing down at Giancarlo's legs, muscular, dark, and hairy.

Giancarlo walked toward Oliver; his eyes fixed on Oliver's blue eyes. He extended his hand and took Oliver's firmly. "Good to see you again. Did you have a nice afternoon?"

"Yes. I went to the Palazzo Altemps. It was a surprising gem of a museum."

"Yes, it's often overlooked. You don't seem to be an ordinary tourist."

Oliver blushed. "I don't know about that. This is my first visit to Rome and to Europe."

"You're kidding!" Giancarlo said with surprise.

"No, it really is my first time."

Giancarlo stepped back slightly and looked at Oliver. Oliver's skin had tanned since he arrived, making his blonde hair even more pronounced. He had changed to a blue pullover and had slipped on some dark jeans. He had brilliant blue eyes and, for a moment Giancarlo thought he recognized Henry's eyes. There was something in the way Oliver held his head, the breadth of his shoulders, and the sophistication of his movements that reminded him of Henry. Giancarlo furrowed his forehead contemplating the idea then said, "You seem so at home here – like you are a native – not like a typical American college student."

"Thanks. It's been eye opening. I'd prefer to blend in, but I feel so conspicuous."

"If Fr. Henry hadn't told me you were visiting, I would have thought you had been living here."

Oliver smiled then said, "Can I offer you a drink or some coffee?"

"Let's have you sign these papers then I'll take you up on a drink."

Giancarlo opened a folder, laid some documents out on a table, and gave Oliver a pen. "Here's the main place to sign and date. You just have to initial these pages. Make sure your birth date and address are correct."

"It all looks good," he replied, signing and initialing the pages. "I still can't believe Henry's doing this."

Giancarlo looked at Oliver, hoping there might be more information disclosed. Oliver felt the under-the-surface curiosity, but he was hesitant to disclose anything more. He thought Henry and Giancarlo must know each other well, but it was clear Henry didn't want to disclose their relationship to Giancarlo.

Giancarlo said, "Thanks. This all looks good. I'll make copies after Fr. Henry has signed and notarized them, and I will mail them to you in the States."

Giancarlo collected the documents and slid them into the folder. Then he said, "So, what about that drink?"

"Yes. Do you have any suggestions?"

"I know a little wine bar not too far from here. They serve appetizers and a nice selection of wine. They have tables outside. There's always a nice crowd there, too. Lots of fun."

"Sounds great. Lead the way."

Giancarlo slipped the folder into his shoulder bag and said, "*Andiamo.*"

They walked out of the hotel, took a right turn and then meandered along several small roads or pedestrian areas until they entered a triangular square where a number of small establishments had taken over the pavement and had erected platforms with small candle-lit tables spread over the decks. At one of the wine bars, a young waiter recognized Giancarlo and waved them toward a free table.

"Is this okay?" Giancarlo asked Oliver as he nodded to the waiter.

"It looks great. I didn't know any of this was here."

"Yes, over the years Rome has begun to develop these charming little wine bars. The young people love them."

"I can see why," Oliver noted as he looked at the young crowd assembled at the adjacent tables. Most were couples, and many were same-sex couples. Oliver wondered if this was a gay bar or at least gay-friendly bar. He took another look at Giancarlo and thought, 'Hmmm, maybe he's gay.'

Giancarlo was looking around and spotted two male friends a few tables away. They nodded at each other and took a long look at Oliver. The waiter approached. He was tall, lean, and young – not more than twenty-five. He had a cute face – round button nose and dimples. He smiled warmly at Giancarlo and asked, "*che desiderate* – what do you desire/want?"

Oliver couldn't help picking up on the double meaning of the phrase even with his rustic Italian. He looked up at the waiter who, at that moment, winked at him.

Giancarlo reached over, placed his right hand on Oliver's and leaned over the menu pointing at a Sicilian Nero d'Avola. "This is quite nice. Should I get us a bottle?"

At first Oliver thought a bottle was excessive and wanted to protest but, when he saw the cost – only the equivalent of 15 US dollars - he decided to go with the flow. "And how about some pro-sciutto and formaggio?"

"*Va bene*," Oliver responded, trying to use the little Italian he had begun to pick up. He realized Giancarlo hadn't retrieved his hand yet, a gesture he originally chalked up as Italian tactility but now wondered if it might be more. He shifted in his chair, finding a subtle way to extract his hand from under Giancarlo's.

The waiter nodded as Giancarlo specified what they wanted and retreated to the kitchen. Oliver continued, "So, do you come here often?"

"Yes, it's a nice casual place to gather with friends. It's not far from my office and on my way home."

"So, you work in the bank?"

"Yes, I'm a financial advisor. That's how I know Fr. Henry. By the way, what do you do?"

"I'm still a student, but I'm studying to be a financial advisor, too."

Giancarlo beamed a big smile. "What a coincidence."

"Yes, indeed," Oliver continued. "I still have a year or two more of school."

"You seem more mature, older than that."

Oliver blushed. He was often told that, and he wasn't sure what to make of it.

The waiter returned, opened the bottle of wine, and poured each a glass. A woman came out at the same time with their prosciutto and cheese. "*Salute*," Giancarlo proposed as he raised his glass.

Oliver raised his in unison and took a sip, letting the velvety red liquid swirl in his mouth. "Hmmm, good choice with the wine."

Giancarlo looked over his glass at Oliver, his face bathed in the late afternoon sun.

"So," he began, "this is your first trip to Rome. What is the occasion?"

Oliver was instantly alarmed, and his hesitation was not lost on Giancarlo. "Hmmm, I had some friends who were here on a semester abroad and wanted me to meet them."

"And how do you know Fr. Henry?"

"He's an old family friend," Oliver said, avoiding any specification of the relationship.

"So, you're family?" Giancarlo pressed.

"Yes," Oliver said, "distant."

"He's a nice man," Giancarlo added. "I've had the privilege of working with him for the past several years."

"And your parents – what do they do?" Giancarlo continued his slow investigation.

"They're managers – for pharmaceutical companies."

"Both your mom and your dad?"

Oliver was now at that moment where the truth of his family was either concealed or revealed, where shame or pride stepped in. He liked Giancarlo, and he wanted to protect Henry, but he was feeling increasingly guilty as he stepped deeper and deeper into Henry's life and further and further away from his own. He decided to be open, "My ma and my mom – yes both."

Giancarlo raised his eyebrows and smiled, a smile of satisfaction as he realized he was onto the scent of Oliver and Henry. "Oh, sorry, I shouldn't have presumed."

"No, it's quite alright. It's still rather unique – even in the States."

"It's even more unique here," Giancarlo began and then strategically added, "It's too bad that Italy is so uncomfortable with diverse families and diverse sexualities."

Oliver decided to deflect attention as long as he could, so he launched into a philosophical rather than personal line of conversation, "So, it's difficult here? I wasn't aware."

"Well, the Church is pretty conservative, and the Church has a lot of sway over local culture. Fr. Henry is no exception. He works for a Congregation that continues to harass gay teachers. How is he with your family?" Giancarlo continued to press, returning the conversation to personal matters.

'He's good,' Oliver thought to himself of Giancarlo's persistence. "Well, he was uncomfortable at first, but he seems to be coming around," Oliver explained.

"I'm glad to hear. I wouldn't have expected it from him," Giancarlo continued. "It's hard for us."

Oliver gulped. Either Giancarlo had just come out or he was making a cryptic remark about his and Henry's philosophical differences. He decided to ask for clarification, "You mean you and Henry?"

"Well, yes – Henry and I have our philosophical differences, but we don't broach them. Our relationship is purely professional aside from a mutual interest in Renaissance art and history. What I meant by it's hard for us is - that for someone like me – in Italy – things are challenging."

"Ahh," Oliver said, "sorry I was so dense."

"No need for apologies. You're being very respectful. Italians like that. They like to leave things ambiguous. It's a kind of don't ask don't tell sort of ethic. But it comes at a cost."

"Yes, I can imagine. I often feel the same way about my family. Do I self-disclose, or do I keep things vague and concealed?"

"It must be easier in the States."

"It is, or at least I imagine it is. It's easier being gay, too."

"Yes, I can imagine."

"So, when did you come out?"

"I haven't really. I mean I have to my friends," he said as he glanced at the couple a few tables over. "But I'm not out at work."

"I guess the banking and financial world are rather traditional."

"Very, and I don't want to lose clients."

"That's too bad."

"And you, do you have a special someone?" Giancarlo finally broached the topic, using gender neutral language.

"Not at the moment," Oliver answered evasively at first. Then the words came to him, "I'm in flux," he said, embracing the uncertainty of his own identity.

Giancarlo nodded and smiled warmly. Then, from Oliver's vantage, Giancarlo said something very insightful, "I imagine it is as challenging making sense of your sexuality in a same-gender family as it would be in a heterosexual one. There are expectations and presumptions and, even in a welcoming environment, it can't be easy."

"I've never had anyone articulate what you just said quite so well. It's not so much that I would be ashamed of being gay or straight – it's that if I end up gay, I feel people will think it was because of my moms. If I end of straight, I feel others will think I'm just trying to distance myself from my parents' orientation. I just want to be me.

I guess no matter what kind of family you're raised in, our identities – not just sexual but also personal – are a challenging process."

"Yes. My father was very exacting. He would have rejected my sexuality but would have been even more critical of my liberal political and social leanings."

"Was? Has he passed?"

"Yes, a year ago, from cancer."

"I'm sorry," Oliver said, taking a sip of wine then resting his hand just next to Giancarlo's – not touching - but close enough to feel heat emanating from Giancarlo's hand.

"And yours – do you know your biological father?" Giancarlo continued, reaching for a slice of formaggio, gently grazing Oliver's hand.

Oliver froze. Giancarlo noticed the hesitation and alarm. Again, he wondered if there was a relationship between Henry and Oliver. "I'm sorry, Oliver, I didn't mean to pry. Please, don't feel like you have to answer the question. I have no right to inquire into your personal life."

"It's okay," Oliver began. He was feeling more comfortable with Giancarlo. However, he still wasn't sure it was okay to disclose his relationship with Henry, so he said, "I'm in the process of finding out who he is."

"Ah," Giancarlo said, sensing something concealed in Oliver's response. "Let's talk about more pleasant things. What do you think of Rome?"

Oliver was relieved at the reprieve and began, "The city has been much more impressive than I had imagined – from the historical monuments to the dense urban life – like this," as he glanced around the bar.

"It is a special city. I grew up here, right in the city. I love it."

"I can tell. It's written all over your face."

"I have an idea. Why don't we get some dinner, and I'll take you on a walk to see some other sites?"

Oliver looked apologetic at first and said, "I don't want to take up your time."

"It's no bother. I like talking with you and would love to show you around."

Oliver nodded. "Sure, why not?"

Giancarlo waived down the waiter, paid the check, and they stepped out onto the street. Giancarlo looked right and left and then said, "This way."

8

Chapter Eight

Giancarlo led them down a narrow road, passing restaurants and small boutique shops. He passed a small broken statue propped up against a wall.

"This is Pasquino, a statue from the Middle Ages – or actually an ancient statue found in the Middle Ages," he began. "They found him in an excavation. He was too ugly and broken to include in any private collection, so he was left on the street. Over the centuries, he has been a sort of spokesman, someone who can say things no one else can. People post pasquinades or sayings on him, essentially town gossip. Many a pope, priest, or noble was defamed by Pasquino."

Oliver nodded. "I think I read about him. It looks like he's still being used that way," as he pointed to some bright colored pieces of paper taped to Pasquino's chest."

"Yes, Rome still likes its gossip."

They continued down the road, passing restaurants filled with people sitting under festive lights strung between poles, sipping wine, eating pizza, and gesturing to one another as they spoke.

"So, in Italy it looks like you have to learn more than Italian to communicate. There's a whole repertoire of gestures that are required as well, right?" Oliver inquired playfully.

"I don't know what you mean," Giancarlo said as he raised both hands in a sign of bewilderment and tilted his head back.

Oliver pointed at him. "See – there's another!"

"Be careful when you point. If you see this," Giancarlo noted as he pointed his index and little finger toward a wall with the other fingers curled underneath, "it's the *malocchio* – a curse."

Oliver chuckled.

"Or this," Giancarlo continued, biting his hand held horizontal in front of his face.

"What does that mean?"

"I think in English you say, 'bite me.'" Giancarlo suggested. "It's a gesture of frustration and rebuke."

They laughed. They dead ended into another street lined with antique shops and art galleries. Most were closed for the evening, but Oliver could see inside the windows. They looked like still life paintings; priceless art objects placed on dark cloth covered tables under spotlights.

"This is one of my favorite streets," Giancarlo said.

"I can see," he said, noticing Giancarlo's broadened smile as they passed several prominent shops. "I noticed the nice furniture in your apartment. Did some of the pieces come from here?" Oliver said as he stopped in front of one of the shops pointing to an antique desk, like Giancarlo's.

"Some, yes. But my grandparents had been collectors, and much of the furniture was theirs."

"You must miss them and your parents?"

"Very much."

"Do you have any siblings or cousins?"

"I have a sister and lots of cousins."

"Is your sister in Rome?

"No, she is a lawyer in Milan. She's very successful. I don't see her often."

"And your cousins?"

"I see them more often. They are all here in Rome."

They began to approach the embankments of the Tiber River. They continued to follow the small lane and a large modern monument appeared in the near distance. "What's that?" Oliver inquired, surprised by the modern architecture.

"That's a new building that houses the Ara Pacis, Augustus's Altar of Peace."

"What's the Ara Pacis?"

"It is perhaps one of the most important monuments we have from the first century. It was built after Augustus's death to celebrate the peace and stability he had established in the 1st century. It includes incredible carvings of the emperor's household going to offer sacrifice. Since these were not idealized portraits but actual representations, it is the closest thing we have to a photograph of them. In the past, the altar had been broken apart and taken to museums around the world. Eventually the pieces were reassembled and placed in this special exhibition hall built just opposite Augustus's mausoleum."

"Can we see the altar?"

"Certainly – let's walk up these steps," Giancarlo said, as he led Oliver up the marble steps to the glass wall behind which the monument stood. The soft spotlights on the piece created a mystical glow in the evening light. Oliver stood at the window mesmerized.

"And, over there, is Augustus's tomb," Giancarlo added, pointing to a circular mausoleum of brick topped with trees. "It is being renovated now. It is the same style as Hadrian's tomb over which the Castel Sant'Angelo was built."

"Ahh, yes, I see. And this wall?"

"That's the Res Gestae – the declaration of the great deeds of Augustus – a kind of Gospel of Augustus, you might say. Some think the Christian Gospels were deliberate attempts to compare and contrast Jesus with Augustus, the Emperor who created the Pax Romana and Jesus who, the Christians claimed, brought the true peace, the peace of God. Of course, both Augustus and Jesus were described as sons of God and appointed to bring about a new golden age. It's fascinating."

"Indeed," Oliver said, his mouth agape. "How did you learn all of this?"

"Well, my father insisted that I get a liberal arts education. He said you can always learn finance and numbers but education in the humanities is critical to becoming a well-rounded human being."

"That was very visionary of him."

"One would have thought," Giancarlo said, "but he wasn't exactly the most warm or big-hearted man."

"I'm sorry."

"It's okay. I've made my peace," Giancarlo said with a bit of chagrin. Then he continued, "It sounds like your moms are really great."

"They are. They are very progressive, visionary, and forward thinking. They have been great role models for me. I'm lucky to have been raised by them."

"Did you ever get teased in school for having two moms?"

"A little - although we grew up on a city where being raised in a non-traditional family was more common. I had a lot of friends raised by two moms or two dads."

Giancarlo smiled and then said, "Let me show you one more thing, and then I promise we'll eat."

Oliver smiled, "I'm enjoying this. No hurry."

Giancarlo led him a bit farther down the narrow roadway and entered a large square. It was circular with a large obelisk in the center. The square was surrounded by a steep hill on one side, a large gate on another, and then twin churches and twin roadways leading away from the square on the far side.

"This is Piazza del Popolo. It was the main square welcoming people who arrived from the north. The ancient Via Flaminia passed through the gates here and then continued straight to the Capitoline Hill. The obelisk was placed here by Sixtus the V to create markers for pilgrims. There's one here, there's one further up the hill. Wherever you go in Rome, there are obelisks that serve as markers – so people wouldn't need maps. They could just look up and follow the routes pointed by the obelisks."

"That's very cool."

Giancarlo nodded and then said, "Let's head down this way. There's a great little restaurant. I'm sure you'll love the food."

Giancarlo took Oliver's hand and led him down a small pedestrian path to a small tavern-like trattoria. Oliver liked the feel of Giancarlo's hand and the security he felt being held and led by him. They approached a small doorway with a lamp hanging over a menu and a few potted geraniums. Giancarlo pushed through the door and pulled Oliver in behind him.

The interior was a small intimate dining area that opened to a courtyard where tables were spaced around a small fountain. "Outside or in?" Giancarlo asked Oliver.

"Outside. We don't get to eat outside too often in Boston."

Giancarlo approached the maître d' who he obviously knew. "*Buona sera, Bruno.*" They kissed each other's cheeks.

"*Ciao, Giancarlo.*"

"*Bruno, questo e' Oliver – dagli Stati Uniti.*"

"It's a pleasure," Bruno said in English.

"*C'e uno tavolo a parte – uno piu tranquilo?*"

"*Certo, Giancarlo. Qualsiasi cosa per te, caro!*"

Bruno winked at Giancarlo and showed them a small quiet table at the edge of the courtyard. "Is this good?" Giancarlo inquired of Oliver.

"Great," he said. The courtyard was surrounded by old stone buildings covered in vines. There were ten or so tables spaced far apart and already filled with couples leaning over candlelight, sipping wine, and chatting quietly. Each table was covered in a starched white linen tablecloth and the waiters wore black aprons over white dress shirts and bow ties. It was a classy place, and Oliver felt apprehensive.

They sat. Giancarlo unfolded his napkin and ceremoniously placed it on his lap. Oliver did the same, conscious of the need to carefully follow protocol. He was in a foreign country with a financial advisor in a small restaurant and mistakes would be easy to spot.

Bruno brought them menus and bottled water. Giancarlo asked for a special bottle of wine and looked over at Oliver and smiled warmly.

Oliver began to relax. He gazed at Giancarlo as he opened the menu. He had a gentleness to him that was surprising given his tall muscular frame. His deep-set brown eyes were warm and inviting as he glanced up over the top of the menu and said, "The saltimbocca is exceptional, here. Do you know it?"

"No. Unfortunately, I'm not very well versed in Italian cuisine."

"Saltimbocca is a veal dish sautéed in a sweet wine with prosciutto and sage. It's nice with spinach and roast potatoes."

"Sounds delicious. What about pasta?"

Giancarlo set the menu down on the table and smiled affectionately, pointing his index figure up as if to make a point. "Well in Rome, you usually have a little pasta as an appetizer. The meat is the main course. It's not like in the States where you get served a huge bowl of pasta as your main course."

"It sounds more civilized. I'm eager to try whatever you suggest."

Giancarlo smiled. There was an innocence to Oliver that he

found enchanting. He was young, curious, and eager to soak up new information and new experiences.

Bruno brought the wine, uncorked it, and poured the dark ruby liquid into their glasses. "This is a Brunello di Montalcino – a nice heavier red wine from Tuscany. I hope you like it."

Oliver swirled the wine in the glass, sniffed it, and then took a sip. "Very nice," he said. "It has an earthy taste to it – a hint of mineral. It is fuller bodied than most reds I've tasted in the past, and it has a nice hint of cherry flavor."

"I'm glad you like it. It's one of my favorites."

Giancarlo paused and looked affectionately at Oliver whose face was bathed in the glow of the candle on their table and the ambient light from the strung pendants stretched between two walls. "You're very sophisticated for your age," he noted. "You mothers must have exposed you to a lot of nice things as you grew up."

"I had a good life, no doubt. But my moms were rather frugal. There were no extravagances or indulgences. I like to read. I think I picked up a lot of things as I traveled in my mind."

"It seems like it comes natural to you."

"Perhaps it does, although I think of myself as awkward, as always feeling things are tentative."

"What do you mean?"

"I don't feel certain of myself or of the path I'm on," Oliver tried to explain.

"Who does?"

"You seem like you do."

"I wasn't always like that."

"What happened?" Oliver pressed.

"I think it was the death of my father that created a new sense of urgency – that I have to become myself. I can't be what someone else wants me to be since that person is no longer around."

"Did his death create space for you, a certain freedom from the fear of disappointing him?" Oliver inquired with a rare psychological observation for someone his age.

"Yes, but more importantly, I couldn't blame him anymore for my unhappiness. Life was in my hands. Happiness was mine to create or destroy. No one else could be blamed."

Oliver began to think about what Giancarlo was saying and realized that his moms had never put pressure on him to make them happy. They were paradigms of encouraging their son to pursue his own dreams and constitute his own happiness. "But," Oliver began timidly, "what if you don't have anyone to blame and you still can't be definitive?"

Giancarlo looked at Oliver and detected his dilemma, a young person haunted not by an abusive or overbearing parent but by the demons inside, the fear of disappointing himself. He said, "There are still the internalized expectations our society casts on us and sometimes we don't even recognize them. They feel like voices in our head, our own voices."

Oliver nodded thoughtfully, recognizing that Giancarlo had uncovered his dilemma, and his eyes began to water. "I'm sorry," he apologized as he rubbed tears from his eyes, not knowing why he was becoming emotional.

"It's nothing to be ashamed of," Giancarlo said as he put his hand on top of Oliver's. "You're in Italy. It's a place where we encourage the expression of emotions!"

Oliver chuckled. "I know, but it's still embarrassing."

"Why?"

"I just met you, and I'm tearing up. That's ridiculous."

"Maybe you just feel comfortable. I'm glad you do."

Oliver looked over at Giancarlo and felt an intense longing – something he had never felt for anyone else before. His pulse raced and he felt a stirring deep within. His heart pounded. He was conscious of his own breathing, almost as if time were standing still, and he looked down at Giancarlo's hand resting protectively over his own.

Giancarlo was speaking, but Oliver didn't hear any sound. He explored his face, the deep brown eyes, the dark lashes, the stubble around his mouth. His lips were full, and he had small dimples that deepened as he spoke. Through the thin linen shirt, he detected the dark contours of his hairy chest, rising and falling as he breathed. He observed his broad shoulders and the strong muscular arms reaching across the table, one of them resting on his hand.

He realized, for the first time, that perhaps he was gay. It wasn't a hit-you-across-the head kind of recognition. It was a gentle and subtle sense of a shift, a relaxing of the defensive walls he had erected around his sexuality. He no longer felt that he had to play the part of the enlightened strait kid who grew up in a gay family. He could be the gay kid who grew up with gay parents. That was okay. He felt a sense of relief.

He began to say the words in his head – 'you're falling for someone – a man – you're gay – that's okay.' It was hard to hear them, to feel them, to register them against the chatter in his head, the rules and norms that raced through his mind. When he was with his friends, he played the part, memorized the script, and paired off with the beautiful and playful girls. It was only now that he recalled more vividly the furtive glances at his male companions, the admiration of their physiques, the mimicking of their gestures, and the longing for their companionship.

He continued to gaze at Giancarlo. He was surprised at how comfortable it felt sharing thoughts and emotions with him, and it made him nervous. He had just met him and wondered how it was possible to feel so comfortable with someone so quickly. Perhaps it was because he was a stranger that he could let his guard down. He wouldn't have to face him in the neighborhood, at school, or at parties. This was a unique moment in time, an opportunity to open the secret door. No one would have to notice it had been opened. If needed, he could close and secure it before he returned to Boston. But as he stared across the table, he felt the swirl of impressions – an imposing and intense masculinity. He was gentle, compassionate, warm, and thoughtful. Yes, he could close the secret door before returning to Boston but, at this moment, he wanted it to be fully open.

In his mind, Oliver began to imagine making love to Giancarlo. He felt himself get hard as he pictured ripping off his tight-fitting shirt, caressing his muscular chest, and breathing in the moistness of his mouth as he kissed him. The thoughts were new but not alien. His heart began to pound even more heavily, and he felt his skin become moist and flush.

Bruno brought out two plates of carbonara, a classic Roman dish of pancetta, egg, and pecorino romano cheese. Giancarlo removed his hand from Oliver's and picked up his fork, twirling the spaghetti skillfully and lifting it to his mouth. Oliver watched Giancarlo carefully, and he dipped his own fork into the egg coated noodles. Giancarlo rested his arm on the side of the table and waited for Oliver to take his first bite. Oliver smiled as the silky sauce awakened his taste buds and slowly slid down his throat.

"It's good, isn't it?" Giancarlo inquired.

Oliver nodded, "It's delicious. I've never tasted anything like this before. It's creamy but has a little crunch with the pancetta. It's salty but smooth. The spaghetti gives it body, and the cheese keeps it velvety."

"I'm glad I could initiate you," Giancarlo said as he twirled another fork full of pasta and lifted it to his lips.

Oliver wondered if there was a double meaning in Giancarlo's remark, and he blushed.

Giancarlo noticed and, with only a slight hesitation, leaned over the table and said, "You're very handsome, you know."

Oliver could have melted in place. He felt a flutter in his stomach and his legs grew weak. "So are you," he said quickly in return, as if the words had been sitting on his tongue ready to blurt out.

It was now time for Giancarlo to blush. "This is turning out to be a very surprising evening," he said looking tenderly at Oliver.

"Agreed," Oliver said in return. He took another forkful of the carbonara and lifted it to his mouth. The texture and flavor of the eggs, cheese, and crunchy pancetta were heavenly, but the candle-light, the robust wine, and the warm exchange with Giancarlo felt like a wave of sensations washing over him.

They continued to eat their carbonara, looking at each other quietly, awkwardly. Then Giancarlo carefully posed the following question, "What did you mean earlier today when you said your sit-uation was in flux?"

Oliver paused, looked off in the distance and then looked back at Giancarlo and said, "That I wasn't sure of my sexuality, that I was trying to figure things out."

"And?" Giancarlo pressed, waiting for him to explain further.

"Well, it doesn't seem to be as much of a question now," Oliver said with a sheepish smile.

"Hmmm. I thought that might be the case. And – do you have a boyfriend or a girlfriend?" Giancarlo asked.

"No. Nothing has ever clicked," Oliver said. He then paused and with perfect timing said, "Until now."

Giancarlo looked incredulous, even a bit frightened. All day Oliver thought to himself how aristocratic and self-assured Gian-carlo appeared – the high cheek bones, the solid jaw, the dark thick tousled hair, and the graceful mannerisms. Now he looked vulnera-ble.

There was a quiet pause and Oliver felt himself take the initia-tive. He said, "And you?"

Two words came out of Giancarlo's lips, two words spoken solemnly and definitively, "The same."

Both stared at each other in an extended reverent silence, neither wanting to disturb the delicate gift laid out before them. They finished their pasta, and Bruno came to retrieve their plates. He could sense the intense energy between them and quietly took them and walked away without a word.

Giancarlo poured wine into their glasses and asked pensively, "When do you have to go back to Boston? Can you stay awhile?"

"I'm supposed to go back in two days."

Giancarlo looked alarmed. Oliver noticed and continued, "I do have an option to delay the flight."

Giancarlo relaxed. "Could you stay? I would like that."

Oliver just nodded. He was at a loss for words.

Bruno came to their table with their main entrees – a saltimbocca for Oliver and a veal chop for Giancarlo. "*Buon appetito*," Giancarlo stated.

"*Grazie*," Oliver responded.

The delivery of their main courses broke the magic spell that had been cast, and Giancarlo began another line of inquiry, "So, what attracted you to finance?"

"My moms were good at investment. They had an advisor, and I was always impressed with the service he offered them. It seemed like a good life. In retrospect, now that I think about it, he was probably one of their gay friends. Maybe I identified with him even without knowing it."

"I had a similar situation," Giancarlo added enthusiastically. "My father was a banker. There was a part of me that didn't want to be like him. I wanted to do anything I could to be different from what he wanted me to be. But there was a financial advisor at his bank who he invited to dinner from time to time. He was straight – I'm convinced. He had a lovely wife, two kids, and a nice condo in our neighborhood. But it felt like the kind of work I could do that would make my father happy and get him off my back so that I could pursue other interests, if you know what I mean?"

"So, you had it all figured out early?" Oliver remarked.

"No, actually I didn't. I wasn't that self-aware. I just see now in hindsight that by becoming the kind of professional my father would have liked, I had more freedom to pursue other things – things that I didn't even know I wanted at that time."

"So, when did you come out?" Oliver inquired.

"Again, I haven't – at least not to my colleagues. Friends yes, but not others. But I recognized it in myself when I was 16 during a summer camp where one of my campmates came onto me. I knew then."

"And what happened to him?"

"He's a politician now. He's deep in the closet, although everyone suspects."

"He must be sad."

"I'm sure he is. But he's very popular, and he has a nice life."

"So," Oliver continued, "you seem to know a lot of people around town – Bruno, the waiter at the wine bar, a couple at the wine bar. Don't people eventually notice, figure it out?"

"They do and, in Rome, if you're not married by a certain age, it can be a problem."

"So, what are you going to do?"

"I'm hoping cultural norms will change before I reach the age where they start whispering. Since my parents are deceased, at least I don't have them breathing down my neck."

"By the way, this is delicious," Oliver continued, taking another bite of the saltimbocca.

"Do you want to try my veal chop?"

Oliver reached over, cut a small piece of Giancarlo's steak, and placed the morsel in his mouth. It was juicy and savory. "Oh my god, that's delicious."

"Yes, simple but delicious."

"They usually put a little oil, lemon, salt, and pepper on the chop and then grill it. The tender meat and the char of the fire bring out the simple flavors."

They finished their entrees and Giancarlo asked if Oliver wanted desert. He nodded and said, "What's on the menu?"

Giancarlo caught the implication and said, "Whatever you'd like."

Oliver smiled and said, "Let's get the bill."

Giancarlo waived Bruno down, got the check, paid it, and led Oliver out the front door and into the cool night air. They walked back toward the center of town. Giancarlo cleared his throat and said hesitantly, "Would you like to come over to my place?"

Oliver nodded. "Can I stop at the hotel first?" he said as they approached the front entrance.

"Certainly. I'll wait for you here."

"No, come up."

Giancarlo smiled and followed Oliver into the hotel. The night clerk glared at Giancarlo who said something in Italian about retrieving something. He nodded.

Once inside the room, Oliver turned to Giancarlo and pulled his head close and gave him a deep moist kiss. "I've been wanting to do that all night."

Giancarlo kissed him back, rubbing his hands on Oliver's chest. "Hmmm," he moaned.

Oliver blushed and said, "Let me get a few things, and we can be off."

Oliver went into the bathroom and threw a pair of shorts, a shirt, a toothbrush, and toothpaste into a small bag. As he walked back into the room, Giancarlo took hold of his shoulders and held him firmly in front of him and said, "You are so fucking sexy."

Oliver felt himself get hard as he looked into Giancarlo's eyes. He reached up to him and gave him another deep kiss. Giancarlo gently nudged him toward the bed. Oliver sat down on the edge, and Giancarlo pushed him back, straddling him with his muscular legs.

Oliver reached up into Giancarlo's shorts legs and felt his warm hairy thighs.

"*Oh, Madonna*," Giancarlo exclaimed as he used one of his arms to raise Oliver's pullover and began to stroke his abdomen. Giancarlo let himself fall onto the bed next to Oliver and reached over to pull him toward him, giving him a warm kiss.

Oliver had never made love to a man before and, at first, he began to tremble as the adrenaline raced through his blood. Reflexively, he began to reach for Giancarlo's zipper and grazed the hardness pressing against the fabric. He heard Giancarlo ask, "Are you okay?"

Oliver nodded, reaching over to give Giancarlo another kiss and rubbing his hands along Giancarlo's hip and around the back of his legs. Giancarlo wrapped his legs around Oliver and nuzzled his nose into his neck, licking his ear and playing with his blonde curly hair. "How did you get a dark complexion and blonde hair and blue eyes? It's a killer combination."

"I don't know. I only know my biological father. He's French. Perhaps my mother was Swedish or Danish or even Dutch."

"Well, it's sexy as hell," Giancarlo emphasized, rubbing his hand up under Oliver's shirt. "Let's go to my place."

"Okay," Oliver replied, pulling himself up on the bed and adjusting his shirt. Giancarlo stood and tightened his belt. His erection began to relax.

They walked out into the hallway, Oliver locked the door, and they took the elevator to the lobby. Oliver nodded to the receptionist as they headed out the door and onto the street. They followed the same path Oliver and Henry had traversed earlier in the day, and shortly they were in Trastevere in front of Giancarlo's apartment.

Giancarlo fished for a key, unlocked the outside door, and then took hold of Oliver's hand, leading him up the stairs towards his unit.

Once inside, Giancarlo turned on a few lamps, closed the shutter to the terrace, and asked Oliver if he wanted a drink. Oliver nodded. "I have wine, brandy, and several liquors," Giancarlo offered.

"A brandy sounds great."

Giancarlo opened a door to an antique chest in the dining room, pulled out a bottle of brandy and filled two glasses. He walked back into the parlor and offered Oliver at seat on the sofa. Giancarlo sat next to him, lifted his glass, and said, "*Salute.*"

"*Salute,*" Oliver said in reply, taking a long slow sip of the brandy. "Hmmm," he said.

"Hmmm, you," Giancarlo said, leaning toward Oliver and rubbing his hands on Oliver's legs.

Oliver set his glass down on the coffee table and leaned toward Giancarlo who took another sip of his brandy and rested his glass on the table as well. Oliver then pressed himself further onto Giancarlo's chest, breathing in his masculine scent and tugging at the fabric around his pecs with his teeth. Giancarlo leaned his head back and let Oliver slide his hands up under his shirt. Giancarlo moaned as he felt Oliver's warm hands.

Giancarlo laid back on the sofa and Oliver climbed on top of him, opening his mouth wide to receive Giancarlo's – their tongues moist, warm, and playful.

"You taste so sweet," Giancarlo said as he began to kiss Oliver's neck and nibble at his ear lobes. He ran his hands over Oliver's back, pulling the fabric of his shirt up onto his shoulder blades and feeling the intense heat of his bare skin. He slid his hands down under Oliver's waist and felt his firm round buttocks and squeezed them. Oliver pressed his pelvis against Giancarlo, letting out a moan.

"Let's go upstairs," Giancarlo proposed, sliding out from under Oliver and taking his hand. They stood up and traversed the parlor, taking the staircase up to Giancarlo's bedroom. He turned on a small lamp that cast a diffused light through the space. Giancarlo approached Oliver. He lifted his shirt over his head and ran his hands over his chest. Oliver sighed.

Giancarlo then unzipped Oliver's pants. They fell to the floor. He stroked Oliver's erection pressing against the soft fabric of his undershorts. They kissed.

Oliver reached around Giancarlo's back and pressed his hands down into the folds of his shorts and rubbed his fingers into Giancarlo's crack. He moaned, "*Mi farai venire se non ti fermi.*"

Oliver had no idea what Giancarlo had said but felt encouraged to continue exploring Giancarlo's body. He unzipped his shorts and pulled them down. Giancarlo pulled off his undershorts, his erect and engorged penis now fully exposed. He slipped off Oliver's undershorts, and they stood facing each other, their respective erections pressed against each other.

Oliver reached down and held them both together, rubbing slowly, rhythmically – an intense heat rising in both. Giancarlo opened his mouth and breathed in Oliver as they kissed. And, for the first time in his life, Oliver knew who he was and who he wanted to be. He fell backward onto the bed and let Giancarlo make love to him.

9

Chapter Nine

Oliver awoke to the intense aroma of espresso. He looked down at the floor near the edge of the bed and found his undershorts. He slipped them on, found his dark jeans and slipped them on as well. He went into the bathroom to pee and straightened the errant curls of his blonde hair with wet fingers. He headed down the stairs to the kitchen and dining room where Giancarlo was pouring coffee and laying out some croissants on a platter.

"*Buon giorno, caro.* How did you sleep?" Giancarlo began, walking toward Oliver and giving him a kiss.

Oliver sighed, "Dreamy. And you?"

"The same. Here, come sit and have some breakfast."

Oliver took a seat and gulped down the small cup of espresso. The croissants were warm, flaky, and full of chocolate. "Hmm," he said. "These are delicious."

Giancarlo had on a pair of loose shorts and a pullover and stared at Oliver who felt self-conscious. Oliver said, "I'll get out of your way soon. I'm sure you have to go to work."

"*Pazienza, caro.* We're in Italy. Time is different. It's not as regimented as in the States. No one is watching whether I arrive at a certain time or not. Besides, I want to savor every minute I have with you."

Now Oliver really felt self-conscious, realizing he had stepped over a line he had never crossed before. He was not a virgin, but he had never spent the night with someone. His only real sexual experiences had been with women. He had fooled around with a few guys, but nothing serious happened. He was now having breakfast across from his first real male partner and first overnighter, someone who made his heart pound and his pulse race. Was it too late to escape, to retrace his steps, to take things back a few notches?

He smiled at Giancarlo, not knowing what to say. Giancarlo looked alarmed, sensing Oliver's reticence. "Oh, I'm sorry. Maybe I've overstepped things a bit."

"No, not at all," Oliver assured him finally. "This is all a bit new for me."

"If it's any consolation, it is for me, too."

Oliver looked incredulous. Surely Giancarlo had slept with men before. Giancarlo noticed Oliver's furrowed brows and fumbled for something to say, "You're very different. There's a thoughtfulness and depth to you that I find enchanting and disorienting." He thought to himself, 'that felt lame.'

Oliver wasn't sure how to react and continued to stare at Giancarlo who then said further, "You're much more mature than your age, and you bring out things in me that I have kept under cover for so long."

Oliver took a deep breath, relaxed, and realized Giancarlo was being sincere. He smiled at Giancarlo as he took a big bite of the croissant and said, "All things aside, I'm sure you have to work. I'll go back to the hotel soon."

"I do. I have several appointments including one with Fr. Henry."

Oliver's heart skipped a beat at the mention of his biological father. "I assume he's coming to sign the trust papers and have them notarized?"

"Yes. By the way, do you want to go out to lunch with him and me? We were going to get a bite to eat after our meeting."

"I don't want to intrude."

"Why would you be intruding? I'm sure he wouldn't mind."

Oliver realized Henry would be delighted to have lunch with him and Giancarlo. He was just nervous that their real relationship would eventually become known to Giancarlo and create problems for his father. "I insist," Giancarlo emphasized. "I'll text him now."

They finished breakfast, showered, dressed, and began to walk toward the historical center. Oliver went back to the hotel and Giancarlo to the bank. Oliver fell into his hotel bed and began to contemplate what had just happened. He was already aching for Giancarlo, obsessing about when he would see him again, and worried about how he could contain his excitement in front of Henry. He glanced at his watch and realized he still had three hours before he would meet them. He pulled out the guidebook and flipped the pages, looking for something to distract him.

An insert popped out with large photos of the Palazzo Massimo alle Terme, another ancient Roman museum. He looked at the map and realized that even though it was a mile away, he could use the exercise and distraction. He put on a cap, tucked the book under his arm, and headed out the door of the hotel. The walk was good. He hiked up a steep hill and continued along a busy boulevard lined with shops. In a short while he approached another square circling a fountain, some large Roman ruins, and a graceful Renaissance building tucked away with the sign, "Palazzo Massimo."

He entered the front door, purchased his ticket, and went inside. The galleries circled a tall glass-covered courtyard filled with ancient Roman sculptures. Each floor included masterpieces he had read about but never dreamed of seeing such as the life size "Seleucid Prince" and the "Boxer at Rest." He couldn't help but chuckle at the vast amount of naked male statues in Rome, an ocean of male eroticism that seemed to dominate museums and public places. He was surprised everyone in Rome wasn't gay.

As he reached the upper floors, he realized that the museum was known for its collection of ancient Roman mosaics and frescos. Each room on the upper floor was more dazzling – colorful floor tiles depicting hunting scenes, gardens, and gladiators. There was an entire wing recreating the dining room of Livia, the wife of Augustus. The delicate frescos of ferns, flowers, and orange trees made the room feel as if one were eating outside. It was breathtaking, and Oliver couldn't contain his excitement at seeing an entire 1st century room in perfect condition.

He finished exploring the museum and walked across the street to Santa Maria degli Angeli, a church designed by Michelangelo out of the ruins of the baths of Diocletian. He walked into the main nave and almost wet his pants. The soaring ceiling and arched walls were original to the baths, built at the end of the 3rd century. The space was larger than any he had ever seen even in a modern building – apart from, perhaps, the inside of the Boston Garden. He wondered how the Romans, 2000 years ago, had been able to create something so spacious and enduring.

He glanced at his watch and realized he had only a half hour to meet Giancarlo and Henry. He opened a map on his phone, walked toward the Spanish Steps, descended them, and then meandered through the boutique shops below until he found Giancarlo's bank. He walked inside, and a receptionist asked if she could help him.

"*Giancarlo Russo, per favore.*"

She looked across the spacious lobby and pointed him out, sitting at a desk behind a plexiglass wall. Henry was with him. "I believe he's expecting you," she added.

Oliver walked across the space. Giancarlo looked up and smiled. Henry stood and extended his hand to Oliver as he walked inside the enclosure. "What a pleasant surprise to learn we're having lunch together," he said warmly.

Although Henry was dressed in a black suit and clerical collar, he seemed uncharacteristically affable and relaxed.

Oliver nodded, reached out his hand to Henry, and then to Giancarlo. "*Giancarlo, piacere.*"

"It's all mine," he said pointedly, looking penetratingly into Oliver's eyes.

"What did you do this morning?" Henry began.

Oliver cleared his throat, trying to get past the memory of having woken up in Giancarlo's arms. "I went to the Palazzo Massimo and to Santa Maria degli Angeli."

"Ah, yes, our common love of ancient history," Henry remarked.

Oliver blushed and looked at Giancarlo who smiled discretely. "Well, gentlemen. I think everything is in order. Henry has signed the trust, it was notarized, and I can mail you a copy, Oliver. Are you both ready to go to lunch?"

"By all means. Thanks for your assistance, Giancarlo. You're the best," Henry said.

"You're welcome. My pleasure."

They exited the bank and made their way to a small trattoria, one of Henry's favorites. "Oliver, you're going to love this place. They have the best carbonara and saltimbocca. You have to try some before you leave."

Oliver glanced over to Giancarlo who avoided his gaze nervously. They stepped inside a nondescript façade and into a traditional looking dining space. Several elderly waiters welcomed them. "*Monsignore, benvenuto. S'accomodi.*" They pointed to a table and the three sat.

Henry ordered wine and explained to Oliver what carbonara and saltimbocca was. Oliver responded, "They sound delicious. I can't wait to try them."

Giancarlo was quiet and had his head buried deep within the menu, afraid to catch Oliver's eyes. He began to second-guess having invited them both to lunch. "Giancarlo," Henry began, "you've been here before. Isn't the rigatoni carbonara incredible?"

"Yes. Oliver should try it. Carbonara is a unique Roman dish. It's like nothing you've had before."

Oliver glanced up and wanted to wink but maintained composure. He noticed Giancarlo was distressed and decided to cut the tension with some questions. "So, Giancarlo. How long have you been a financial advisor?"

Giancarlo thought to himself, 'Oliver is good. He's clever. He's going to totally steer the conversation to avoid any accidental disclosures.'

"My father was a banker. I began to think about it when I was a teenager and studied it in college. What about you? Didn't you say you were studying finance?"

Henry smiled as he looked at Oliver and Giancarlo and realized they had a lot in common.

"Yes, I'm hoping to be an advisor, like you," Oliver replied.

"It's nice work. I would encourage you."

The waiter came and took their orders. "So, Fr. Henry, you'd suggest the carbonara and the saltimbocca?" Oliver inquired. "I hope there's not too much pasta. I'm not that hungry."

"They're small portions here in Rome," Henry noted. Oliver looked over at Giancarlo who maintained his head bowed into the menu.

"Giancarlo," Henry began, "what are you going to have?"

"How are their veal chops?" he inquired of Henry, looking up at Oliver and winking discretely. He felt more relaxed and less concerned that something would spiral out of control.

"They're delicious. Oliver, maybe you should try a veal chop instead of the saltimbocca."

"Maybe I can try some of Giancarlo's?" he asked. "If he wouldn't mind? I've never had saltimbocca and would like to try it."

Giancarlo realized Oliver was going to play with him and decided a few double entendres wouldn't be too dangerous. "I don't like to share my meat but, given the occasion, maybe Oliver could have a bite or two."

Oliver blushed and, fortunately, Henry couldn't see his face. Henry was still looking at the menu and hardly noticed the banter between Giancarlo and Oliver. The waiter came and Henry ordered carbonara and saltimbocca – as did Oliver. Giancarlo ordered amatriciana and a veal chop.

Henry leaned back, poured some wine into their glasses and offered a toast, "Thank you Giancarlo for your work. And thank you Oliver for your visit to Rome. I'm very happy. *Salute!*"

"*Salute,*" they all said in unison.

"So, Oliver, when do you have to go back to Boston?" Henry inquired.

"My flight is scheduled for tomorrow but I'm thinking of perhaps extending my stay a bit. There are other cities in Italy I would like to see, and I might as well take advantage of the time I have."

"Splendid idea," Henry said. "Maybe I can take some time off and show you around."

Giancarlo and Oliver glanced at each other, and Oliver began, "That's a generous offer. I've actually made some plans with some classmates of mine who are in Italy. Maybe we can visit before I leave."

Henry looked disappointed but then looked over to Oliver, "That would be nice. Just let me know."

Giancarlo glanced over at Henry and Oliver and, as they looked at each other and smiled, he was struck by the similarities of their mouths and eyes. Both had deep set eyes with a unique arch of brow and large sensual noses. Both their mouths were framed by a pair of identical dimples particularly pronounced when they smiled.

"*Dio mio,*" he murmured under his voice. He began to scrutinize them more carefully and noticed the similar hue of their complexion, the slightly darker olive skin characteristic of the French. 'Ah, yes,' he said to himself, 'Montpierre, French Canadian.'

"Fr. Henry, you've never told me where you're from. I know you're from the States, but what is your ethnic heritage?" Giancarlo inquired.

"My grandparents on both sides of my family are French Canadian. They migrated to the States after the arrival of the English in Quebec – thus my surname, Montpierre."

"Interesting," he said. "That must be where you get your dark complexion," he noted, looking intensely at Oliver.

"My parents were lighter, but my grandparents darker. I must have gotten it from them."

Oliver decided to jump in and take control of the conversation. "It's amazing how similar the French and Italian characteristics are. I really can't tell the difference."

"Oh, we know," Giancarlo noted, tossing out another double entendre. "There are slight variations in hue. It's obvious to us."

Oliver blushed and Henry seemed oblivious, checking his phone for messages. He looked up at Giancarlo, "So, what will you do this summer in your free time?"

"I usually meet my cousins at the beach for long weekends and for the month of August. And you?"

"I have a busy agenda through July. We have several cases we are wrapping up with some schools in Italy."

"Anything you can share?"

"Not really. It's all confidential at the moment. It will probably hit the press. They aren't too friendly to us."

Giancarlo knew Henry was conservative and had remained with the bank because of its conservative leanings. Henry always presumed Giancarlo had similar political views, the apple not falling far from his father who had been a staunch Catholic. He said, "That's too bad. But you have to admit, the Church's policies don't seem to line up with current trends."

"They never have," Henry underscored. "We aren't here to be popular. We're here to defend the truth."

Oliver bristled. His family was precisely the kind of thing people like Henry sought to undermine. Although Henry had softened his rhetoric the other day, he was now taking a more traditional approach. Oliver interjected, "Sometimes the truth is not what we think. It can be uncomfortable and force us to rethink our assumptions."

"Well put, Oliver," Henry said, remembering their exchange just a few days before. "You've helped me appreciate that. Thanks."

The waiter came with their pasta, and they began to eat. The pasta courses were followed by the main entrees and more wine. Giancarlo was impatient to leave. He glanced at his watch and announced, "I have several meetings this afternoon. Can you both excuse me?"

"Certainly, Giancarlo," Henry replied. "Thanks for your work. Can you send Oliver copies of the notarized trust?"

"Absolutely. I have his address."

Giancarlo reached his hand across the table and shook Oliver's. "It was a pleasure meeting you. I hope the rest of your stay in Italy is good."

"Thank you," Oliver replied, smiling warmly at Giancarlo.

Giancarlo left. Henry and Oliver enjoyed an after-dinner drink and then Henry said, "I'll walk you to your hotel on the way to my office."

They left the restaurant and began to meander through several small narrow roads through the historical center. "Oliver, thanks for coming to Rome to meet me. It has been the dream of my life to finally know who you are and make the connection. I'm sorry for our initial exchange, and I hope I can learn to appreciate who you and your moms are."

"Me, too. Love is love, and I would hold my family up to any other in comparison."

"I'm proud of you. You're a smart, thoughtful, and principled person. Let's keep in touch."

"And thanks for making me beneficiary of your trust. That means a lot."

"It's only appropriate," Henry concluded. He reached over and gave Oliver a hug.

Oliver went inside this hotel, and Henry continued walking toward the Vatican. A few minutes later Oliver got a text from Giancarlo. "Can you meet me?"

"When? Where?" Oliver texted back.

"Is Henry gone?" Giancarlo inquired.

"Yes, he's heading to his office."

"I need to see you right away," Giancarlo texted.

"Okay. My hotel?"

"Yes. I'll be there in 15 minutes."

Oliver went downstairs and waited in the lobby. When Giancarlo appeared in the door, his heart pounded with intensity. He stood up and signaled for him to follow. They went upstairs and entered Oliver's room, flooded with light and air from the terrace. Oliver offered him a seat. Giancarlo said, "Let me stand awhile." He was pacing nervously.

"Oliver, Fr. Henry is your father, right?"

Oliver was startled by the directness of Giancarlo's question. He hesitated. Giancarlo jumped in, "Don't worry, I already figured it out. You don't have to answer."

"How?"

"I was sitting across from you. Your facial features are too similar. As you both smiled, it became apparent – the arch of your eye and the dimples on both sides of your mouths."

"I didn't notice," Oliver said.

"No, you probably wouldn't have."

"This is a problem," Giancarlo added, pacing again.

"How is it a problem?"

"My bank has a lot of clients who are well-placed Vatican officials."

"I thought the Vatican had its own bank."

"They do," Giancarlo continued. "But when they want to be discrete and hide their assets, they come to us."

"So, what's the problem."

"Henry is very conservative. If he finds out about me, I'm finished with the bank."

"Why does he have to find out about you?"

"I don't know. I'm just nervous. There's too much hidden information. It's bound to come out in the wrong place."

"It doesn't have to."

"Rome is a small place with lots of eyes."

"I'm beginning to surmise," Oliver continued.

"So, Henry is your biological father?" Giancarlo pressed.

"Yes, I'm afraid so."

"When did you find that out?"

"Just recently, after a DNA test on an ancestry site. We met for the first time this week."

"Wow, that must have been life-changing for you both."

"Yes. At first it didn't go well. He found out that when he and the woman he had an affair with put me up for adoption, the adoption agency placed me with two women. He was furious. We almost parted ways acrimoniously but, he had a change of heart. We met again and had a nice discussion. I think he's more appreciative of me and my family."

"I'm not convinced. The cases he mentioned have to do with some teachers in Catholic schools who will be removed from their positions because they are gay, lesbian, and coupled."

"Are you telling me his change of heart is a façade?"

"It could be – or you may have had an impact on him."

"Sit down, you're making me nervous," Oliver said to Giancarlo.

He sat in one of the lounge chairs and looked sad. "Why are you so sad?" Oliver pressed further.

"I was on such a high last night and this morning. This discovery just makes me feel uneasy."

"But what's the problem?"

"Okay, listen. Maybe I'm a little ahead of myself. I've just met you but I'm already crazy in love with you. I know – it doesn't make sense and sounds adolescent – but it's true."

Oliver nodded. "I feel the same."

"Okay. So, let's say this continues to develop. Then what? I can't move to Boston, but you could spend more time in Rome. But, if you do that, what's Henry going to think? Once it's out that his biological son is a poofter and shagging the financial advisor at the bank, it's over – for all of us!"

"Yes, I can see that is a problem. What if we take this a step at a time? Let's get to know each other. See if what we're experiencing has legs. If so, then we look at the next step – admittedly more challenging. Henry doesn't have to know anything at the moment. We can also see what he does with these cases at the Vatican. Maybe he's had a real change of heart, and we can trust him, confide in him?"

"You're more optimistic than me. I see a catastrophe written all over this."

"I think there's a term in Italian I've heard on the streets – *piano piano* – take it slow, easy."

"You're one cutie!"

Oliver smiled and walked over to Giancarlo. He squatted down near his chair and leaned into him, giving him a warm kiss. "*Ti voglio bene!*"

"Now you're softening me up in my own language. You're a clever one!"

"I'm not sure I know what you mean," Oliver said with a twinkle in his eye.

"You're the master conversation manipulator. I could have strangled you."

"And you're the double entendre master. Not wanting to share your meat. Please, no one's fooled. Just remember, I'm the only one with sharing privileges now."

Giancarlo nodded and leaned over to give Oliver a long moist kiss. He looked up and asked more seriously, "What are you doing about your flight?"

"I've postponed it. My ticket is open ended, so I can call the airline when I want to return."

Giancarlo looked pensive. Oliver continued, "What's the matter?"

"I'm just thinking. Are you going to stay in the hotel, or would you like to come to my place?"

"I don't know. I can stay here. It's not a problem."

"Let's think this through," Giancarlo began. "We need to avoid Henry and other clerical clients who know me. The hotel is too close to the center and to the clerical shops nearby. My place is outside their usual stomping ground, as you say in English. Maybe it's safer there."

"Safer in what sense?" Oliver smiled sheepishly.

Giancarlo chuckled. Oliver was glad he was finally relaxing and could find the humor in the situation. Oliver continued, "I can always get a wig and pretend to be your girlfriend."

"I'm afraid the neighbors would be the first to report something suspicious. They've never seen a girl cross the threshold."

"Would you be okay with me spending time there? I might have some bad habits that would drive you crazy."

"The only thing driving me crazy is your sexy smile, your blonde wavy hair, and a nice package I discovered last night." He looked down at Oliver's crotch.

Oliver blushed. Giancarlo continued, "If you're not comfortable, that's okay, too. I realize this is all new for you."

"Let's give it a try. I can always check back into the hotel if things don't work."

"I can't imagine they won't."

"Me, either."

"By the way," Giancarlo interjected, "we could travel this weekend. I could take off Friday and Monday and we could go someplace. There's so much to see in Italy. Where would you like to go?"

"What do you suggest?"

"There are the classic tourist places – Florence and Venice. Any interest?"

"I was in Florence last weekend with friends. Venice sounds nice but is pretty far away, right?"

"Well, with the fast trains, it's not bad."

"Really?" Oliver replied, obviously intrigued by the idea of seeing Venice.

"I'll check into it – see if we can find a nice hotel and book some tickets. In the meantime, I could show you more of Rome. I can tell my boss I'm consulting with clients which, technically, is true."

"I'm fine entertaining myself during the day."

"And at night?"

"I think that's your department," Oliver said again with a sheepish grin.

"What now?" Giancarlo inquired. "I can't concentrate at work. Why don't we go do something?"

"Fine with me. How do we avoid Henry?"

"That's relatively easy. I know where his office is, where he lives, and the usual places the priests hang out for dinner. They rarely move outside of that and, if they do, they don't want to be spotted."

Oliver chuckled. "How do people take them seriously? Sounds like they live double lives."

"They do. They have for centuries. It's just the cultural backdrop here. No one bats an eye."

"But the damage they do to others – to women, to gay people."

"Unfortunately, Italians are rather conservative on these issues, too. The Church gets by with it because the people don't challenge them."

"But it must be changing?"

"Slowly – as you said earlier, *piano piano* – slowly, carefully, cautiously."

"Let's get you checked out and moved into your new quarters."

Oliver smiled warmly, gave Giancarlo a big hug, and began to throw things into his suitcase. "I better text my moms and let them know what's up."

"You mean about us?"

"Not yet. I just want to let them know I'm not at the hotel – that I'm hanging out with a friend I met in Rome. I'll let them know I'm extending my stay. It will provoke questions, but they won't pry."

"I can't wait to meet them some day."

"That would be nice."

10

Chapter Ten

A few days later, Giancarlo sat facing Oliver on the fast train to Venice. The Tuscan landscape passed swiftly past their window. Giancarlo attended to some work emails, and Oliver read up on the history of Venice. It was his first trip with Giancarlo, and he couldn't have been more excited. A text popped up from his moms. "Hope you're doing well. We miss you. Send photos."

Oliver replied, "Miss you too. I'm heading to Venice with a friend."

They replied, "You keep referring to a friend. Who?"

Oliver hesitated. The last couple of days with Giancarlo had been more than he anticipated. They got along well. It was easy to talk with him about all sorts of things. He was handsome, affection-ate, thoughtful, and generous. He was now racing off to Venice and wanted to share his excitement and joy with his moms. Slowly he typed in the letters, GIANCARLO, in the text and sent it.

He knew his moms would be intrigued and, within seconds they replied, "Giancarlo who? Did you meet someone? Call us. Right now."

Oliver pushed their number on the phone and waited for them to pick up. "Oliver?" they asked as they picked up.

"Ma and mom – why are you up so late?"

"We couldn't sleep."

"Why?"

"You tell us." His moms were intuitive and were always picking up on things – even remotely. He knew they had to know something was up.

"I met someone."

"Well?"

"His name is Giancarlo." Oliver could hear their muffled voices concealed with their hands covering the microphone.

Rita then said, "Congratulations. This must have been unexpected."

"Yes, very much so."

"How did you meet?"

"He is Henry's financial advisor. We met when Henry named me his beneficiary."

"We're still troubled by that. I hope he doesn't try to nuzzle his way into our family."

"He won't. Trust me."

"So, tell us more about Giancarlo."

"Well, he's handsome, about thirty,"

"Thirty? You're only twenty. Oliver, are you sure?"

"Yes, mom. He's been nothing but gracious and caring and respectful."

Anna then jumped in, "A man, then?"

Oliver knew this was the big question. At some level he didn't want to self-identify, to fall into categories of straight, gay, or bi. He just loved Giancarlo. It wasn't about being gay or not. But he had to admit to himself that what he felt with Giancarlo – both emotionally and physically – was so radically different from anything he had ever felt with or for a woman. "Yes, ma. A man. I think I'm gay."

"Are you sure?"

"After this week, yes. I'm pretty certain. I finally feel myself."

"Oh, we're so happy for you," they both said in unison on the phone. "Can you send a picture?"

"When we're finished talking."

"So, what does Henry think?"

"He doesn't know. He's kind of conservative and Giancarlo has to be discrete."

"Sounds complicated."

"It is, but it's fine."

"Well, we don't want to keep you. Have fun on your trip and send us photos."

"Love you."

"Love you, too."

After Oliver hung up, Giancarlo looked up at him and said, "You just came out to your moms. Wow!"

"Yes, it was both less momentous and more profound than I anticipated."

"In what way profound?" Giancarlo inquired, looking across at Oliver who had turned his head to watch the landscape outside.

"It was the first time, other than to you, that I've disclosed who I am. I've always avoided categories, but it felt good. I felt like I was finally in sync with myself."

"Hmmm," Giancarlo murmured contently.

Oliver continued, "I didn't think it would be so powerful, so energizing. It's like a big burden and dilemma has been lifted."

"I can see it in your face, in the way you hold your body. You're lighter."

Oliver smiled. The train passed through Florence, Bologna and then began to cross an expansive lagoon with fishing boats, remains of old viaducts, and the faint outline of Venice in the distance. It felt good to be near the water, reminding him of his summers on the Cape. Oliver's face was pressed against the glass window as the train pulled slowly into Santa Lucia station.

Throngs of tourists descended on the platform and made their way to the piazza facing the grand canal. The bright sunlight glistened on the turquoise water, choppy with the chaotic comings and goings of barges, water taxis, and gondolas. The first view of Venice was everything Oliver had imagined, multicolored medieval buildings rising from canals, arched bridges under which gondoliers passed, the aroma of sea air, and a muffled quiet in the absence of car traffic. Giancarlo pulled their suitcase while Oliver took photos.

"We're not far from here. Let's walk," Giancarlo noted, looking at his phone for directions.

They crossed a small but crowded bridge to a residential section, meandered through several tight pedestrian passageways, crossed another bridge, and took a narrow walkway that was perched over a picturesque canal. Barges of fruit and vegetables passed beneath them as they crossed another span and entered a quiet square. "I believe the hotel is here, nearby."

Giancarlo looked at his phone, pulled up the address, and then pivoted in place. "There," he said, pointing to a blue doorway on the corner with a sign overhead, *Chez nous.*

"*Chez nous*? Isn't that French? We're in Italy and we're staying at a French Inn?"

"*Calmati, caro.* It's a gay inn, and the *chez nous* is code for our place."

"Oh." Oliver said, more relaxed.

They pushed open the door and a handsome man, about forty, greeted them with a warm smile.

"*Sono Giancarlo Russo. Abbiamo una prenotazione.*"

"Sì – *per due notti.*"

The receptionist looked at Oliver with intrigue. Oliver wasn't sure if it was his being American or his being so young that startled him.

"*Voi avete prenotato la camera quattro – un suite king con balcone.*"

Giancarlo nodded. Oliver looked perplexed but stood patiently while Giancarlo took care of the paperwork. The young man handed Giancarlo the key and said in English, "Have a nice stay."

They took a small elevator to the fourth floor where they found their room and unlocked the door. It was an expansive space with tall ceilings, venetian furniture, and a large terrace overlooking nearby rooftops and St. Mark's tower in the distance.

"Oh my God," Oliver began, leaning on the edge of the marble balustrade. "This is beautiful. It's so serene and quiet up here."

"I'm glad you like it. Venice is an odd place. It's very busy during the day but, at night, the tourists leave, and the city is reclaimed by the residents. We can rest here and take a stroll later."

"I'm ready to go out sooner than later," Oliver said, anxious to see the sights.

"Well, let's go then."

They walked outside the inn and began to follow the signs on the corners of the building, some pointing toward the train station, others to San Marco, and a few to the Rialto bridge. Giancarlo avoided the main path and led Oliver through the quiet side streets and neighborhoods. "This is the real Venice," he said to Oliver.

"It's so quiet."

"Yes, there are no cars. If you're near the Grand Canal, it's noisy given the boats, but here in the neighborhoods, it's incredibly peaceful."

"It's so romantic," Oliver said, taking Giancarlo's hand. Giancarlo squeezed Oliver's hand warmly and then let it drop, conscious of the conservative views of local Venetians. They continued to walk toward the Piazza San Marco passing small boutique shops and artist galleries. As they got closer to St. Mark's Square, more of the shops displayed hand blown glass made on the island of Murano. All-of-a-sudden, the small walkway passed under a covered arcade and into the main square, a vast space lined with cafes. "Oh my God," Oliver exclaimed. His eyes began to tear up, emotions welling up within him.

"Yes, the first time is moving," Giancarlo said tenderly as he watched Oliver rub his eyes. "There's nothing like it."

Oliver felt the flood of sensations overwhelm him, the orchestral music filling the sprawling square, the flocks of pigeons soaring into the blue sky, the multiple domes of San Marco glistening in the sun, the red brick tower looming overhead, and the church of San Giorgio across the lagoon in the distance. He was choked with emotion. Giancarlo reached his arms around Oliver and gave him an affectionate hug.

"Let's walk out toward the lagoon, take a stroll inside the basilica, and then have something to drink."

Oliver nodded.

They made their way across the square and approached the vast lagoon filled with gondolas, vaporetti, water taxis, and private yachts making their way to the exclusive docks of luxury hotels. The choppy water surprised Oliver, imagining the lagoon to be more placid. The beautiful façade of the Doge's Palace stood majestically on the edge of the expansive body of water where larger boats and yachts were moored.

They made their way inside the basilica, every inch of the walls covered in gold and chromatic tile images of sacred stories from the Bible. Oliver's neck stretched upward to take in the Byzantine-style images lining the walls, arches, and ceiling.

"They say much of the interior was inspired by Hagia Sophia, the basilica built in Constantinople in the 6th century. It is now a mosque or museum but for centuries it was one of the oldest churches in Christendom, richly decorated in frescos and mosaics. Venice always had a close connection with Byzantium, and many artifacts were brought here by the doges," Giancarlo explained.

"It's amazing. Every inch seems covered in gold mosaics."

"Yes, it's probably one of the most important examples of Byzantine religious art, although the nearby city of Ravenna includes a lot as well."

They spent more time wandering through the basilica and then went back out into the sunny square. They took seats at a café along the shady side of the piazza. They ordered drinks and savored the warm sea air and the soothing music played by a classic quartet orchestra on an elevated wooden stage. The music echoed off the walls and filled the square.

Giancarlo excused himself to go to the bathroom while Oliver took more photos and texted several to his moms. When Giancarlo returned, he had a newspaper in hand.

"What's that?" Oliver inquired.

"That's right – you're so young you don't even know what a newspaper looks like anymore."

"Hey," Oliver protested. "I know what newspapers look like."

"Well, I thought you might find this interesting," Giancarlo said as he tossed the paper toward him, the paper folded in half with a photo of Henry on the front.

"Oh my God. What does it say?" Oliver inquired, alarmed.

"It would seem our Henry is a leopard whose spots don't change."

The creases on Oliver's forehead deepened as he looked at the photo and then looked up at Giancarlo.

Giancarlo began to translate the main points outlined in the article. "The Vatican has removed a dozen gay teachers in Catholic-sponsored schools across Italy and issued an explanatory document that sets out several key points. The Church claims that these teachers' lifestyles contradict Church teaching about the morality of same-sex relationships, setting a bad moral example. Moreover, their families endanger the upbringing of their children who need a mother and a father for their proper human formation."

"How horrible! How's Henry involved?"

"It would appear he is their spokesperson and main author of the supporting documentation."

Oliver's face became red with anger. "And all of this after putting on a pretty face for me."

"It must feel like a gut punch to you."

"You've described it perfectly. I feel like someone punched me in the stomach and kicked the legs out from under me."

"I'm sorry."

"It's not your fault. I just can't believe he can say what he's saying after having met me, learned about my family, and praised me for turning out so well."

"It's dishonest, to say the least," Giancarlo noted solemnly.

"Let me see that," Oliver said, as he reached for the paper. He traced his fingers over the image of Henry in his collar, standing in front of a church, reading from a document.

"Does the article report any pushback from students, parents, or the government?"

"In fact, it does. Students organized a protest since, in all the cases, the teachers were well liked and exceptional in their fields. The government says it is discrimination, and believes it is wrong, but their hands are tied since these are religious institutions."

"So, it's okay for the Church to discriminate?" Oliver asked angrily.

"Apparently so."

"That's not right."

"Well, they claim they have a right to promote their beliefs – the freedom of religion argument."

"But, if I'm not mistaken, they claim their views are based on research. Does it mention that in the article?" Oliver asked, leaning over the paper.

Giancarlo continued to skim the article, turning the page to the continuation of the report on subsequent page replete with pictures of the teachers and students protesting. "Hmmm, it does quote Henry saying, 'research shows that kids are at a disadvantage when they do not have a father and a mother.' He claims they are basing their views on reason, on scientific research."

"Bullshit," Oliver blurted out, a few people at nearby tables looking over. Oliver put his hand up to his mouth and said, "*Scusi.*" He then continued saying to Giancarlo, "As the child of two mothers, I've read up on all the research. Kids are better off when they have two parents. But, even with that data, it has to do with economic and social advantages, not necessarily that kids can't be raised successfully with one parent. Moreover, none of the research that talks about the importance of two parents controls for gender. The assumption is that kids will have a mother and father, but all of the research that compares kids raised by two moms or two dads with those raised by a mother and father show that kids raised in same-sex families score equal to or better than their counterparts in terms of psychological development, maturity, integration, self-esteem, regard for others, sense of gender identity, and clarity about sexual orientation. In fact, in many areas they score higher than their counterparts."

Giancarlo grinned at Oliver's passion and knowledge. "Take a breath," he admonished him playfully.

"Moreover," Oliver continued without a pause, "in studies of family function comparing straight families with gay and lesbian families, gay families are indistinguishable, scoring as high if not higher than straight families in all sorts of areas that determine the health and well-being and functionality of families. So, I don't see how Henry can say research backs up their view. It doesn't. He's being dishonest."

"Welcome to the Catholic Church."

"Maybe that's why my moms converted to the Episcopal Church."

"That's why so many Italians don't go to church anymore. The hypocrisy and dishonesty are all too apparent."

"Even in the area of homosexuality? I thought Italians were traditional, even conservative in that area."

"You're right. They are still traditional, but they don't like institutional dishonesty. When they see it, even if they are sympathetic with the cause, they object to the misuse of reason and the abuse of authority."

Oliver took a long sip of his drink and looked off in the distance. He looked troubled, sad, deflated. Giancarlo reached over and took his hand. Oliver turned back toward Giancarlo and said, "What am I going to do? I can't let this go without some kind of response. It's personal. Henry, my biological father, has just insulted me and my family. That's unacceptable."

Giancarlo looked deeply into Oliver's piercing blue eyes and detected a passion for justice he hadn't noticed before. He realized this young twenty-year-old was formidable and ready to convert his life experiences into action. It was inspiring and frightening at the same time. Giancarlo realized Oliver's activism might spill over into his life and unsettle the cart of apples he had balanced carefully at the bank.

"Let's use our time here in Venice to think about what we can do. I want to support you. We need to think strategically," Giancarlo said carefully.

Oliver nodded and said, "I feel like the first thing I want to do is call him and ask him to remove me from his trust. I'm embarrassed to be associated with him and want to sever all ties."

"I'm not sure I would do that."

"Why?" Oliver inquired.

"Henry's trust is huge. You'd be throwing away a lot of money."

"How huge?"

"Close to a million euros and growing."

"You're kidding?"

"No, and that's why he and some of his friends are so important to the bank. These are not small accounts. They are significant and, since we get a small percentage of the growth of their funds, it's lucrative."

"Wow. I never realized."

"You have to keep this confidential."

Oliver nodded.

"No, we have to find a way to corner and challenge him in such a way that he doesn't have many options, certainly not options that would hurt you or me."

"What do you propose?"

"Well, the only thing that comes to my mind at the moment is that we have a lot of information about him, about his past."

"You mean that he had an affair and a child?"

"Not only that, but that the child was placed for adoption with two women."

"Yeah, he was pretty upset when he found that out."

"This would be an embarrassment for him on multiple layers – his affair, the pregnancy, the placement and then – back to the point of honesty – you. If people were to find out how well you turned out being raised by two women, they would have to challenge Henry's narrow mindedness, one that is dishonest given what he knows about you."

"Hmmm," Oliver mumbled under his breath. "So, essentially a form of blackmail."

"Yes."

"But what would we want him to do? Retract his statements, reinstate the teachers, refrain from future removals. How is he going to agree to that? How is he going to explain that to higher ups and get their approval?"

"We have to show him the way, provide him with a blueprint."

"I'm listening," Oliver said attentively.

"First, we challenge him – or rather, you challenge him. Call him and tell him you are hurt and disappointed. He might do the right thing without pressure. However, that's unlikely."

"So, then what?"

"You hint that you can't let this go unchallenged. That the real truth needs to be shared."

"A double entendre."

"Precisely. Priests are masters at that. He'll pick up on it right away."

"What will he do next?" Oliver asked excitedly.

"He's likely to try to buy you off, give you some of his trust now."

"Shit, that would be hard to pass up."

Giancarlo looked disappointingly at Oliver who then grinned and added, "Of course I wouldn't take it."

Giancarlo continued, "At that point, he will get nervous that you will go public and will be more desperate. He's likely to try to buy time – to engage you in a protracted debate, one that he will say he's going to take seriously and, if persuaded, seek to change the position of the Church."

"That's good, no?"

"If it was sincere, yes. But it won't be. You'll have to put pressure on him. Tell him this will only work if he puts the removals on suspension until further investigation and study can take place. He might go for that, but his superiors may not. It depends on whether he's part of a conservative group that's trying to consolidate and pre-serve power in the curia or whether he is surrounded by progressives who can't seem to stop him."

"You've done some thinking about this."

"Unfortunately, I overhead my father's conversations with colleagues and learned the art of political maneuvering. Now, if none of these tactics work, we have to be ready to go public. I have some editor friends at several newspapers who we can rely on to help us get the message out."

"What about you? Eventually Henry will learn about us and threaten you as a way to pressure me to back off."

"Yes, I thought about that. Once that happens, I will have to come out. People will be surprised but, their greatest fear is the loss of money. I have a lot of rich gay friends who know other rich gay friends who would be willing to support the cause. Some are already clients of the bank and could threaten to pull their money. Others could promise to deposit funds if the right things took place. The loss of the priests' funds has to be met with an equal amount of resources from progressives."

"Wow!"

"Yes, the unfolding of this could be quite interesting but, it's about time people began to challenge things. People like you are hurt. Families like yours are weakened. We need people to understand that the Church's policies are not just wrong - they are dangerous, hurtful, and unjust."

Oliver looked relieved and more relaxed. Giancarlo looked into his eyes and asked, "Are you okay now?"

"Better. I think I want to call Henry sooner than later."

"Do you want to tell him about us, to take some of the pressure off?"

"Not yet. He's not trustworthy with respect to the people I love."

Giancarlo smiled warmly.

The next morning, Giancarlo and Oliver went out on the terrace to call Henry. Giancarlo sat in the wings, and Oliver pushed the button on his phone to dial Henry's number.

"*Pronto*," Henry responded.

"Hello, Henry. This is Oliver."

"Oh, Oliver. Great to hear from you. I hope you're having fun with your friends. Where are you?"

"In Venice at-the-moment. It's quite nice."

"Ah, yes. Venice. I hope it's not too crowded."

"It is, but I'm finding my way along less traveled routes and neighborhoods."

"Good for you. So, what I can do for you?"

"Well, I'm calling because I saw the article about the dismissals."

"Ah, yes. I wondered if you might have seen that."

"I'm very disappointed in you. Explain to me how you could say the things you said given our recent conversations."

"Oh, Oliver. I'm sorry. Don't take it personal. It's Church policy and teaching. I have to promote and defend it. I'm sure you understand."

"No, I don't understand. What you've done hurts me personally. It directly undermines and weakens families like mine and kids like me. What do you think a 12- or 13-year-old kid thinks when the Church says he's being harmed or abused by not having a mother and father? What do you think a 12- or 13-year-old kid thinks when his sexuality is shamed, when he's told he's a moral disgrace, when his role models are embarrassed and dismissed? Have you ever thought why gay teenagers commit suicide at such high rates?"

"Slow down, Oliver. I think you're exaggerating."

"Actually, I'm not. It's worse. Not only does it hurt the families and gay kids you've targeted, it's an assault on truth and an assault on the Church."

"I don't know what you mean."

"You say that your positions are backed by research – that you're just standing up for the truth. That's not true. You know – or should know – that the research says just the opposite. Kids do better with two parents, but the gender of those parents doesn't matter. All of the research and tests on kids raised by gay parents or on the function of gay families is normal or exceeds normal."

Henry was quiet.

"I assume your silence suggests you know that to be the case. So, if what you claim to base your positions on isn't true, and other people know it, what do you think that does to the credibility of the Church. Why do you think people are leaving? The Church is dishonest, and people know it. It's not only dishonest, it's hurtful."

"Are you finished?" Henry said angrily.

"Well, do you have something to say?"

Henry began slowly, deliberately, thoughtfully, "Truth doesn't change by polls, research, or cultural trends. God who is eternal spoke on the matter of gender, family, and parenting. It's in the Bible, it's eternal."

"So, why is it that we no longer allow slavery, but it was allowed and discussed in the Bible?"

"Sometimes one draws on deeper and more substantial truths to find new conclusions."

"So, why couldn't we do the same regarding homosexuality?"

"God created man and woman as complementary. Men achieve their well-being in relationship to women and vice versa. In relationships involving two men or two women, there is no gender complementarity, and thus no authentic sexual love."

"So, my moms don't love each other authentically?"

"That's not what I'm saying."

"What are you saying then?" Oliver insisted forcefully.

"That even as hard as they try, they don't have the gender complementarity that would ground true love."

"Then that is what you're saying – that they don't really love each other."

"Hmm," Henry mumbled.

"So, you'd have me believe that my mothers have been using each other for 24 years just for pleasure, just to satisfy their sexual needs? Do you really think two people would commit to each other, be faithful to each other, sacrifice for each other, take care of each other for 24 years just for sex, just for pleasure? That's beyond believable."

"So, Oliver. It sounds like you've given this some thought. How do we respond to the book of Genesis in the Bible?"

"First of all, there are two stories of creation in the Bible, not one. So, which of these would you like me to consider? It would appear that the truth of the Bible is poetic not singular."

"Whatever you'd like," Henry said with disdain.

"I believe God said it is not good for the human being to be alone. Sexuality is about the importance of companionship, love."

"Good."

"And so gay people have the same need for companionship and love as straight people."

"Go on."

"If we see the same evidence of authentic love in gay people as we see in straight people – and we do – then love must be built on more than gender complementarity."

"I don't understand."

"For heterosexuals, the complementarity of gender is significant. But if gender complementarity was all that was needed for love to arise, then we could expect any man and any woman to be able to love each other, but we know that isn't the case. Love is grounded in something deeper - interpersonal complementarity. It is the rich constellation of personal features of one person in relationship to another that grounds a life of love."

"But if you eliminate gender as a key ingredient, you dismantle procreation and many other things."

"Not all marriages result in children. We know that some people are infertile. How do such couples sustain their marriage? They are generous and life giving in other ways."

Henry was increasingly quiet. Giancarlo, listening in on the call began to nod affirmatively to Oliver. Oliver continued, "Think about my mothers. They gave a child a home – your child – a child you were embarrassed about. Think how generous and life-giving they were. And I want to ask you point blank, can you honestly say I turned out bad because of their love?"

"No, you are a loving, thoughtful, principled, and smart young man. But think about what you might have been had you had a father and a mother. That is what the Church is standing up for - your right to being brought up by a man and a woman so you understand who you are as a man, as a heterosexual."

Oliver gulped. He hadn't expected that. He pondered what to say next. Giancarlo noticed his hesitation and shook his head no. He knew Oliver wanted to come out, to blurt out to his father that he was gay. "Don't do it," Giancarlo whispered to him.

"I think this conversation is over for the moment," Oliver said. "The hypocrisy of your saying I would have turned out better with a father and yet my father abandoned me and abandoned the woman who loved him – that hypocrisy is astounding. Great job Henry. I'm sure the world would congratulate you on a job well done."

Oliver hung up.

"Wow. I wasn't expecting that," Giancarlo interjected.

Oliver began to cry. Giancarlo reached his arm around him, gave him a squeeze and said, "*Caro*, you were incredible. Where did all of that come from?"

"When you grow up in a family that is often assaulted by religious conservatives, you do your research."

"I think you landed a good punch at the end. If I were Henry, I'd be shaking in my boots. He's got to know you are contemplating outing his past."

"Let's get out of here. I need to take a walk, distract myself. I'm raging on the inside."

"Good idea. Let's take a ride to some of the lesser-known islands in the lagoon – or maybe even go to the Lido, the beach."

"Perfect. A little water and sunshine will help heal my frayed nerves."

They walked to the vaporetto stop near San Marco and picked up a boat for Lido. Soon they were gliding across the lagoon toward the beaches of Venice. They disembarked at Lido and walked past several historic hotels to the Adriatic Sea where large waves were rolling up on the sandy shore.

They took off their shoes and began to walk along the edge of the water, passing neat rows of chaise lounges filled with tourists. Oliver leaned his head back and let the warm sun caress his face. He could feel the tension and anger leave his body with each step on the coarse sand.

"Giancarlo, I'm sorry you got dragged into all of this."

"*Caro*, I'm so grateful to have met you. We'll sort this all out."

"But I don't want this to become a problem for you."

"We'll handle it," Giancarlo said, rubbing his hands over Oliver's shoulders.

Oliver wondered if Giancarlo would have second thoughts about their budding relationship as things unfolded with Henry. He was not confident of Giancarlo's affection yet and, out of curiosity asked, "So why is a handsome, smart, and thoughtful person like you single?"

"I told you the other day, I was waiting for you."

"Ahh, that's very sweet but really – why hasn't someone snatched you up?"

"Someone tried, but he wasn't successful."

"Who?"

"It's a long story."

"We've got time," Oliver replied, nodding for Giancarlo to begin.

"A few years ago, I met someone through some mutual friends. He was a schoolteacher, so he appreciated the need to be discrete which was good for me at that time in my career."

"What was he like?"

"Playful, affectionate, social, and handsome."

"Sounds amazing! But?" Oliver pressed.

"Unfaithful."

"You're kidding."

"No, I wish I was. We dated for about six months. Things seemed to be going well. We spent the weekends together – alternating between his and my place. He seemed really into me. He was thoughtful, generous, surprised me with gifts, and we enjoyed similar pastimes. One weekend I had to travel for work for a big account we had in Milan. Martino, his name, stayed behind in Rome. I finished work early and took the fast train back to Rome to be with him. I went to his place, and he was there with another guy – actually, one of our friends. I was devastated."

"How horrible. What did he say?"

"He apologized but then tried to argue that gay people aren't bound by the same rules as straight people – that we don't have to buy into the heterosexual coupling paradigm."

"What did you do?"

"I ended it right away. I get it. There are guys who have open relationships, but that's not for me," Giancarlo said, looking intensely at Oliver.

"Me either," Oliver replied. "Or at least that's not what I imagine for myself."

Giancarlo seemed to sigh in relief and then he continued, "For me, when I form a relationship, I feel like there's a kind of emotional vulnerability that goes with it. You become vulnerable to the other person, and one of the ways you honor that is by being faithful, by creating a safe place for the other, letting them know you are committed to them."

Oliver nodded. "So, anybody else?"

"Not really. I've gone out with a few guys here and there, but nothing has ever clicked, as you say in English. I think maybe I was overly cautious, not wanting to get hurt again."

"That makes sense. But why me? Why so fast?"

"I've been asking myself the same question. It's not like me to dive in like this. Maybe it's the age difference that makes me less nervous."

"Or is it that I live in the States? That this could be over sooner than later?"

Giancarlo nodded. "I've thought of that, too. But surprisingly, I don't see that as a real problem."

"Me either," Oliver added, smiling.

"You're very cute. I love your wavy blonde hair, your dark complexion, your blue eyes, and your lean lanky body. I like how insightful you are. You're smart, curious, and sophisticated yet playful, spontaneous, and innocent. Your innocence isn't naïveté but rather a warm-hearted enthusiasm for life. You're passionate - both in terms of love and affection as well as for justice. You're like a young wine that has complexity and the promise to age well, to become more flavorful and multifaceted with time. I feel like I could grow with you – that you could inspire me and invite me to be the best I could be. Shall I go on?"

"No, I think you've made your point. I'm humbled."

"And you – have you been in love before?"

"As I said the other day, not like this!"

"Surely you must have had a boyfriend or girlfriend?"

"With guys I just fooled around. I think I was curious about the sex but never felt any connection with anyone. There was a girl I dated in high school for a few months. We ended up going to the prom together."

"What's a prom?"

"Oh, it's a big deal in the States. At the end of your senior year in high school, there's a formal dance. Everyone dresses up in tuxes and gowns. You go out to dinner, you go to the dance, and then you go to after-prom parties."

"So, who was this girl?"

"Her name was Anita. She was very popular."

"You must have been, too!"

"Well, I was on the lacrosse team and, seemingly, the girls thought I was a catch."

"They weren't mistaken," Giancarlo said, winking at Oliver.

"Anyway, Anita and I dated for a while. She was very excited that we were going to the prom together. It was a status thing for her."

"You mean going with you?"

Oliver blushed and nodded timidly.

"And?" Giancarlo pressed for more information.

"There just wasn't anything there. She was beautiful, affectionate, brilliant – she was accepted into Yale – but I just didn't feel anything deep down."

"So, no guys either?"

"No, although in retrospect I think the physical stuff with the guys was more appealing. But, in the end, no one really connected."

Giancarlo began to feel sweaty, and a knot formed in his stomach. As they talked, he began to realize how new this all was for Oliver – how he was probably Oliver's first real love – male or female. Giancarlo began to rethink things in his head. Maybe he should take this more slowly, create some distance between them, give Oliver space and time to get used to his new identity. Was it wise to date a 20-year-old, he asked himself?

Oliver could see the reticence in Giancarlo's face, and he said, "Do you believe in soulmates?"

Giancarlo was surprised by the question. He gazed at Oliver, looked out over the water, and then turned back to him. "In general, no. I think it's a notion concocted by film producers and novelists to hook us on romance. There are people with whom you are compatible, and you make them your mate, your companion. But it's not like there's someone you were destined to meet, if that's what you mean."

Oliver went blanch, and Giancarlo noticed right away. He realized that for Oliver their meeting had been unexpected and thus a kind of fortuitous or providential moment, something fated to happen. He had to admit that for him it had been the same and that perhaps he was wrong about the idea of soulmates. Maybe there was something like destiny, and maybe it was hitting him over the head.

"How do you explain our meeting?" Oliver asked pointedly.

"Well," Giancarlo began, "you have to admit it was unexpected."

"It was more than unexpected. It was unlikely. There's no way we should have met, but we did. And, when we met, there was an instant connection."

"I admit that."

"What, that we shouldn't have met or that there was an instant connection?" Oliver inquired.

"Both," Giancarlo answered.

"Isn't that significant and meaningful?"

"Or, playing devil's advocate, maybe it was just a random but nice accident."

"There are things that are random but when they are meaningful, it's hard to say they are just an accident, even if a nice one."

"True," Giancarlo nodded.

"And if the randomness is extraordinary – something very unlikely to have occurred – doesn't that add to the meaningfulness?" Oliver pressed further.

"Maybe."

"You don't persuade easily," Oliver noted.

"I think I inherited my father's skepticism."

"Let me take another line," Oliver continued. "Maybe the idea of soulmates has to do with someone who gets you, someone who recognizes who you are and awakens a deeper part of you than anyone else has."

Yes," Giancarlo murmured, "continue."

"Well, that's what I feel about us – that somehow we awaken something in each other that is profound and new and enriching."

"Yes, but that doesn't necessarily mean that it has to do with providence or destiny."

"But, whether it's providence or not, isn't it worth pursuing?"

"Yes, as long as," Giancarlo began until Oliver interrupted him.

"Shhhh. There's no 'as long as' here. Didn't you just say I was like a wine that could mature with age? Don't we owe it to what we have discovered to follow it through?"

"Who said we shouldn't?" Giancarlo protested.

"The look on your face earlier when you realized how new this was to me."

"I didn't say that."

"You didn't have to."

"I'm scared but excited."

"Me, too. Isn't that wonderful?" Oliver remarked, reaching over and giving Giancarlo a warm kiss.

Giancarlo nodded. He grabbed Oliver's hand and the walked forward in silence.

Later they took a vaporetto back to Venice, disembarked at the Rialto bridge, and walked back to their hotel.

11

Chapter Eleven

Giancarlo and Oliver enjoyed the rest of their time in Venice, each trying to dispel any second thoughts or doubts about their budding relationship.

Oliver had expected some kind of response from Henry after their heated exchange and only got a cryptic text from him: "When you're back in Rome, let's talk."

They returned to Rome Sunday afternoon. Giancarlo had taken Monday off, and they were going to explore more of the Roman Forum.

That Monday morning, Oliver was seated at Giancarlo's dining table, sipping espresso, enjoying a croissant, and slicing a fresh pear that he ate with a little goat cheese. He checked emails and texted his moms. Giancarlo was finishing up with his shower and came down the steps dressed in shorts and a light pullover, ready for a day in the Forum.

"Are you ready to head out, soon?" he asked Oliver.

"Yeah, just give me a moment. I'm checking my mail."

Giancarlo picked up his phone off the kitchen counter. There was a text from Henry: "Giancarlo. I hope you are well. I have a question for you. How much money can I liquidate from my trust?"

Giancarlo said to Oliver, "Hey dear, I just got a strange message from Henry asking about liquidating some of his trust."

Oliver responded, "I just got an interesting email from him, too. He wants to meet with me before I leave for the States, something about some assistance he would like to provide for my education."

"He's going to try to buy you off," Giancarlo said.

"How much do you think he's going to offer?" Oliver inquired.

"He could withdraw about 200,000 euros now. That's a large sum, but he might know that he's in deep trouble if you decide to challenge what he's doing."

"200,000 euros. Incredible!" Oliver said excitedly. "However, he could offer me a million, and I wouldn't back off."

"Dear, let's be rational. Why should you pass up a million euros to make a point that few will even notice?" Giancarlo proposed.

"First of all, he probably won't offer a million," Oliver continued. "Second of all, he may not offer anything. He could retire and walk away from it all. I don't see what's in it for him to continue if he faces a scandal."

"You're right. Does this mean he might be more useful as an insider seeking change than as someone exposed who might simply give up?" Giancarlo considered. "If that's the case, we need to be careful how hard we push him."

"Agreed," Oliver replied. "Why don't you text him your answer, and I'll propose he and I meet tomorrow. Right now, we should enjoy your day off and head to the Forum."

"Wonderful idea!"

They sent Henry their messages, grabbed their phones and wallets, and headed out the door. They walked across the Tiber River past the Theatre of Marcellus. It was an ancient structure that had been converted into apartments during the Middle Ages but recently restored by archaeologists to its original form. They meandered up the inclined road to the Capitoline Hill, the original summit of Rome where the magnificent temple of Jupiter once stood. They climbed the broad ramp, passed under the colossal statues of Castor and Pollux, and stood in the small piazza designed by Michelangelo.

"Michelangelo was given the task of reorienting the Capitoline Hill. For centuries, the focus had been on the Forum – the center of ancient Rome. But in the 1500s, the idea was to celebrate a new Rome – Christian Rome. The Catholic Church saw itself as the inheritor of the grandeur of Rome and the Vatican was its center. So, the piazza and its buildings face away from the Forum and toward St. Peter's in the distance," Giancarlo explained.

They made their way down toward the entrance of the Forum, bought their tickets, and then began the long walk up the Palatine Hill.

"Tell me again why you wanted to come back to this part of the park?"

"I don't think I fully comprehended the significance of it. I need to see it again and put the pieces together," Oliver explained.

"You're fascinating," Giancarlo exclaimed. "Most tourists rush to the other side of the hill, get a glimpse of the massive Circus Maximus, and then head to the Colosseum. What's your interest in this?"

"My conversations with Henry sparked all sorts of questions. When I was here the other day, I felt something emotional. I can't put my fingers on it."

"Well, let's take a look."

The walk up the hill was relaxing. The temperature was pleasant. Shade cast by the mature umbrella pine trees lessened the intensity of the bright sun. They passed under ancient arches, standing solitary amongst the trees, sentinels to another age. They followed a beaten path of gravel and clay to a crest filled with active exca-vations. Just below the path was a structure of rooms lined with frescos. "This is the so-called house of Livia, the wife of Augustus," Giancarlo began. Oliver leaned over the railing and peered into the dark cavernous space.

"Why so-called?"

"As with a lot of archaeology, we only have conjecture based on a few fragments of information or remains. These structures date back to the 1st century and were apparently preserved even when the area was rebuilt by later emperors."

"So, they were seeking to preserve the heritage of Augustus and his family," Oliver guessed.

"Exactly. But, more importantly, just below this area – see over there – are the excavations of huts from earliest Rome." They de-scended the steep walkway and gazed into the excavation site. There were numerous foundations of round structures. Giancarlo noted, "These date back to somewhere between 700 and 900 BC."

"Wow!" Oliver said, tears welling up in his eyes.

Giancarlo noticed and rubbed his eyes affectionately. "Why so emotional?"

"I don't know. I'm asking myself the same question," Oliver said, now smiling in embarrassment. "So, when was Rome founded – or I should ask – when was the date of the story of Romulus and Re-mus?"

"Traditionally, it is alleged to be 753 BC. There are other dates given by historians in ancient times, but this seems to be the gener-ally accepted one."

"And these huts?"

"They date to that same age. They even found a trench that cor-responds to the legend of Romulus tracing out the boundary of the city, although there are questions about its authenticity."

"And the legend?"

"Well, historians have always had to grapple with the two stories of Rome's founding – the flight of Aeneas from Greece and the legend of Romulus and Remus – a local story. The Roman myth focused on the birth of the twins by Rhea Silva, a vestal virgin, and the god Mars. With many mythological stories, the idea is that great peoples or nations arise from divine and human origins. Belief in their divine ancestry inspires people to work together to achieve their lofty destiny."

"What is the story of the she-wolf?"

"The king of the surrounding tribes at that time, Amulius, feared that the twins would challenge his authority and had them cast into the Tiber. Some legends describe a peasant putting them in a reed basket so they would be safe, like the story of Moses in Egypt. Other legends suggest that the twins were abandoned in a cave, the Lupercal, and suckled by a wolf."

"How did they become founders of Rome?"

"A shepherd raised them, and when they were older, they began to distinguish themselves as leaders. They got involved in a dispute between two rival kings of the local tribes. Several leaders suspected their origins and supported their cause, leading to their ascent and the founding of Rome as a new city."

"But only Romulus survived, right?"

"Yes. When they were seeking to establish Rome, there was a dispute about where to locate the city – on the Palatine Hill or the Aventine Hill. The twins got involved in a contest of auguries and Romulus won, allegedly killing his brother afterwards."

"So, this must be the most sacred place in ancient Rome?"

"Well, in some sense yes. Although the temple of Jupiter on the Capitoline was probably more important. We know this area was considered important since Augustus built his palace here. Prior to Augustus, the area was a wealthy residential district. But, after Augustus, it was the location of imperial palaces. Augustus clearly

wanted to associate himself with the history of Rome – that somehow he embodied Rome and its greatness and that he and his successors were there to preserve the heritage."

"The Pax Romana, the peace and prosperity that had been established by Augustus in the 1st century."

"Exactly. And there's even a legend that Livia's house was built
over the Lupercal – the cave of the she-wolf – further association
with the origins of Rome."

"I find it fascinating how the legitimacy of a nation or religion or
people is often tied to a location like this. The ideals are reinforced
in connection with the story – in this case the story of the union of a
mortal woman and the god of war – or at St. Peter's – the authority
of a simple Galilean fisherman who carries on the mission of Jesus
who is son of a mortal woman – Mary - and God," Oliver noted.

"The shrines preserve the original founding myth and the ideals
of the people. The authorities seek to reinforce their authority by
proximity to these places."

"But what if the practices of the leaders betray the original ideals
or the original story?" Oliver mused, thinking of the inconsistency
of Catholic views on gay people and Jesus' inclusive love?

"That's where those who challenge corrupt authority can also ap-
peal to the original founding stories. Change is often a matter of
unveiling the implications of a founding myth or ideal for shedding
light on contemporary concerns. Most moments of transition are
not a radical rupture with the pass but a transformation or even a
return to the original principles."

Oliver rubbed his chin as he looked down at the huts. He felt a
flutter in his chest, an unconscious reaction to something. It was almost as if he were looking at a mirror, that the passing of history
and the shift of historical moments wasn't something that had happened in the past in another place, but was something he was fully
part of, something happening here and now. The huts before him,

the foundations of Augustus's palace nearby, and the dome of St. Peter's in the far-off distance were monuments to pivotal moments in history, each involving continuity and change. He realized he was standing in a new pivotal moment, and he shuddered in both excitement and apprehension.

They were alone, and Giancarlo noticed Oliver's pensiveness. "Are you okay?"

Oliver nodded without saying anything, overcome with emotion.

Giancarlo put his arm around Oliver's shoulders and pulled him close. "There's something happening to you here."

Oliver nodded again. Timidly he said, "This is just so moving. I don't know why. It feels a part of me."

"I understand. Growing up in Rome, I often had similar feelings."

"Have you ever thought about living anywhere else?" Oliver asked.

"Not really. I studied in Milan, but this is my home. I feel a part of it."

"I can see that in you. Did you like Milan?"

"Yes, although aside from the skiing nearby, there's nothing much that draws me to the northern part of Italy."

Giancarlo's reference to skiing jolted Oliver out of his pensive trance. He asked, "You like to ski?"

"I love it. Do you?"

"Yes. My mothers and I go skiing a lot in New Hampshire and in Vermont. Where do you ski?"

"When I was in Milan, there were a lot of places within a short drive. I guess my favorite areas were in the northwest of Italy – Cervinia, Courmayeur, and places like that."

"Did you ever go to Switzerland?"

"At Cervinia you can ski from Italy to Switzerland. It's very cool. Nearby is Verbier. I speak French, and it's a wonderful resort."

"I'd love to go sometime."

"We will," Giancarlo said, smiling warmly at Oliver.

"You ready to head back?" Oliver suggested, taking a protracted look at the huts and then slowly pivoting, taking in the surroundings as he did.

Giancarlo said, "Sure. We can always come back."

They walked back to Giancarlo's apartment and checked emails.

Henry wanted to meet him the next morning at the Hotel Santa Chiara where he thought Oliver was staying.

"What should I tell him?" Oliver asked nervously.

"Tell him you are going to be over in the St. Peter's area – that maybe you could meet at a café in the area," Giancarlo recommended. "I would also encourage you to take your phone and record the conversation. It might prove useful later."

Oliver arranged the meeting. Oliver and Giancarlo took the afternoon easy, each doing a little reading and work. Giancarlo prepared a nice pasta dish for them, and they settled on the sofa afterwards to watch some movies on TV.

The next morning, Oliver woke early, his heart racing in anticipation of his meeting with Henry. He tiptoed downstairs, made some coffee, and checked emails. A little while later, Giancarlo appeared. He had just rolled out of bed and was wearing only a pair of shorts. His hair was tousled, and he yawned as he looked out the window at the morning light. "Hey dear," he said as he approached Oliver and gave him a kiss.

Oliver had been unsettled and distracted but, with Giancarlo standing next to him, he began to relax. He looked up at Giancarlo's muscular chest, broad shoulders, and his alluring eyes. He rubbed his hand over the soft dark hair running from his abdomen up across his pecs and gave each a squeeze. He noticed Giancarlo getting a little hard and ran his hand around the back of his buttocks, pulling him up close to his face and tugging at the fabric of his shorts with his teeth.

"Don't start something you can't finish," Giancarlo admonished him.

"Oh, I can finish it alright. The question is whether you're ready for it or not."

"Let me get some coffee first," Giancarlo winked at him. He made a cup of espresso and then came and sat next to Oliver at the table. "How are you doing?"

"I'm nervous. I didn't sleep well."

"I know. You were stirring a lot."

"Sorry."

"It's okay," Giancarlo said. "This is a big deal. Is there anything I can do?"

Oliver nodded no and turned his head back to the computer screen to check more emails.

"So, what's the plan?" Giancarlo asked.

"Well, I'm going to meet Henry at a café on the Borgo Pio, near the Vatican. I'll listen to what he has to say and record our conversation. I imagine he's going to directly or implicitly bribe me, and I need to decide what I want to do – or rather, what we want to do."

"What's your thought?"

"The more I think about it," Oliver began, "the more upset I am. I'm not upset so much for me. I'm upset for the harm the Church is doing to gay families and to gay adolescents who internalize the shame and are at greater risk for suicide or decisions that put them in danger. This needs to stop."

"So, practically speaking, what does that mean?"

"I think I need to press Henry hard. I'm in a unique situation to challenge someone who is in a position to change the actions of the Church. I can't pass this up."

"So, what are you going to do?"

"I don't know yet. I think I will know in the situation. I know that's not much of a plan, but I need to trust my gut."

"I'll support you whatever."

"Thanks. You're incredible," Oliver said as he looked affectionately at Giancarlo.

"No, you're incredible both in terms of your principles and in how you have totally changed my life in such a short amount of time. I love you."

"I love you, too," Oliver said in reply.

Oliver excused himself and went upstairs to shave and shower. Giancarlo followed. They both dressed, Giancarlo in a suit for the bank and Oliver in jeans and a dress shirt for his meeting with Henry. They headed out the door and walked across the river to the historic center. Giancarlo continued to the bank, and Oliver walked down the Corso Vittorio Emmanuel toward the Vatican.

He found the small café on the Borgo Pio and picked out a table for their meeting, one that was a bit removed from the others. He ordered an espresso and waited for Henry.

Henry approached, dressed in a dark suit and collar. Oliver stood and shook his hand and invited Henry to take a seat. "Can I order you a coffee or something else?"

"I'll have a cappuccino, thank you."

Oliver waived down the waiter and ordered a cappuccino for Henry and another espresso for himself.

"Well, Oliver," Henry began, nervously wringing his hands. "I have been thinking about what you said the other day on the phone. It's all very well thought out and probably well founded. Unfortunately, change in the Church is slow and that can be frustrating. I want to promise you I will do what I can to move that change along, but I need you to be understanding and patient."

Oliver nodded.

"I know it's not much of a consolation, but I'm prepared to offer you some resources for your own studies in the hope that you recognize it as a gesture or pledge on my part. I am able to liquidate some of the trust and give it to you sooner than later. I would like to give you 100,000 euros as a pledge of my sincerity and hope that you will be patient."

Oliver didn't respond at first. He looked pensive and rubbed his chin to signal his consideration of Henry's offer. He continued to remain silent, looking for words he would like to express. None came. Henry began to get nervous and impatient and said, "Well, what do you think?"

"I'm at a loss for words. Essentially, if I understand what you're proposing, you're asking me to stand aside as the Church continues to ruin people's careers and create internalized shame for adolescents who are more at risk of committing suicide or harming themselves if they think their sexual orientation is perverted, unnatural, and immoral."

"I'm asking you to be patient. Change is slow."

"Why?" Oliver asked, "Why is change slow? The information is there to support change – the research you chose to ignore in your document."

Henry bristled. Oliver was convinced he didn't accept the evidence of current research. He then began to speak, "I'm just one man. I can't change the institution."

"But you're one man who is at the center of that institution and at the center of this particular set of events. Your action is the direct cause of harm and, it would seem, you have the power to reverse that or soften it."

"I can't."

"You can't or you won't?" As he spoke, Henry stiffened, his shoulders arched forward and his neck muscles flexing with tension. Oliver looked straight into his eyes and asked, "Why can't you do anything?"

Henry lowered his head. "I can't say."

"Who are you protecting?"

Henry shook his head no.

Oliver looked at him intensely and a thought came over him. What if Henry was about to be promoted, perhaps become a bishop or head of a congregation? If he were to challenge things now, his career would be finished. He wasn't prepared to sacrifice that.

"Help me understand what happens behind the scenes," Oliver began. "If evidence contradicts what the Church teaches, how is that handled? Why doesn't it change the equation? If I recall, Pope John Paul II said, when he apologized for how the Church treated Galileo, that if clear and certain reason contradicts the teaching of scripture, we have to find a new way of understanding the scripture so that our interpretation lines up with reason, right?"

"Yes, I believe he said that."

"So, if clear and certain reason shows that being gay isn't a pathology and that gay relationships and families bear the same marks of love, commitment, happiness, and other qualities as heterosexual relationships and families, why doesn't a congregation like yours take that into account and seek to interpret scripture or even church teaching in a different way? Aren't you refusing to follow papal teaching and refusing to follow the principles of Catholic theology?"

Henry nodded, "I guess you could say that."

"So, help me understand why that doesn't happen."

"I don't know. I guess we're afraid of change."

"Let me venture a guess. I suspect that the Church with its teachings has created a comfortable place for men who are uncomfortable with their sexuality. They cloak themselves in piety to conceal the shame they feel about themselves. If the Church changed course, they would have to look afresh at their sexuality, and many are not willing to do that."

Henry bristled again.

"And let me venture another guess. You're not willing to challenge things because the system is a comfortable place for you, too. You cling tenaciously to the idea that your affair with my biological mother makes you a heterosexual, but that's not the case, is it?

Henry remained speechless, his head hanging down.

Oliver continued, "You mentioned to me that your father had made fun of you, had called out your intellectual, artistic, and sensitive tendencies. You mentioned that you wanted to prove that you were different from your colleagues. But, in the final analysis, you're not. You are just like them – self-loathing and using the Church as a comfortable closet."

Henry shook his head. He slowly stood up and glared at Oliver. Then he tossed his napkin down on his chair and began to walk away. Oliver looked at him incredulously.

He sat quietly for a moment and then when Henry was out of sight, he texted Giancarlo: "Call me when you can."

A few moments later, Giancarlo called, and Oliver explained what had transpired. "So, what are you going to do now?" he inquired of Oliver.

"I don't know. I feel sorry for him. But I also don't want to drop this."

"Why don't you go home, relax, and I'll be there soon."

A few moments later, Henry walked to the bank, entered the lobby, and asked for Giancarlo. Giancarlo put down his phone and stood, waving Henry over to his desk.

"Fr. Henry, what I can do for you?" Giancarlo inquired.

"I texted the other day about a withdrawal. I'd like to withdraw 100,000 from my trust."

"Ok. Let me get a form out for that." Giancarlo opened a drawer in his desk and pulled out a pad of forms, ripped one off and laid it on the top of the desk. Then he continued, "As your financial advisor, I'm curious. What do you have in mind?"

Fr. Henry replied, "I have an opportunity for an investment, and I'd like to use some of the trust for it."

"Do you have an account you want us to send the money to?"

Henry hesitated then said, "Can I get it in cash?"

"We have to be able to account for that large a sum of money. It either needs to be in a cashier check made out to you or we have to deposit it directly into another account with the account holder's name and bank number."

Henry rubbed his chin. "Let's do a cashier check made to me. I assume I can then endorse it to someone else, right?"

"Yes, you can."

Giancarlo typed in Henry's account number on his computer and began to complete the form. He looked up from time to time, and Henry seemed nervous. Giancarlo interjected, "So, Fr. Henry, how have you been doing since I last saw you – I believe last week with Oliver?"

"Fine," Henry replied without elaboration.

"He seemed like a nice young man."

"Yes."

"So, all of the fields on the form are complete. I need your signature and date." Giancarlo rotated the form and placed it in front of Henry.

Henry signed and dated it quickly.

"It will just take a few moments for me to get one of the tellers to issue a check."

Henry nodded.

A few moments later, Giancarlo returned with a check, placed it in an envelope and handed it to Henry who swiftly slipped it into his jacket pocket and extended his hand to Giancarlo. "Thank you." He then headed for the door.

When Henry was out the door, Giancarlo texted Oliver, "Henry just withdrew 100,000 euros."

"Wow. Interesting," Oliver replied.

"Don't go out till I get home."

"Ok."

Around 6, Giancarlo left the bank and walked across town to his apartment. He walked up the stairs, unlocked the door and found Oliver seated on the sofa reading his iPad.

"Hey, *caro*," Giancarlo said as he closed the door and walked toward Oliver.

"It's good to see you," Oliver said. Giancarlo could see that Oliver was unsettled and nervous. "I'm worried about Henry," he added.

"Henry's a big boy. He can take care of himself. You just need to worry about you," Giancarlo said as he sat next to Oliver and placed his hand on his thigh, giving it a tender rub. "Are you hungry? Why don't we go out?"

Giancarlo changed into a pair of jeans and a long-sleeve pullover. Oliver washed his face, brushed his hair, and put on a pair of shoes. They walked down Giancarlo's street and crossed a busy boulevard into an older section of Trastevere. "Where are we going?" Oliver inquired.

"A little trattoria run by some friends of mine. You'll love it."

They walked farther, made a few turns, and ended in front of a small cluster of buildings, one of which included a spotlight over a doorway and a glass-covered menu. They walked inside and the maître d's eyes lit up. "*Giancarlo, carissimo. C'e stato molto tempo che no ci vediamo.*"

"*Antonio, questo e' Oliver, il mio compagno.*"

"A pleasure," Antonio said, giving Oliver a kiss on both cheeks.

"*Compagno come?*" Antonio pressed Giancarlo, trying to figure out in what sense he was referring to Oliver as his companion.

"*Come amante,*" Giancarlo said with emphasis, "he's my lover."

Antonio looked at Oliver. Oliver blushed and smiled. Giancarlo put his arms over his shoulders and squeezed him tightly. "Your best table, please."

Antonio winked at Giancarlo, grabbed two menus, and showed them a quiet table. "*Grazie*," Giancarlo said, giving Antonio a kiss on the cheek.

The intimate room was filled with 10 tables all occupied by gay couples – at least that was Oliver's impression. "This is one of my favorite places. It feels like home. Everyone is very friendly," Giancarlo said as he took Oliver's hand and kissed it.

A couple from across the room waved at Giancarlo. He waved back. They got up and approached Giancarlo's and Oliver's table, "*Giancarlo. E' passato molto tempo.*"

"*Si, sono stato molto occupato.*"

"*Si vede* – one can certainly see you've been busy." They winked at Giancarlo and stared at Oliver.

Giovanni e Tomasso, questo e' Oliver. Oliver, questi sono due amici – ma *stai attenti –* be careful – they are prone to bite."

They extended their hands to Oliver who shook them and said, "*Piacere.*"

"*Piacere nostro*," they added, emphasizing that the pleasure was theirs. They said a few more things to Giancarlo, smiled, and returned to their table.

"You're obviously making a good impression. Everyone's talking about you."

"What do you mean?" Oliver inquired.

"Giovanni and Tomasso mentioned in a whisper that they had heard about us, that everyone has been talking."

"Is that okay with you?"

"Yes, although it's a bit disconcerting. I guess they're all surprised. I haven't dated much."

"Anything else?"

"Well, they say I've robbed the cradle and that you are a hottie."

"They're very observant."

"Hey! Yes, you are a hottie but no, I didn't rob the cradle. You're way more mature than your age. I think you're pulling my leg about being 20."

Oliver blushed.

They ordered dinner, slowly finished a bottle of wine, and discussed what had occurred during the day.

"So, he essentially offered you a bribe," Giancarlo noted at one point in the conversation.

"Yes, but I didn't respond as he had anticipated."

"So, what do you think he's going to do with the 100,000?" Giancarlo pressed further.

"Maybe he'll make another try. I fully expect the conversation is not over."

"I imagine you are right. He is in a tight corner, and he's trying to figure out how to navigate it. So, you think he's about to be promoted?"

"That would be my guess," Oliver noted.

"And you think he's gay?"

"That's when he got up. I think I hit a raw nerve. I was thrown by the whole affair with a woman thing, too. But he's too fastidious to be straight, and there were too many things he recounted from his childhood that suggest his father feared he would be queer."

"You're probably right, although I've never heard anything regarding him. My sources are usually forthcoming, and no one has mentioned Henry."

"We'll see."

They finished their meal, said goodbye to a few couples, and then began to walk home. Back in the kitchen, both Oliver and Giancarlo checked phone messages and emails. There was nothing from Henry.

They went upstairs. Oliver went into the bathroom and, when he came out, Giancarlo was leaning against the headboard of the bed without anything on, the sheets draped provocatively over his groin.

"Well, this is a nice surprise," Oliver said, leaning on the edge of the bed and slowly tugging at the sheets, revealing Giancarlo's erection underneath. Giancarlo grabbed his hand and pulled Oliver toward him, giving him a warm kiss, and stroking the small of his back. He tugged at Oliver's shirt and pulled it up over his head. His shoulders gleamed in the soft light cast by the bedside table lamp, and his piercing blue eyes sparkled, sending chills down Giancarlo's back.

Oliver stroked the edges of Giancarlo's pecs, hardened by his state of arousal, and he gave them a squeeze. He then ran his hand down Giancarlo's side and over the top of his legs, grazing his erection. He tugged on Giancarlo's right leg, lifting it over his own torso, massaging the calve and the bottoms of his foot as he let it rest between his own legs.

"Oh my God. That feels so good," Giancarlo moaned. "Can you do the other side?"

Oliver pulled himself up over the bottom half of Giancarlo and ran his hand down the back of his left leg, massaging the calve and the bottom of the foot. He then knelt at the edge of the bed and warmly massaged the bottom of both of Giancarlo's feet. As he did so, Giancarlo's erection stretched higher in the air. Oliver's heart raced as he glanced at the beautiful body laid out before him.

Oliver stood up and pulled down his pants, standing at the edge of the bed in his undershorts, stretched by the hardness underneath. Giancarlo leaned forward and kissed the front of Oliver's shorts, tugging playfully at the flesh beneath. Breathing in Oliver's scent, he sighed and ran his hands down the back part of Oliver's legs, finally pulling him up close. He then held him carefully and fell back on the bed, Oliver remaining on top of him.

Giancarlo reached his hands behind Oliver and felt the warm

moistness in his crack, squeezing his firm round buttocks, slowly pressing the undershorts down his legs until they were hanging on his ankles. Oliver kicked them off and crawled further up on top of Giancarlo. He stared into his deep-set brown eyes and ran his hand through his dark hair, tracing his fingers along his brow and over his cheeks, flush with desire.

"I want to eat you up," Oliver said as he opened his mouth and gave Giancarlo a long moist kiss, their tongues tenderly exploring the wet cavernous space between them.

Giancarlo ran his hands over Oliver's back and then up his neck, grabbing hold of the hair on the back of his head. He nuzzled his nose in the small of Oliver's neck and kissed him, Oliver arching his back in ecstasy as he felt Giancarlo's warm tongue explore the space behind his ear. Giancarlo whispered, "*Quanto sei bello* – you're so handsome."

Both Giancarlo and Oliver were lean and, as their bodies became more aroused, their torsos became increasingly taut, pressing firmly against each other. Giancarlo felt particularly turned on as Oliver moved nimbly over him, muscle against muscle. He pressed his hands deeper and deeper into the folds of his back and Oliver resisted playfully.

Giancarlo spread his legs and felt Oliver press himself closer, burrowing his hardness against Giancarlo who moaned. He wrapped his legs around Oliver's back and leaned his head back. Oliver began to kiss the underside of Giancarlo's jaw, moistening the carefully trimmed dark stubble covering the caramel skin below. He ran his wet lips over Giancarlo's Adam's apple and then further down his neck, tenderly kissing his collar bone and shoulders.

They both were sweating as the adrenaline and blood rushed to the surface of their bodies. Neither wanted to bring their passion to a climax, preferring to explore each other's bodies with abandon. Giancarlo held Oliver tightly and rolled them both over so that he was top. He pulled himself back slightly and stared at Oliver. Then he kissed his eyes slowly and tenderly. He continued kissing Oliver's nose, its sensual lines pointing toward his dimpled mouth and angled jaw. He opened his mouth widely to give Oliver another kiss, inhaling Oliver's warm breath racing in the heat of the moment.

He began to kiss the sides of Oliver's pecs, savoring the salty sweetness of his skin. He could feel Oliver become more aroused. He rode up and down over Oliver's hardness and felt Oliver doing the same under him. They both began to lose control of themselves and exploded in spasms of intense pleasure, Giancarlo collapsing on Oliver in exhaustion. He laid his head on Oliver's chest and listened to his heart slowly return to normal. Oliver rubbed his hand through Giancarlo's dark hair and whispered in his ear, "I love you."

Giancarlo said in reply, "*Ti voglio bene.*"

They smiled at each other, and Giancarlo murmured, "Are you sure you haven't had much experience?"

Oliver nodded no.

"Is that a no you're not sure or a no you haven't had experience."

"No experience."

"Well, you're some neophyte!" Giancarlo said, rolling off the bed and walking into the bathroom.

Oliver grabbed his shirt and undershorts and slipped them on, walking into the bathroom behind Giancarlo. They stood in front of the mirror, Oliver behind Giancarlo, his arms reaching around his waist. He whispered to him, "You're so handsome."

Giancarlo turned around and said, "Those blue eyes!" He traced his fingers over them and down his cheek. He then tugged on his ear lobe and said, "What a wonderful surprise you are."

"You, too!"

They cleaned up and then slid under the covers, falling quickly asleep.

12

Chapter Twelve

The next day, Giancarlo went to work, and Oliver walked toward the Colosseum where he was to meet an archaeologist who was going to take him on a tour of an early Christian site, the Basilica of San Clemente. The mid-June day was already heating up as the sun beat down on the dark cobblestone sidewalks and street. He had decided to wear jeans to avoid problems at the church, and he was beginning to rethink that decision as he felt his legs sweat in the humid heat.

Just beyond the Colosseum, at a small café facing ruins of a gladiator training ground, a young woman stood waiting, looked up at him and asked, "Are you Oliver?"

"Yes. You must be Flavia."

"*Piacere.*"

"The pleasure is all mine. Thanks for agreeing to take me on a private tour."

"*Andiamo?*" she asked, pointing in the direction of the basilica.

Oliver smiled and followed Flavia's lead. It was a warm day.

Flavia had on a light cotton skirt, comfortable shoes, and a light blue blouse with a silk scarf loosely draped around her neck.

As they walked up the hill toward the church, she began, "This area was all owned by the imperial Flavian family, the ones who built the Colosseum after Nero's death. Archaeologists have found all sorts of structures – some to support the events at the Colosseum and others for independent use. The current basilica was built in the 12th century. During the last century, the Dominicans who run the church began doing excavations. They found the remains of a 4th century church under the current one and, under that, remains of 1st and 2nd century Roman buildings."

"So, on one site, we have all of the layers of Roman history."

"Yes, it's quite exciting!"

Flavia pushed open the nondescript green door on the side wall of the church and waved Oliver into the cool dark nave of the basilica. It took Oliver a few minutes for his eyes to adjust and quickly he noticed the gleaming gold mosaics over the apse. "Wow!" he said enthusiastically.

Flavia walked over to a machine and dropped in a few coins. Lights illuminated the curved apse, and the beautiful images came into focus. Flavia explained that this is considered one of the nicest examples of mosaic art in Rome. She pointed out the symbolism of the artwork – the cities of Rome and Jerusalem, the twelve lambs, Peter and Paul, the martyrs, the rivers of paradise, and the tree of life. It was an encyclopedia of religious art all in one place.

"This looks like the same style of art as in San Marco in Venice," Oliver noted.

"Precisely. They are of the same artistic period and influence, and both used gold leaf and multi-colored mosaics to create the beautiful effect you see."

"It's incredible," Oliver said, gazing at the magnificent images stretched out before him.

They walked to the back of the church and descended a marble staircase to an excavated area under the church. Oliver could smell the earth as they proceeded deeper underground. His pulse raced in excitement at exploring another ancient site. Flavia explained that the 4th century church was built just after the Christianity began to enjoy freedom in the Empire. One could argue it was one of the earlier parish churches – different from so-called monumental churches Constantine had built over the tombs of St. Peter and St. Paul. The apse of the 4th century church wasn't built until later since it would have required the destruction of a Mithraic temple on the lower level and, until other religions were banned, Christians and members of the Mithraic religion coexisted.

They explored the 4th century level, Flavia doing her best to help Oliver envision the space since it was interspersed with supports for the upper level, making the layout confusing.

"Why are all of the columns different?" Oliver inquired.

"Since this was a more modest structure, funds were probably limited. Recycling architectural pieces from other buildings was a way to economize. And even in the 4th century, there was some decline in the affluence of the city of Rome."

"Come, let's go to the lowest level!" Flavia said with excitement as they had finished visiting the 4th century level.

The stairway down was narrower and, as they arrived at the bottom, the floor was irregular, a compressed form of tufa or volcanic soil. Flavia explained that the 4th century church was built on top of a warehouse with a series of storage rooms encircling a courtyard. Some archaeologists suggested that early Christians may have met here, but Flavia disagreed.

She then led Oliver to the Mithraeum, a nice example of a Mithraic temple. Oliver peered through the iron gate that protected the room and noticed the reclining triclinium – dining table – and the constellations etched in the ceiling and the statue of Mithras slaying a bull.

Flavia explained that In Mithraism, members were "reborn" through a ritual bath, were received into the community with a ritual handshake, and were then part of the community that shared in a sacred meal of bread and wine consecrated by "fathers" in intimate cave-like rooms where the story of Mithras was retold and reenacted. Mithras was born from a rock, miraculously produced water, wrestled a wild bull back into the cave, and slayed it. The bull was sacrificed so that new life could be produced. There were mythological connections between the bull and the moon and Mithras and the sun – so that the story of Mithras involved a cosmic struggle and sacrifice, not merely an earthly one. The Christian writer Tertullian believed that the similarities between Christianity and Mithraism were so close that the devil must have invented Mithraism to dupe people away from the true faith.

"So, who was Clement since this place was named after him?" Oliver inquired.

"That's a good question," Flavia responded. "He must have been someone associated with the imperial household to have been able to use the area as a place for Christians to meet. There is speculation that he was a Jewish ex-slave who converted to Christianity. Also, there was a Flavius Clemens who was a senator and cousin of Domitian. He was condemned to death for being atheist, suggesting that he was, in fact, a Christian."

"You mention women as benefactors. I read someplace that early Christianity was popular, in part, because it offered opportunities for leadership to women," Oliver inquired of Flavia.

"*Appunto!*" She said excitedly. "In fact, in Paul's Letter to the Romans, he addresses women who were apostles and deacons. Some archaeologists believe that wealthy widows offered their homes to early Christian communities and even presided over their banquets, what we would today call the Eucharist or Mass."

"What happened?"

"After Constantine, when Christianity became official and began to merge with the dominant Roman imperial culture, women were prohibited from holding official leadership positions as this offended the patriarchal culture of ancient Rome."

"Things haven't changed much, have they?" Oliver asked.

"Only that Christianity had been revolutionary at one time and has now become the preserver of male privilege in another time," Flavia added.

They finished the tour, and exited the basilica, blinded by the bright sun outside. "Let me show you one of my favorite bookstores," Flavia said enthusiastically. She walked down the street and entered a small shop full of manuscripts, maps, and artifacts.

"Wow!" Oliver exclaimed as he began to trace his fingers over countless titles - special studies on Roman history, archaeology, and art.

"I knew you would like it! I have another appointment. Can I leave you here?"

"Flavia, you've been incredible. Thank you. Can I call you later for another tour?"

"Absolutely. It would be my pleasure. I always like clients who are genuinely interested in history."

Oliver nodded, handed Flavia her stipend, gave her a kiss on the cheek and then turned back toward the center of the bookstore. He began to take several volumes off the bookshelves. Many were in Italian, and with his Spanish background, he could make some sense of them. There was a limited-edition book of photos of underground sites in Rome. He decided to get it as a gift for Giancarlo. It would look great in his parlor on the coffee table. He put back a few books but kept four. He paid the bill and then headed down the street. He found a taxi and returned to Giancarlo's apartment.

Once inside, he decided to text Henry. He wanted to continue their exchange.

"Henry. I'm sorry if I upset you yesterday. Let's talk. Are you free?"

There was no response. Oliver took his shoes off, laid on the sofa, and began to read the new books he had purchased. Around 4, Giancarlo texted that he had finished work early and wanted to meet Oliver in the historical center. Oliver slipped on a pair of shoes, changed into a fresh pair of pants, and headed out the door.

Giancarlo was sitting at a small table in the Piazza Rotonda, in front of the Pantheon. The sun was just far enough down on the horizon to begin to create shade on the north side of the square. They sat under a large umbrella and ordered a round of Camparis and soda.

"So, how was the tour with Flavia? Isn't she great?"

"She was incredible. I learned so much, and I didn't realize there's so much of ancient times still able to be seen on site."

"Welcome to Rome!" Giancarlo said enthusiastically.

"I started thinking. Maybe I should switch to archaeological studies."

"And give up a career in finance? I don't think so."

"Why not. I'm sure Flavia does well giving tours."

"It's a long process. You have to study, then pass exams, and then get on a special list of licensed guides. It's an arduous process."

"I'm young."

Giancarlo nodded and took a sip of his Campari. He grinned. "You're so cute when you're animated. It's inspiring."

Oliver blushed.

"So, any word from Henry," Giancarlo inquired.

"No, it's very strange. I texted him and didn't get a response."

"Did he get your text?"

"The phone said it was delivered. I couldn't tell if he had read it or not."

"Hmm. Well, we just need to wait and see."

As they discussed Henry, Oliver felt an unsettledness in his stomach. Something wasn't right, but he couldn't figure out what it was. His intuition was generally good, but he couldn't get a clear read. They finished their drinks, got a pizza at a local pizzeria, and then returned home.

The next morning, Oliver got up early and went downstairs to make coffee and eat a little cereal with yogurt. He checked his emails and messages. Nothing from Henry.

Giancarlo woke, joined Oliver downstairs, ate breakfast, showered, and went to work. Oliver remained in the apartment, sat on the terrace under the umbrella, and read his books. He was energized as he poured over them and was increasingly curious about the idea of switching careers. Around mid-morning he decided to call Henry's office to see if he could connect with him.

He dialed the number of the Congregation for Education and a receptionist answer. "*Pronto.*"

"*Si, voglio parlare con il Padre Enrico Montpierre.*"

The receptionist put him on hold. A few moments later, a male voice came on the line. "Can I help you?"

"I'm Oliver Monte-Fitzpatrick. I had met with Fr. Henry last week, and I was wanting to thank him for the visit before I returned to Boston."

There was a delay on the other end of the line and the voice began timidly, "I'm sorry. Fr. Henry isn't in the office."

"When might you expect him?" Oliver inquired.

"He was supposed to be here already for a couple of meetings, but he hasn't arrived. Can I take your name and number and let him know you called?"

"Yes, please do." Oliver gave his contact information and hung up. As he did, he felt a sense of dread.

He texted Giancarlo: "*Caro.* I called Henry's office, but he hasn't come in today. He was expected."

"Hmmm." Giancarlo texted back.

"I'm not feeling good about this."

Giancarlo replied, "Let me see if there's anything I can do to trace him."

"Thanks. Let me know what you find."

Giancarlo typed in Henry's name into his computer and noted his address. It was a side street off the Borgo Pio, near the Vatican. He decided to take a taxi there and knock on his door. About a half-hour later, he buzzed the door. There was no response. An old man approached the main door of the building and began to unlock the door. He looked at Giancarlo suspiciously. Giancarlo inquired in Italian, "Do you know Fr. Henry Montpierre. He was supposed to be at a meeting earlier."

The man responded in Italian, "He left early this morning."

"Okay," Giancarlo said. "I was just worried about him."

The man nodded and waited for Giancarlo to leave.

Giancarlo texted Oliver to let him know that Henry wasn't at home. They decided to wait to see if he surfaced in some way. Surely, he would be in touch with Oliver knowing that he needed to resolve their dispute.

The next morning, they still hadn't heard from Henry. No messages. No emails. Giancarlo pulled up the electronic version of one of the Italian newspapers and began to scan the headlines. As he scrolled down, a small article popped up. The headline read, "Vatican priest found dead in his apartment off the Borgo Pio. Police are investigating the circumstances of his death."

"Oh God. Oliver, I think this may be Henry. Brace yourself."

Oliver leaned over Giancarlo's laptop and Giancarlo read the small news blip. "Oh my God," Oliver began. "Do you think he committed suicide? Oh no."

Giancarlo reached his arm over Oliver's shoulder and squeezed him tightly. "First of all, we don't know if it is Henry. But, even if it is, let's not jump to conclusions yet. Maybe there was foul play or a heart attack or something else."

"I know it's Henry. I've been feeling it for the past twenty-four hours."

"Let me make some calls."

Giancarlo called the reporter at the newspaper who confirmed it was Fr. Henry. "Do you know anything else about the circumstances?"

The reporter noted that since the Vatican police were the initial responders, there hadn't been any information released yet. "They are usually very protective of the circumstances of deaths like these," the reporter said. "However, a friend of mine at Santo Spirito hospital tipped me off. It looks like it was a suicide."

Giancarlo's face went blanch. He looked at Oliver who noticed the alarm.

Giancarlo said, "*Grazie*," and hung up the phone.

"Oliver, *caro*. I think Henry committed suicide."

Oliver began to break down in tears. "I can't believe it. I shouldn't have been so hard on him."

"It's not your fault. He was haunted by his own demons."

"He had found a way to deal with them."

"Yes, at others' expense. It's tragic, I realize. But think of the harm and deaths he may have caused by his actions. It's one thing to be self-loathing and cause harm to yourself. It's another to project that onto others. You were simply holding a mirror up for him to see."

"I know. But I could have been more understanding or diplomatic."

Giancarlo and Oliver hugged.

"What are we going to do?" Oliver asked, looking with teary eyes at Giancarlo.

Giancarlo looked off in the distance as if he had a thought. "Hurry. Let's get dressed," he said to Oliver, taking his hand and leading him upstairs. They showered and dressed and then went to the bank. Once inside, Giancarlo sat Oliver across from his desk and began to type in some information.

"Just as I thought. The check for 100,000 has been cashed."

"What do you mean?" Oliver asked, perplexed.

"The check we issued Henry the day before yesterday has been cashed."

"Do you know who cashed it?"

"I think I can find out, but I'll have to ask a colleague to take a look." Giancarlo stood up and went back into one of the offices in the senior management section of the building. After a few minutes, he returned with a piece of paper in hand.

"This is very confidential. We could be in trouble if someone found out we had this information. The check was cashed and deposited into an account here. That's how we know who it is."

"Well?" Oliver said, waiting for Giancarlo to continue.

"It's a doctor. Doctor Giacomo Salvatore. He runs a small clinic in the Prati neighborhood of Rome. I have his address."

"Do we go there. Say something to him?"

"No, that's too risky now. Let's see how things unfold."

"What do you think is up?" Oliver asked.

"I think you were right. Our Fr. Henry was gay. He must have had a relationship with Dr. Salvatore. Maybe he was his physician. Perhaps that's how they met."

"Can you look up any information about him?"

"I'm typing in Google as we speak."

"And?"

"Well, there's not much here. He's a general practitioner. He has an office in the Prati – not far from Henry's apartment. He's married and has two children who are 16 and 18. And, he's very handsome. Look at this picture."

"Son of a bitch!" Oliver shouted as he looked up from Giancarlo's computer.

Giancarlo looked at him incredulously. Oliver noted his consternation and said, "I feel sorry for him. But all the while that he's removing gay teachers, he's having an affair with a man."

"Let's not jump the gun yet. I agree, that's what it looks like, but he could have just been paying old debts or something like that."

"100,000 euros? Come on." Oliver said.

Giancarlo nodded. Then he began to type in more information into the computer. He smiled and looked up at Oliver, "You know what all of this means?"

"What?" Oliver asked.

"You just inherited nearly a million euros and an apartment in Rome."

"The trust, right?"

"Yep. I don't see any documentation revoking it. It's on file. You're the beneficiary. If Henry had intended to remove you in revenge, he would have done so, just as he handed Giacomo a check for 100,000 euros."

"Oh my God."

Giancarlo nodded, choked with emotion. "It's sad and momentous at the same time."

Oliver sat mesmerized in his chair, rubbing his hand through his thick blonde curly hair, and shaking his head.

Oliver's phone vibrated, a call announced on the screen, "*Citta del Vaticano.*"

He looked up, showed the screen to Giancarlo. "Should I take it?"

"Yes."

"*Pronto*," Oliver said as he pressed the button to respond to the call.

"Oliver Monte-Fitzpatrick?"

"*Sì, sono io.*"

"This is Monsignor Flanagan from the Congregation for Education. I work with Fr Henry Montpierre. I believe you know him. Can you come to my office to meet with me?"

Oliver looked over at Giancarlo who shook his head no. He wrote a message on a piece of paper and shoved it over to Oliver, "Ask to meet him at a local café."

"Monsignor Flanagan, can I suggest that we meet at a café, perhaps one on the Borgo Pio. I met Fr. Henry there the other day."

There was a pause and then monsignor Flanagan said yes and suggested they meet in a half hour.

Oliver hung up and gave Giancarlo a hug. "Do you want me to go with you?"

"No, I think it's better this way."

Oliver took a taxi to the Vatican and made his way to the little café where he had met Henry a few days before. A portly Irish priest sat at a small table at the edge of the café and nodded to him. He was wiping perspiration from his forehead and stood as Oliver approached.

"I'm Monsignor Flanagan. You look just like your picture. Thanks for coming."

"Oliver. Nice to meet you." He extended his hand and then took a seat opposite Flanagan who lowered himself onto his wobbly chair.

"I presume you might be aware that Fr. Henry was missing. Someone mentioned you had called our office."

"Yes."

"Well, Fr. Henry was found dead in his apartment yesterday evening."

"Oh my God," Oliver noted, pretending surprise. "What happened?"

"We don't know yet. We're still trying to figure that out."

"That's terrible. He seemed fine the other day."

Flanagan nodded then asked, "What is your relationship to Fr. Henry?"

Oliver hesitated, looked down at the table and slowly began to say, "We had just met last week."

"Yes?" Flanagan mumbled, looking inquisitively at Oliver.

"Well, it would appear he was my biological father."

The priest nodded, as if he already knew the information and handed him an envelope. "Open it."

Oliver flipped up the cover of the envelope. It had already been opened. He pulled out a piece of stationary with the logo of the Congregation at the top of the page and beautiful script below.

"Dear Oliver. You are a very smart, thoughtful, and beautiful person. I am so glad we had a chance to meet. I'm proud of you. I wish you success in your future endeavors and in your passion for social justice. Love, Henry."

Monsignor Flanagan looked at Oliver whose eyes began to water, a tear streaking down his cheek. "I'm sorry," he said warmly and continued, "I understand you are his beneficiary."

"How would you know that?" Oliver said, looking up at Flanagan with alarm.

"We found a copy of his signed trust in his apartment. It's suspicious that he signed it so close to his death."

Oliver realized Monsignor Flanagan was insinuating foul play or at least that the Vatican could make that argument.

"If you need witnesses to his decision to execute the trust, I can provide them and more."

Monsignor Flanagan bristled, realizing the Vatican was more vulnerable than Oliver. He then reached into his pocket and pulled out a chain of keys and slid them across the table at Oliver. "Here are the keys to his apartment. Our police have already searched the place."

Oliver starred at Flanagan in disbelief. It seemed odd that in less than twenty-four hours he was being informed by a Vatican official of Henry's death and being handed keys to his apartment. Oliver realized Flanagan and his men had probably searched Henry's apartment thoroughly, removing any embarrassing evidence.

"Good day, Mr. Monte-Fitzpatrick," he said as he stood, extended his hand, and shook Oliver's forcefully. He then walked down the road.

Oliver texted Giancarlo: "Can you come to the Borgo Pio now?"

"Sure, *subito*. I'll take a taxi."

In about fifteen minutes, a taxi pulled up to the beginning of the pedestrian zone of the Borgo Pio and Giancarlo, dressed in his banking suit, stepped out, paid his fare, and waved to Oliver.

"What's this about. I was worried."

Oliver dangled the keys in front of him. "Henry's apartment."

Giancarlo's eyes widened and he said with concern, "We shouldn't go in there yet. It's a potential crime scene."

"The Vatican Police have already cleared it. Monsignor Flanagan said as much."

They walked down the Borgo Pio and turned down one of the small side streets, found Henry's building, unlocked the main door, and walked up the marble steps to the next floor. They unbolted his unit and walked inside.

It was a modest apartment but fastidiously maintained and decorated. The front door opened to a parlor that stretched the length of the building, overlooking a small space between adjacent buildings. On the right of the parlor was a kitchen and dining area and, to the left, a bedroom, bath, and small study.

The furniture was modern, something Oliver hadn't anticipated.

The sofa was grey, low to the ground, and shaped in an "L." There were two low rise comfortable chairs and two small end tables. The lighting was primarily recessed spotlights in the ceiling. The walls were covered in original oil paintings, mostly representational and impressionistic rather than modern.

Oliver strolled around the main area, picking up a few small table-top photos that stood on a buffet chest. There were several with Henry, his arms slung around a handsome somewhat younger man. Oliver wondered if it was Giacomo.

He wandered into the bedroom, opened the armoire, and rummaged through the suits hanging neatly – some traditional black for his clerical work and others tan and blue for his days off. He had a range of slacks – both jeans and casual dress slacks. The shelves in the armoire were full of carefully folded sweaters and pullovers.

"If you had any doubts about Henry before, they're dissipated now, right?" Giancarlo said as he watched Oliver examine the room.

"Yes, he appears to have had impeccable taste, and the gay gene is quite evident in the way things are arranged, decorated, and organized."

"He also had the means," Giancarlo noted. "He had inherited a large sum of money from his father, despite their estrangement."

"It's interesting to note the same thing happening now - his and my estrangement and the passing on of Henry's estate."

Oliver sat down in one of the chairs in the parlor and lowered his head. The idea that Henry had committed suicide over his being gay was disturbing, and he thought how much pain Henry must have been feeling to have gone to that point. He began to sob.

Giancarlo approached, knelt next to him, and rubbed his hands over Oliver's knees. "Caro, it's not your fault."

"I know that intellectually, but emotionally I feel like I pushed him. It's awful."

"Hmmm," he murmured, "I can see how you would feel that way, but maybe there's more to the story." Giancarlo looked across the room and then turned back toward Oliver and said, "What if we had a talk with Giacomo. Maybe we can find out more from him."

Oliver looked up at Giancarlo. "How do you propose we do that?"

"We call him and ask to see him."

"Under what pretext?"

"Maybe we can just be honest. We can tell him we found his contact information and that you are his son and wanted to be in touch."

Oliver nodded. Giancarlo searched Giacomo's contact info on his phone and dialed his office. A receptionist answered. "I'm calling on behalf of an Oliver Monte-Fitzpatrick. He's the biological son of one of Dr. Salvatore's patients, Fr. Henry Montpierre. He'd like to visit with the doctor."

The receptionist asked to put Giancarlo on hold, and in a few minutes, an older male voice came on the line. "Hello. This is Dr. Salvatore."

"I'm calling for Oliver Monte-Fitzpatrick. He's Fr. Henry's biological son, and he was wondering if you might have time to speak with him. I'm sure you're aware that Fr. Henry was found dead yesterday."

"Yes, and I expected a call from Oliver. Can he come over in a half hour? I have some free time."

"Sure. We'll be there shortly."

Giancarlo and Oliver made their way across the Prati area of Rome to a beautiful building full of professional offices – physicians, lawyers, psychologists, and accountants. They made their way to the third floor and pressed the intercom, saying, "Oliver Monte-Fitzpatrick for Dr. Salvatore."

The door buzzed open. They walked inside the reception area and a middle-aged man, in good shape and attractive, walked into the room and extended his hands to Giancarlo and Oliver. "I'm Dr. Salvatore. Nice to meet you."

"I'm Oliver, and this is Giancarlo who called earlier."

"Come in. Let's talk."

Oliver and Giancarlo sat in larger chairs facing Giacomo's desk. He wore a long white coat, a tie, a white dress shirt, and dark slacks. He had tan skin and dark cropped hair. Oliver thought he was attractive and could envision him and Henry together.

Giacomo began, "I understand you are Fr. Henry's biological son. He mentioned you a few weeks ago and was eagerly anticipating your visit."

Oliver relaxed as Giacomo conveyed the information.

"I'm sure you are distraught at his death and are looking for some information."

Oliver and Giancarlo both nodded.

"Fr. Henry and I have known each other for at least 10 years. He's been a patient and a confidant. We shared an interest in art and history."

The information didn't surprise Oliver who smiled.

"I can't say too much, but I think some information is owed you. Fr. Henry told me about your disagreements and warned me that you would be upset when you found out about his death."

Oliver's forehead creased and Giancarlo leaned forward in his chair. Oliver asked, "He told you in advance that he was going to commit suicide?"

Giacomo nodded. "He had late-stage cancer – metastatic cancer that had spread to his bones. It had begun to compress parts of his spinal column causing excruciating pain."

Oliver looked at Giancarlo dumbfounded.

Giacomo continued, "We treated his symptoms and pain well enough for a while, but it was beginning to get worse. I don't know if you noticed a change of pallor from time to time or even weakness, lightheadedness?"

Oliver said quietly, "Now that you mention it, there was an episode at the Vatican Museum the other day, and another one afternoon when we were visiting. He didn't look well."

"He faced a terrible death, and he decided to ask for assistance."

"Assistance in dying?" Oliver inquired.

Giacomo didn't elaborate but nodded. He cleared his throat and then added, "As you can imagine, there's not a lot I can say without violating doctor-patient confidentiality. But I want to assure you, Fr. Henry's death has nothing to do with your visit or what transpired between you. What happened was in the works for some time."

Giancarlo nodded, realizing the 100,000 euros was probably a payment to Fr. Salvatore to assist in his death – something that was illegal but not entirely uncommon with end-stage cancer patients. Giancarlo decided to see if he could extract any more information and said, "I'm sure given your long relationship with Fr. Henry, this must have been hard for you, too. We're sorry for your loss."

"It's always difficult when one's patient dies. Over the years, Fr. Henry and I dealt with a lot of his health issues. He's always been a thoughtful patient, probably due to his pastoral background."

"So, you had a personal relationship with him?" Oliver inquired further, hoping more information might be shared.

"Not exactly. We shared some common interests, and we had a lot of interaction around his illnesses, but our politics were quite different - in fact - quite opposed," Dr. Salvatore said.

"In what sense?" Giancarlo asked further.

"He's very conservative. I have a gay son, and I have expressed disagreement to him about his views and actions. The other day, he recounted that he had discovered that his biological son had been raised by lesbians. He was upset by that but also confounded by how bright, thoughtful, well-adjusted, and passionate you were."

Oliver then asked, "Why do you think he took the action with the teachers the other day – knowing what he knows about you, your family, and me and my family?"

"I was disappointed by that, as well. This is only conjecture, but I think he was under a lot of pressure from a faction within the Church. He's conservative but capable of thinking critically and creatively. I have a feeling the removal of the teachers was in the works for some time, and there was little he could do to stop it," Giacomo elaborated. He paused and then looked up at Oliver and said pensively, "I tried to read between the lines and, I know this is little consolation, but the way he framed the rationale leaves it open for review, for a reconsideration. I think he left a Trojan Horse in the documentation that, once someone notices, will make the decision and action vulnerable to reversal. Henry was clever in that way."

Oliver nodded and then smiled, reassured that perhaps Henry wasn't as vile as he had come to think. He then said, "Why did he go through with his suicide precisely at the time of the removal and after meeting me?" Oliver inquired.

"It was purely coincidental. The disease and pain had begun to mount considerably. Maybe the stress of the action he was going to have to take coupled with meeting you accelerated things but, if so, only by a week or so."

Oliver looked off in the distance, rubbed his hand through his hair, then turned back to Dr. Salvatore. "You said he was conservative. Wouldn't that preclude suicide?"

"Ordinarily, yes. I happen to be an advocate for physician assisted suicide, and he and I had long conversations about it. I think he eventually justified it not so much as suicide but as a form of self-administered pain management," Dr. Salvatore explained.

"A fatal dose of a pain killer."

Dr. Salvatore nodded.

"Is there anything we can do for you?" Oliver said, realizing Henry's passing must have been stressful for his physician.

"No, but I do want to say something to you. Henry and I spoke the other day. He expressed remorse for what he had to do in removing the teachers. He apologized to me and my son. He also said that you had been a surprise and had been enlightening. He realized the Church was citing research very selectively and that perhaps it was wrong, that a correction might be needed."

"But he went through with it anyway."

"I'm afraid so. Institutions don't usually change from within. They have to be shown the way from without. I think it's ironic that the place most impacted by his disease was his spine – that it was being eaten away by the cancer and then crushed by the weight of the burdens he carried."

Giancarlo looked at his watch and then said, "Doctor, we don't want to take more of your time. Thanks for being so honest with us. Here's my card in case you need to get in touch." Giancarlo handed him a business card. Oliver nodded in support.

"Thank you for meeting with us," Oliver added.

"It's been a pleasure despite the circumstances. Maybe we can meet again socially. I'd like for my son to meet you. He continues to struggle with the fear that being gay will put him at a disadvantage. The fact that your moms are successful and happy in Boston is impressive."

"That would be an honor," Oliver said.

Oliver and Giancarlo shook Dr. Salvatore's hand and then exited the building.

"Wow! That was an eye opener," Oliver began as he and Giancarlo began to walk down the sidewalk.

"I never knew Henry was sick. This must have developed

quickly," Giancarlo remarked, his head downturned. He then added, "What did you think of Giacomo?"

"He's cute," Oliver began, "but I think he's straight. He would have said something about himself if he was open about his son."

"Agreed."

"So, perhaps Henry is straight, too?" Oliver inquired as they crossed a bridge over the river heading into the historical center of Rome.

"Maybe," Giancarlo began tentatively. "But there were some interesting photographs in the apartment. There's more to uncover. He was very discrete. Perhaps for a reason."

Oliver nodded. They both continued to walk quietly, deep in thought over what had transpired.

"Olie, I have an idea. My uncles and I have a villa on the sea. Would you like to get away for a couple of days? I need a break and, if I do, I can imagine this has been even more stressful for you."

"That would be great. We wouldn't impose on them?"

"It's early in the season and midweek. No one will be there. Besides, I have a separate suite. If others are there, we'd still have privacy."

"When do we go?"

"Do you want to go this afternoon. Depending on traffic, we could get there by dinner time."

"My bags are packed!"

"*Andiamo*," Giancarlo said, as he took a turn to the right and headed back toward his apartment.

13

Chapter Thirteen

Giancarlo and his uncles shared a villa overlooking the ocean at San Felice Circeo, south of Rome. It was a block up from the waterfront but, given the slope of the hill, it enjoyed unobstructed views of the sea. The villa had a small pool, a large deck, and a garden filled with herbs. Giancarlo's grandfather had built the house and handed it on to his sons at his death. Now that Giancarlo's father had passed, he had taken over his family's part of the complex.

Each family had their own suite with a large bedroom, bath, sitting area, and balcony. The common areas were shared by all, and the family retained a housekeeper, Margarita, who cleaned, kept the kitchen supplied, and occasionally cooked for the family.

Oliver was laying on one of the chaise lounges under an umbrella. Giancarlo was adjacent to him, doing work on his laptop. Margarita had just left them a tray of croissants, juice, and coffee. Oliver had his eyes closed in contemplation.

Giancarlo reached over for some coffee and smiled at Oliver laying in the shade. He had on a pair of shorts, a blue tee-shirt, and flip flops. His skin had become darker and his hair shinier from the sun. It was hard to imagine they had only known each other for a couple of weeks. It felt as if they belonged, had been partners for years, and shared a common history and life. He realized why all his earlier relationships had failed. This was the one he was destined to embrace and make his own.

He returned to his computer and pulled up several electronic newspapers. He skimmed the headlines and then noticed an article about the Vatican's dismissal of the gay teachers.

"Oliver, you've got to see this."

Oliver stirred, rubbed his eyes, and looked over. Giancarlo began to read out loud, "Today, the Congregation for Education at the Vatican announced its decision to suspend the removal of several gay teachers announced the week before. Spokesman, Monsignor Flanagan said, 'We believe the rationale used for their removal was flawed, and we want to review the procedures. Until further notice, the teachers are in good standing.'"

"Oh my God," Oliver said excitedly. "What do you think this means?"

"Well, either you scared the shit out of old Monsignor Flanagan who didn't want another international scandal drawing attention to the Church or old Monsignor Flanagan may be an ally, someone who was waiting for Henry to move on so that more thoughtful policies could be put in place."

"How do we find out?"

"I propose we talk to Monsignor Flanagan."

"Just like that?"

"Yes, just like that."

Oliver leaned over and asked, "Let me see that."

Giancarlo handed Oliver his computer and Oliver glanced at the article, deciphering the Italian as best he could. "I just can't believe this," he said excitedly.

He returned the computer to Giancarlo and turned, pulling himself up on the edge of the chair, facing Giancarlo.

"I've been thinking."

"Yes?"

"I just inherited nearly a million euros and an apartment probably worth close to that. What if we used that money to form an institute, one that would support research and policies about homosexuality?"

"There is already a dozen of those. How would yours be different?"

"Well, what if the institute was one that sponsored panels and debates between scholars and Church leaders, a kind of collaborative?"

"Hmmm, sounds intriguing," Giancarlo said. He continued, "But how would you get Church leaders to buy in?"

"I've been thinking. Maybe there are people within the Vatican who know things need to change but need pressure from the outside, people who could provide them with the language and framework for change?"

"It sounds nice, Oliver, but nothing is going to change as long as you have a male celibate clerical system that is perpetuated precisely to shield sexually self-loathing men from reality. They won't change the system because it would force them to change."

"What if some of them do want to change? What if there are enough within the hierarchy that are ready? They just need a push from the outside. Other Christian churches have embraced women's rights and the rights of LGBTQ people – not because one day they woke up and said, 'wouldn't this be nice.' They needed a push, from the outside. But there was enough support within to eventually embrace it, but only after those on the outside were able to articulate the soundness of the change."

"Are you sure you don't want to study theology instead of archaeology?"

"Ha, Ha! Seriously. We need to create dialogue, dialogue between those who hold power and those who live reality."

"But if we've learned anything from history, empires eventually shut down dialogue and plurality of views in order to protect the privileged group. And that is why they fall. Maybe the Church is an empire that just has to fall," Giancarlo said thoughtfully.

"But empires become great when they are able to embrace change and new information, when they draw on the richness of diversity. Religions survive when they change, too. We could be at that moment when the Catholic Church finally embraces change."

"Or we could be at the moment when a whole new religious system arises in its place."

"How do we know which is the case?" Oliver pressed Giancarlo.

"Time will tell."

"But in the meantime, can't we do something to create the conditions for change, not collapse?" Oliver inquired.

"Or we can support the conditions for a new religion," Giancarlo added.

Oliver seemed intrigued. He looked out over the deck at the sparkling sea, a hazy horizon stretching away from the shore. He then turned to Giancarlo and said, "Whether we fund the conditions for change within or without, it's the same. By articulating a new paradigm, it can either be embraced by the Church or rejected but, if rejected, it becomes the basis for a new spiritual community anyway."

"You know, you're proving yourself to be quite a philosopher," Giancarlo said as he ran his hand over Oliver's curly blonde head of hair and gave him a kiss. "You're also the cutest one I've met."

Oliver blushed. He was starting to feel more relaxed and lighthearted as some path forward became clearer. "Let's go for a swim," he said, grabbing Giancarlo's hand, lifting him up and pulling him to the pool.

"Let me change into my suit," Giancarlo protested.

"You don't need one," Oliver said, as he tugged hard on Giancarlo's shorts. They fell to the ground. Oliver unzipped his, let them drop, and they both leaped into the water.

The water was soothing as Oliver treaded his way to the other side, Giancarlo following close behind. He pivoted and began to swim toward Giancarlo, wrapping his legs around him as they met. He felt himself get hard and pressed himself up against Giancarlo's abdomen. He could feel Giancarlo's hardness beneath him and leaned his head back and moaned.

Giancarlo opened his mouth and gave Oliver a deep moist kiss. The taste of the saltwater mingled pleasantly with the aroma of coffee and chocolate Oliver had just eaten. Oliver kissed him back, nibbling on his ears and running his hands over his broad muscular shoulders. The contours of his chest, covered in moistened dark hair, emerged and receded as he bobbed in the water.

"How could I have ever been confused about myself?" Oliver said as he gazed into Giancarlo's eyes.

"You just needed to meet the right person!" He winked at Oliver.

They swam to the side, hopped out, and grabbed the towels that were laying on the chairs and dried themselves. Giancarlo spotted Margarita from an upper floor looking down at them. She walked away from the window.

"Let's go into town," Giancarlo proposed as he led Oliver into the house to change clothes.

"Don't you have work?"

"I did most of it already, and I can finish up later. It would be nice to go into town and walk along the water and have some lunch."

Oliver nodded. He slipped on a pair of shorts, a pullover, and some sneakers. Giancarlo rummaged through the closet and found a worn pair of jeans, a linen shirt, and some casual shoes.

They walked down the windy road into town, poked their heads into a few shops, and strolled along the beach. It was early in the season, but many of the bathing establishments were already busy with tourists renting chaise lounges and soaking up the warm sun.

"I feel out of place wearing clothes on the beach," Oliver said self-consciously.

"Don't! You look like you just washed ashore from California. Look at the heads turning," he said, nodding his head in the direction of the beach chairs lined up before them.

Oliver knew he was kidding but looked anyway. No one was looking. He turned back at Giancarlo who was in the process of taking off his shirt. "Well, now they'll start looking," he said as Giancarlo's broad shoulders came out from under the sleeves and began to glisten in the sun.

"They're all straight here anyway," Giancarlo noted.

"Not that one over there," Oliver remarked as a middle-aged but trim man in a Speedo suit began walking their way, his arousal clearly visible.

"He's not looking at us. He's eyeing the women over there with their tops off," Giancarlo said as he looked in the direction of a row of women in the front row of beach chairs propped up on their elbows, exposing their ample breasts to passersby.

"By the way, are you still in flux?" Giancarlo continued, leaning playfully into Oliver's shoulder.

"It's funny you should ask. No – I'm a certifiable poofter as they say in Britain."

"That's good to hear," Giancarlo said.

"Since we met, things have felt good, in sync. It's amazing how we can delude ourselves for so long and then, all-of-a-sudden, things fall into place."

"Have you given any more thought to your plans for the rest of the summer?"

Oliver cleared his throat and paused. "So much has happened. Between meeting Henry, his death, my inheriting his estate, our meeting, and my coming out, I feel like my life has been turned totally upside down." Oliver grabbed Giancarlo's hand and walked closer to the edge of the beach. He pulled off his shoes and stepped into the clear water lapping listlessly on the yellow sand. Giancarlo slipped his shoes off, rolled up his pant legs, and stepped in with him. They both looked down the coastline where soft green hills plunged into the clear blue sea. A light haze concealed the beach towns of Sperlonga and Gaeta far off in the distance.

Oliver continued, "I know this may seem presumptuous on my part, but I'd love to stay."

"I was hoping you would say that. I would love for you to stay, too. But I know you have your life and studies in Boston, and I wouldn't want to get in the way."

"You know when I talked about studying archaeology? We joked about it. But the idea really intrigues me."

"Go on, I'm listening," Giancarlo said as he led Oliver along the shoreline, walking in the shallow cool water.

"Do you think it's too late to matriculate for courses in the Fall?"

"We could find out. Why don't we ask Flavia? She must have connections."

"What about housing? Do you think those things are already settled by this time?"

"What do you need housing for?" Giancarlo said, looking inquisitively at Oliver.

"I don't want to take advantage of your hospitality and Henry's place will be sold by then."

"Are you kidding. I love having you around."

"I know," Oliver began, "but doesn't this seem a bit fast – my moving in and all? Remember our talk in Venice?"

"Yes, it does. All my friends have said, 'are you crazy?' And I say, 'yes, I'm crazy in love with him.'"

"Ahh," Oliver sighed. "But in all seriousness, it's too fast, it's too big of a change – for you and for me."

Giancarlo looked sad and alarmed. Oliver looked out over the water, avoiding Giancarlo's deep brown eyes. Giancarlo put his hand on Oliver's shoulder and turned him toward him and said, "*Resti – ti prego.*"

Oliver could sense Giancarlo's emotion and distress in begging him to stay. Every fiber of his being wanted to say 'yes, I'll stay.' But rationally he couldn't justify it. It was too hasty.

Giancarlo saw that Oliver was about to say 'no, I can't' so he interjected, "Let me make another proposal." Oliver nodded quietly. "Why don't you go back to Boston. You can stay as long as you like here, but at some point, you could go back home. Spend some time with your moms and sort things out with them. We can get you matriculated for classes in the Fall and, if you like, I could visit you in Boston in August. I think with those comings and goings, we'll know what to do."

Oliver smiled. It seemed like a good plan and less impulsive. "I think you're right."

"Could I come see you in Boston?"

"That would be incredible!" Oliver said excitedly. "I would love it, and my moms would be ecstatic. We could go to Provincetown for a visit."

"What's Provincetown?"

"It's a charming historic town at the end of Cape Cod set amongst immense sand dunes and broad open beaches facing the ocean. And it's very gay."

"What do you mean?"

"Well, at the beginning of the 20ᵗʰ century, it became a center for painting, art and theatre and, since then, has been attracting an increasingly gay clientele. It's probably the most important gay destination in the USA – and has countless galleries and artists. It's amazing."

"Sounds wonderful. Should I book an inn or something?"

"That's probably not a bad idea. Let me talk to my moms and see what they suggest. So, you'd really come to Boston?"

"Are you kidding? I can't wait."

They continued to chat, walked along the beach, and then stopped at a small restaurant for lunch. The sun overhead was strong, and people were retreating to the cool shade of the restaurant pavilion. Their table looked out over the beach. A light salty breeze blew across the sand. They ordered a crisp bottle of white wine, an arugula salad with fresh tomatoes, and some spaghetti tossed in fresh crushed tomatoes and basil.

"This is so delicious – simple but the flavors are intense," Oliver remarked.

"How's the food in Provincetown?"

"There's a lot of seafood. Lobsters, seabass, and oysters. There are also great bars on the edge of the water – and the famous tea-dance."

"What's that?"

"Everyone gathers between 5 and 7 to have drinks, mingle and dance on a big deck overlooking the water."

"And you weren't snatched up earlier?" Giancarlo remarked jokingly.

"Officially I couldn't go. I'm underage."

"Oh, that's right. In the States you can't drink until you're 21. What a strange practice."

"I know. But this summer I'll be 21."

"When's your birthday?"

"In July."

"We'll have to celebrate."

Oliver looked nervous, hesitant to make the next statement but timidly said, "But I'll probably be back in Boston then."

"*Ti prego, no!*"

"But I thought we agreed I'd go back soon to sort things out."

"We didn't say soon – just some time." Giancarlo reached over and took hold of Oliver's hand. He ignored the glances from the adjoining table and stroked the top of Oliver's fingers. "*Non c'e fretta.*"

Oliver nodded.

"You know what that means?"

"Yes, there's no hurry."

"You're picking up Italian quickly."

"I have an idea," Oliver said, his eyes widening. "What if I begin to take Italian classes?"

"That's fine with me. If it will keep you here longer."

"Well, it would give me something to do during the day. And, if I'm going to study archaeology, I'll need to know the language."

"You have a good start with Spanish – but you're right – you'll need more background in the Fall."

They continued to chat, plan, and discuss logistics. They walked back to the house and made plans to return to Rome the next morning. Oliver looked online for Italian courses and signed up for a program. He agreed to stay in Rome until early July to celebrate his birthday with Giancarlo and then return home. Giancarlo would fly to Boston in August, and they would both return to Rome later.

Back in Rome, Oliver texted Monsignor Flanagan. They agreed to meet for lunch at a small trattoria in the Prati neighborhood. Oliver found the restaurant. Flanagan was already seated enjoying some wine and checking messages on his phone. He stood up, shook Oliver's hand, and invited him to sit.

"You look very tan. You must be enjoying your stay in Italy," Flanagan began while pouring Oliver some wine.

"I was at the shore for a couple of days."

"Hmmm," Flanagan murmured.

"Thanks for agreeing to meet with me."

"Given all that has transpired, it's the least I could do for you," Flanagan noted.

They ordered their lunches and Flanagan nervously tapped his fingers on the cloth covered table.

"I noticed the removal of the gay teachers was postponed," Oliver began directly.

"Ah yes, I wondered if you might have noticed. By the way, you're very well informed for an American visiting in Rome. I had called the hotel, and they said you weren't there anymore. Where are you staying?"

Oliver pondered what to share with Flanagan and decided to be discrete. "I'm staying with a friend who lives here in Rome. It's been nice to experience Rome like a local, evening reading newspapers. That's how I noticed the postponement."

Flanagan seemed more relaxed as Oliver shared that information. He then said warmly, "How are you doing? It must be difficult with Fr. Henry's passing."

"I have to say I was in shock, and I am sorry if our meeting caused him distress."

"What do you mean?" Flanagan inquired, wondering if Oliver knew that Henry had caused his own death with the pain medicine.

"Fr. Henry and I had a disagreement a couple of weeks ago. He had been upset when he learned that I was raised by a lesbian couple. He eventually apologized but we had a subsequent conversation that got even more heated when I challenged him for what he did to the gay teachers."

"How would that have had anything to do with his death?"

Oliver realized he wasn't supposed to know of Henry's self-administered overdose, so he carefully corrected himself, "I don't know, perhaps the stress of it all causing a heart attack or stroke. By the way, do they know what happened?"

"I'm afraid not," Flanagan interjected matter-of-factly.

"Do you think he was stressed?"

Monsignor Flanagan nodded then said, "Fr. Henry and I were good friends. We both arrived in Rome roughly the same time – he from Boston and I from Ireland. Over the years, we shared a lot about our lives, and he shared the story of his affair and wanting to locate you. I advised him against it, but he persisted."

"So, you must have talked after our first meeting?"

"Yes. He was distraught. He had the press conference coming up, the dismissals, and an imminent announcement of his promotion."

"That must have been hard on him."

"Yes. I tried to get him to postpone the dismissals, but he felt that he was being pressured from above to make it happen."

"And to make his promotion happen?"

Flanagan just starred at Oliver, not admitting anything.

"Let me ask you something, Monsignor. What is your opinion of the dismissals?"

Monsignor Flanagan shuffled in his chair nervously. He wrung his hands slowly, looked off in the distance and then turned to Oliver, "I was against them."

"Why?"

"They don't make sense anymore."

"Go on," Oliver encouraged him to elaborate.

"The majority of reasonable people no longer believe that being gay is a pathology. It's been removed from all the professional manuals of sicknesses. No reasonable people believe that a teacher's sexual orientation is relevant to their job or that their marital status is relevant either. The Church's position on these matters is teetering on twigs. There are no legs to stand on – neither research nor anecdotal experience supports what the Church says officially."

"Then why does the Church continue to pursue this."

"It's afraid of change or, rather, men like Henry are afraid of change." He squirmed in his chair and then continued, "If the Church were to begin to affirm the moral goodness of gay people, he would have to re-examine his life, the reasons he's a priest. I don't think he has it within himself to do so."

"So was Fr. Henry gay?"

Flanagan tensed up even more and looked away evasively. He took a large sip of wine and then looked at Oliver and said, "I'm not sure."

Oliver looked at him inquisitively, encouraging him to elaborate.

"I suspect he was. Even though he had an affair with a woman, I believe it was to try to convince himself that he wasn't gay. But, to my knowledge, after that, he was celibate."

"But there are some photos in his apartment with men who are quite handsome."

Flanagan grinned and said, "Yes, that's true. But I don't think they were sexual relationships. Fr. Henry enjoyed the company of handsome men – men who were athletic, married, and professionals. There was a latent sexual tension in his friendships, one that was certainly – shall we say – homoerotic. But I'm not sure they were physically sexual."

"So, do you think he took his life out of shame?" Oliver said, foregoing the charade of not knowing about his taking his own life.

Flanagan looked at Oliver incredulously. "So, you know?"

Oliver nodded.

"How?"

"I have sources."

This alarmed Flanagan. He didn't like to be out maneuvered and realized Oliver was in even a stronger position to blackmail the Church. "Did you know he was ill?"

"Not until recently."

"Ahh," Flanagan sighed. "I see. Yes, he was quite ill. But he didn't commit suicide."

"No?" Oliver asked suspiciously.

"No. He was taking medicine for excruciating pain and probably took too many pills."

Oliver thought to himself, 'at least everyone's stories are consistent.'

A waiter approached, placing two steaming bowls of pasta in front to them. Flanagan quickly plunged his fork into the pile of spaghetti and began to twirl the tomato coated noodles and lift them to his mouth. He wiped a little sauce off his mouth with his napkin. Oliver slowly began to lift some noodles to his mouth, breathing in the subtle hint of basil and garlic.

"So, Monsignor," Oliver interjected between bites. "What can I do for you?"

Flanagan looked puzzled. "What can you do for me?"

"Yes. He was your friend, and it must be hard on you. And you've undoubtedly taken a risk in putting the removal of gay teachers on hold. Is there anything I can do to support you and your efforts?"

Flanagan placed his fork into the bowl of pasta, paused and took a deep breath, looking intensely at Oliver. "I thought you were going to blackmail the Church."

"What?" Oliver said with alarm.

"Fr. Henry shared with me how upset you were and how the real truth needed to come out. That's why he offered to support your education."

"You mean the bribe – you know about it?"

"Yes, he mentioned it. I advised against it, but he wanted to make some kind of gesture."

"I have to say I was tempted – that is to try to expose him. I was very upset by the harm his actions would cause."

"But?"

"Well, after his death, it didn't make sense."

Flanagan sighed in relief.

"Besides, the way he framed the supporting documentation, it left room for questioning the logic."

"Fr. Henry said you were smart. I see nothing gets by you."

Oliver smiled, blushing slightly.

Flanagan continued, "Yes, I think he intentionally inserted a poison pill into the document. It's not that he disagreed with the teachers' dismissals, but he loved the Church enough and saw the handwriting on the wall to the extent that change was inevitable. It left me with a way to suspend the dismissals and ask for further study."

"That's what I want to help with. How can I support people like you in the Church?"

"I don't know if that's possible or not. I'm actually pretty pessimistic. For every individual like me, there are countless others who think the Church should preserve its archaic views on gender and sexuality. They are also heavily funded. With all the pedophile lawsuits, the Church is bleeding money. Conservative patrons who are against the dismantling of patriarchy and the embrace of gay people are willing to buy bishops. They can bail out dioceses in exchange for the bishops taking more extreme stances – on reproductive rights, women's rights, gay rights."

"So, do they need to be exposed?" Oliver inquired, wondering if hard ball was the way to go.

Flanagan shook his head. "No one bats an eye anymore when a new scandal emerges. People already expect it and know it. The news hits the papers, and within weeks, it's forgotten."

"Fr. Henry said you were interested in ancient Rome and early Christianity."

Oliver nodded.

"Then you must know that early Christianity arose not in direct confrontation with Rome. It arose as an alternative community, an alternative paradigm. Rome fell because corrupt power fed on itself – consumed itself, one corrupt leader after another. There was a vast community of people who lived by an alternative paradigm and, when the old one collapsed, the new one rose in its stead. Spend your time and resources in shaping a new model of gender and sexuality and spirituality. When the time is ready, that paradigm will be embraced and made the norm."

"But doesn't that mean that all of the good that Christianity does, that the Church fosters, will be lost?"

"Not necessarily. In the same way that Roman ideals and institutions continued in Christianity, whatever new paradigm emerges, it will bring with it the perspectives and values of the Church that are enduring. The Gospel will live on, but it will live on in a new form and with a new set of practices. That I'm certain of."

Oliver finished his plate of pasta and took a long sip of his wine. Flanagan took a piece of the crusty bread, wiped the bottom of his bowl, and savored the final bit of sauce, washing it down with a gulp of wine. He rested his elbows on the table and looked over at Oliver contently.

Oliver waved down their waiter and asked for two espressos. He then said, "Monsignor Flanagan, it has been an honor to get to know you. I am surprised by what you have said, but in a strange way, it is inspiring and hopeful."

"As a man of the Church, I'm saddened by the failings of the institution. At this point in my life, I see a lot of decay and decline, and it is depressing. But, as someone who believes in the Gospel – that Jesus taught us to find God in our humanity, to see humanity as the place where God discloses Godself – I am very much inspired. I see a new age in which we take seriously the dignity of every human being – that we seek to provide meaningful work for everyone, that we fight against income inequality, that we affirm the equal dignity of men and women, that we embrace sexual and gender diversity, and that we work toward a sustainable future for the planet. If God created the world and if God became human or incarnate in Jesus – then it is in working for these changes that we are advancing the Gospel. The spread of the Gospel isn't about the spread of the Church. The Gospel is spread by a community that believes in its values – and that may exist more outside the institutional Church today than inside it, I'm afraid to say. But all that means is that a new spiritual community is arising, and that is exciting."

"You are an amazing man, Monsignor Flanagan. You've helped me see so much more clearly."

"And you are an amazing young man. I believe Henry saw this in you, too. The message he wrote to you - cryptic and short – was essentially that. You have a rich life ahead of you in fighting for justice."

"I know what I need to do."

"I'm glad."

The waiter brought their espressos which they finished in single gulps. Both rose, embraced, and walked outside. The Prati neighborhood was quiet, most people finishing lunch, taking a siesta, or returning to work. Flanagan headed back to the Vatican and Oliver to Trastevere.

Oliver unlocked the door to Giancarlo's condo and walked inside. He opened the large glass doors and stepped out onto the terrace. He sat in a chair and leaned back, letting the warm sun caress his face.

I4

Chapter Fourteen

Oliver stood impatiently outside the customs area at Logan airport waiting for Giancarlo. People, groggy from long flights, filed through the automatic opaque doors. He glanced at the monitor. Giancarlo's flight had arrived 30 minutes earlier. A large group of people began to exit the area, and Oliver peered at their luggage tags, looking for FCO, the code for Rome's airport. Slowly a few bags with FCO began to appear. He could feel his heart race in anticipation.

Suddenly, he looked up and saw Giancarlo coming out through the doors.

"Giancarlo!" he yelled.

Giancarlo looked over at him and broke out in a broad smile. He walked briskly toward Oliver and reached his arms around him, giving him a warm kiss on the lips. "Oliver. What a sight for sore eyes."

"I'm so glad you're here. I've missed you," Oliver replied, squeezing Giancarlo within his arms.

"Look at you. You're even more tan than when you left Italy. And your hair – blonder," he said as he ran his hand over Oliver's curly head of hair.

"I've been at the beach a lot the last few weeks."

"*Si vede* – you can see it."

"Let me take that," Oliver said as he took hold of Giancarlo's suitcase and began rolling it toward the skywalk and the parking garage. "We can get the car, and we'll be at the hotel in no time."

They walked toward the garage, each staring at each other, beaming with excitement. Oliver reached over and held Giancarlo's hand. It felt warm and comforting.

"Where's the hotel again?"

"It's actually a gay bed and breakfast in the center of town."

"How are your moms?"

"They're still pretty upset. But once they meet you, they'll be fine."

"Are you sure?" Giancarlo asked, a look of apprehension spread across his face.

Oliver nodded.

They found Oliver's car, exited the airport, and took the tunnel into the city. Once they came out, Giancarlo said, "Wow! I didn't expect this."

"What?"

"The city is so big and beautiful."

Oliver decided to take the scenic route along Storrow Drive. It was dusk, and the sun was setting over the river. A few sail boats were making their way back to the marina on the Charles River. "That's where I live – up there," Oliver pointed at Beacon Hill. They took the exit for the Back Bay and drove past the Boston Garden toward the South End.

"Look at all of these Victorian townhouses," Giancarlo remarked. "One after another."

"It's one of the largest preserved neighborhoods of this type in the country. Back in the 60s and 70s, it was in bad shape. The gays moved in, fixed places up, and now it's one of the most sought-after sections of the city."

"That happened in Rome, too," Giancarlo said as he pressed his face to the window.

They drove down several tree-lined narrow streets, found a parking space, and rolled Giancarlo's suitcase and Oliver's overnight bag toward a red brick townhouse. Oliver pressed the doorbell, and a handsome 30-year-old opened the door. "You must be Oliver and Giancarlo. I'm Sebastian."

Oliver nodded.

"Welcome. How was your flight?"

"The flight was fine. What a nice place you have," Giancarlo responded as he looked around the parlor.

"Let me take you to your room. It's on the top floor with nice access to our roof deck."

They climbed the stairs and were shown into a large bedroom with an en suite bath. It was tastefully decorated with large black and white photos of historic Boston, a rich Persian carpet, and a couple of easy chairs. The bath was spacious – with a large walk-in tile shower, marble floors, and a double sink vanity.

"This door," he noted, pointing to a door just outside their room, "leads to a staircase to the roof terrace. There are tables and chairs there with great views of the city."

"Thank you," Giancarlo said. "This all looks great."

Sebastian exited and walked downstairs. Oliver turned to Giancarlo, pulled him close, and gave him a warm moist kiss. "I have missed you so much," he said as he began to rub Giancarlo's biceps and shoulders.

"Mmmm," he moaned, reaching down for the tail of Oliver's shirt and raising it, sliding his hands up under the fabric and rubbing Oliver's abdomen. "You feel so good."

Oliver grabbed hold of his hand and said, "Let's get you unpacked and then go out to eat. It's getting late."

"Aren't we going to go meet your moms tonight?"

"Not yet. I wanted you all for myself tonight. They're still a little testy."

"I'm sorry I'm causing problems."

"You're not causing anything. They're just having to deal with a lot of change – my meeting my biological father, his death, my coming out, my meeting someone 10 years older than me, my moving to Italy to study archaeology, and our moving in together."

"Now that you frame it that way, it does sound like a lot."

"But we're the ones dealing with it," Oliver said emphatically, "not them."

"Well, they are dealing with it, too," Giancarlo noted. "I hope they will become more comfortable."

"Me, too."

They unpacked their things. Giancarlo freshened up and put on a clean shirt. They headed out and walked down the small side street to a larger boulevard lined with boutiques, cafes, and restaurants. It was a warm night, and many were sitting outdoors.

"Here it is," Oliver said, as he pushed his way through a door and into a classic bistro-style space with small booths and a large marble bar filled with a pre-theatre crowd having drinks and appetizers. The maître d' showed them a booth they had reserved.

"Is this okay?" Oliver asked.

"It looks perfect – particularly with you in front of me."

Oliver smiled then said, "Everything is good here. I thought we could go to a typical American place tonight."

Giancarlo opened the menu and began reviewing the options. He settled on a hanger steak with fries. Oliver opted for the cod. Both ordered salads. Oliver ordered a bottle of Italian red and got carded. Giancarlo looked askance. "What's that all about?"

"In the States, they're strict about the drinking age. They check your IDs."

"That's so strange. In Italy, everyone grows up drinking wine with meals, and it would be considered bad form to ask someone for their ID at a dinner."

Oliver nodded.

"So, tell me how things have been with your moms. This sounds like a problem."

"Well, when I got back, there was a lot of discussion and debriefing, and they were clearly not happy."

"Like what?"

"Well, they were apprehensive in the beginning when I wanted to meet my biological father. The fact that he died while I was in Rome was startling – and his giving me his estate, shocking."

"You have to admit, it was pretty astounding."

"I think they felt betrayed."

"But, in the end, he's out of the picture."

"I know, but they were still unsettled by it all."

"Then there's me," Giancarlo said with a grin.

"Yes, there's you. Ten years older, they keep reminding me."

"Ten years is not a lot of difference," Giancarlo underscored.

"They said that would be the case if I was older, but the fact that I am just 21 makes the age difference more significant, more problematic. And, having just come out, they think I'm jumping into a serious relationship when I should date more."

"I don't disagree with them," Giancarlo said thoughtfully.

"What?"

"I wouldn't change this for anything, but I can see their point. This is all new to you, and you should have an opportunity to date."

Oliver looked at Giancarlo incredulously. "Why would I want to do that?"

"I wouldn't if I had met me, but in theory, it makes sense."

Their salads came, and once the waiter left Oliver said, "Scratch humility."

Giancarlo smiled and then took a bite of the salad.

"But what is really throwing them," Oliver continued, "is moving to Italy, studying archaeology, and moving in with you. It would be one thing to date you. But I'm changing careers, countries, and making a long-term commitment."

As Oliver pronounced the words 'long-term commitment,' Giancarlo felt blood rush to his face. The two of them had never used that terminology. Things had always been framed more as a move-in while you're studying in Italy – not 'we are making a commitment.' He wanted to ask Oliver, 'are we making a long-term commitment,' but decided to save that for a later discussion.

"Well, that is a lot to digest. I suggest we just enjoy our time together this evening and, when I have less jetlag, we can strategize about how to approach your moms."

Oliver reached for his glass of wine and took a long sip. "Agreed. So, how was work this last week?"

"Things are slowing down now that Italians are on the August break. I had a few clients to deal with, but a lot of it involves filing documents and following up on leads."

"Thanks for setting up access to my funds online. It's been fascinating to follow their progress. Your recommendations have been lucrative."

"I try," Giancarlo said humbly. "And you, how are preparations going for your return?"

"I got the acceptance letter from the University of Rome and have filed the residency paperwork. I booked a seat on the same flight as your return. I'm not going to bring much, so we can go shopping for clothes and other things when I get back."

"What about your studies here?"

"They gave me a leave. I can return next year if I want."

"That's good. Keep your options open."

Oliver stared at Giancarlo who was evasively playing with a few leaves of lettuce on his plate. He was worried Giancarlo was having second thoughts about everything. "You okay?" he asked.

"Yes. Why not?"

"Well, this is a big deal for you, too. A few weeks ago, you were a handsome eligible gay bachelor in Trastevere, and now you're just handsome," he said playfully.

Giancarlo looked up and said slowly and deliberately, "I couldn't be happier. No second thoughts."

The waiter came with their entrees. Giancarlo began to cut into the hanger steak and, after taking a bite said, "American steaks never disappoint."

"You should try the cod. It's native to this area and delicious."

Giancarlo reached over and took a bite of Oliver's fish. "Hmm," he said, "delicious – just like you."

They continued chatting, catching up on recent news, and making plans for the upcoming week. They walked back to the inn and, since Giancarlo was feeling tired from the flight, they slipped under the covers and fell quickly asleep.

Giancarlo rose early the next morning, his biological clock still set to Roman time. He checked emails in bed until Oliver woke and then pressed himself against Oliver's side, reaching over and massaging him to hardness.

"I've missed this," he whispered into Oliver's ear, licking his lobes, and then running his tongue down Oliver's neck and onto his clavicle. Oliver shuddered and arched his back as Giancarlo stroked him more firmly.

Giancarlo pressed his own hardness into the gap between Oliver's buttocks that were flexing as he moved back and forth in Giancarlo's hands. He could feel his skin moisten and tighten as he became more aroused.

He loved the feel of Oliver in his arms. He was lean and muscular but had soft supple skin. He savored running his hand over the round of Oliver's shoulder and down the contours of his arms, squeezing his bulging biceps and strong forearms.

Oliver felt secure in Giancarlo's embrace and cherished as Giancarlo played with his arm, stroked his chest, and messaged his erection. He trembled as Giancarlo breathed into his ear and said, "You are so sexy."

Oliver pivoted and faced Giancarlo; their erections pressed against each other. Giancarlo leaned toward him and began to glide his wet lips over Oliver's and then pressed more firmly against him, both opening their mouths widely, relishing the wetness they shared.

Giancarlo continued to massage Oliver's chest, squeezing his pecs playfully. Oliver nuzzled himself into Giancarlo's dark hairy muscular torso, breathing his scent and sensing Giancarlo's increased desire.

They continued to take pleasure in the raw intimacy of the moment, their naked bodies pressed against each other. There was a familiarity they both sought to reclaim after their extended absence, and they continued to learn new ways to arouse and pleasure each other. Each felt increased pulses of heat rising within them as they moved in unison. Then, almost as if timed, they both let out a deep moan and exploded in throbs of pleasure.

They both collapsed on their backs, holding hands, and staring at the ceiling.

"Whew!" Giancarlo said. "I needed that."

"Me, too. I was just stirring from my sleep when suddenly I was being man-handled."

"Any regrets?"

"None." He smiled.

They rolled out of bed, showered, and went downstairs for a

sumptuous buffet breakfast. They dressed in shorts and polo shirts for a hot day in the city. Oliver walked Giancarlo to the Boston Common where they began walking the Freedom Trail and the historic sites of revolutionary Boston.

After a lunch in the North End at a small trattoria, they returned to the inn for a nap. Oliver cranked up the AC and snuggled up close to Giancarlo under the blankets. He loved resting his head on his chest, feeling its rise and fall and the heartbeat below. Around 4, they decided to get up and prepare for dinner at Oliver's moms' house.

"I'm nervous," Oliver said.

"You're nervous. What about me? You're going to your home and to your mothers. I'm walking into a courtroom where a trial is being readied by a bunch of ace attorneys."

"It's not going to be an interrogation," Oliver assured him.

"Are you sure?"

"No."

Giancarlo continued to feel and look anxious.

After dressing, they walked to Beacon Hill. En route, Giancarlo insisted on picking up some flowers and a bottle of wine. Oliver buzzed in the code for the common entry and then walked up to the penthouse, slipped in a key, and opened the door.

"Ma and mom – we're here."

Anna came around the corner from the kitchen and walked up to Oliver, giving him a kiss. "Ma, this is Giancarlo. Giancarlo, my ma Anna."

"It's a pleasure," Giancarlo began, shaking Anna's hand and looking at her warmly. Anna said nothing at first, choked with emotion. Slowly she eked out a timid, "Welcome."

"These are for you," Giancarlo continued, handing her the flowers and bottle of wine. She took them, smiled, and nodded in thanks.

Rita approached from behind her. Oliver was shocked when she first appeared. Her eyes were blood shot and she had rings under her eyes. Her hair, usually curly, was flat in sections, evidence she had been laying down and sweating. "Mom, this is Giancarlo. Giancarlo, my mom Rita."

"*Piacere*," Rita said, surprising Oliver and Giancarlo.

"*Piacere mio*," Giancarlo replied and then added, "I didn't know your mom spoke Italian, Oliver."

"Yes, her family is from the Abruzzi."

Rita produced a fake smile and said, "Why don't you guys come into the living room. What can we offer you to drink?"

"Some wine?" Giancarlo replied in a question.

"And you, Oliver?" Rita asked.

"The same. Let me help you." Oliver went into the kitchen with Rita to open a bottle of wine. "What happened here?" he inquired as he began to tease out the flattened sections of her hair and rub the rings under her eyes.

"It's nothing," she replied stoically, opening the corkscrew, and beginning to insert it into the bottle. "He seems very nice," she said. Oliver nodded.

Meanwhile, Anna sat in one of the easy chairs facing Giancarlo, seated on the sofa. "So, your flight was good?" she began.

"Yes. No problems."

"And the inn?"

"It's very nice. What a beautiful city you live in – and this place – it's incredible."

"We'll have to give you a tour later."

Giancarlo nodded nervously, sweat forming on his brows.

Rita and Oliver returned from the kitchen, pouring everyone a generous glass of wine.

"*Salute*," Oliver said, raising his glass.

"*Salute*," they all said in unison.

Giancarlo decided to take the more direct approach and began, "Anna and Rita, I want to let you know that I appreciate the concern you have for Oliver and for all of the changes taking place. It must be very distressful and unsettling."

Anna and Rita looked at each other, surprised by Giancarlo's forthright admission. Rita began, "Well. Yes. It has been quite a lot to process."

"If there's anything I can do to ease your mind or assure you, let me know."

Oliver nervously took a handful of nuts from a bowl on the coffee table and began to consume them with abandon.

Rita looked at Anna again and said, "Why don't you tell us a little more about yourself. That seems like a good beginning."

Giancarlo nodded and then began, "Well. I'm not sure where to begin. I'm a financial advisor at a bank in Rome. My parents died several years ago. They were young."

"We're sorry," Anna said.

"I inherited my grandparents' home in the center of Rome. I have a sister in Milan and several aunts and uncles and cousins in Rome and its environs."

"Where did you learn to speak English so well?" Anna pressed.

"In school – both in grade school and then in college – in Milan."

"We understand you were Oliver's biological father's financial advisor."

"Yes. Father Henry and I worked together for many years. That is how I met Oliver – when I did the paperwork for the estate."

Anna and Rita looked at each other again. Anna then interjected, "Oliver explained what had happened. It seems a bit unusual to us."

"I'm sure it must. It was all so surreal for Oliver and for me. We were shocked to learn how sick Fr. Henry was. It must have been his illness that prompted him to reach out."

"That makes sense," Anna said. "And have you been in a relationship before?" she continued, going straight for the jugular.

Giancarlo cleared his throat. "Over the years, I've dated. In Rome, you have to be rather discrete. My father was very prejudiced, so I wasn't out to him. There was one person I had a long-term relationship with, but he was unfaithful. We broke up."

Oliver then added, "Ma and mom, Giancarlo has a lot of friends. Everywhere you go in Rome, he knows people."

Anna then continued her line of questioning, "I'm sure you must appreciate that we are concerned about Oliver. He's young and impressionable."

"Ma!" Oliver blurted out in protest.

"Well, let's say he's at least young. This is all new for him, and we don't want him to get hurt."

"Anna and Rita, I assure you that I only have Oliver's best interest at heart."

"Then explain why his moving in with you is a good idea. It's too quick," Rita said emphatically, her hand shaking.

Giancarlo bristled, taken back by Rita's directness. "I think you need to ask Oliver," Giancarlo replied.

Rita continued to press her case. "He's too young. Imagine if he was a college-age woman – your daughter – and informed you she was moving in with a man 10 years her senior?"

Giancarlo nodded in agreement with the point.

"We've suggested he get his own apartment in Rome if he's so intent on studying archaeology. You guys can date and, if things are still good later, then move in together. Give it some time," Rita suggested.

Giancarlo looked over at Oliver who looked at his moms. "Ma and mom. We've been over this a million times. What's the difference if I go to Rome and spend all my time with Giancarlo but live in a separate apartment?"

"It creates some autonomy and perspective," Anna said.

"Let me ask you something," Oliver began, staring at his moms. "Giancarlo doesn't know how you both met and what happened afterwards." Rita and Anna looked at each other nervously. "You met in Spain and, after your semester abroad, moved in together in Boston to finish college. You were the same age I am now and, after a short time, became companions and shared a home. How is that any different from what I'm doing?"

They both looked directly at Giancarlo. "We're sorry," Rita began hesitantly and apologetically, intensifying her stare. "It's your age."

Giancarlo took a long sip of wine, evading their glances. Oliver interjected, "it's only 10 years difference."

"That's a lot when you're young," Anna remarked. "Relationships are healthier when there is equal power. The age difference adds to the power difference. How do you develop your own sense of authority and autonomy if the other person is older, more persuasive, more authoritative?"

"But Giancarlo is very respectful of me, and always involves me in decision making," Oliver said in protest.

"That's nice to hear," Anna continued, "but you've just come out, and you will be a foreigner in Rome. This puts you at a disadvantage."

"So, should I just give up on this relationship and find someone my own age? It doesn't work that way," Oliver began to plead. "It is rare that one chooses whom to love. Love grabs you and thrusts you into a place of vulnerability and, it is precisely in that vulnerability that mutuality and respect and love grow," Oliver stated with conviction.

Anna, Rita, and Giancarlo all looked at each other and then looked back to Oliver. "Honey, where did all of that come from?" Anna inquired. "You sound like a philosopher."

"From you," Oliver said. "Over the years, I've listened to you talk with each other and with your friends. I've followed theories about gender, gender roles, and gender equality. I've heard you talk about emotional vulnerability as the foundation for authentic love. Don't you trust that you've instilled in me the resources I need to forge a good relationship?"

They both nodded.

"I think you've overlooked how vulnerable Giancarlo is. He's in a profession where being in an open relationship is risky. He's willing to get over the hurt from his last relationship and trust again – trust a young man who turns heads everywhere we go."

Giancarlo looked curiously at Oliver who then added, "I know that may sound conceited, but I've noticed your worried look when handsome men cruise me."

"How did you know?"

"I'm observant. And, another point," he began, looking at all three. "I'm financially independent. I'm not in a position where I have to defer to someone else for my livelihood. If I needed Giancarlo to take care of me, then the power difference might be more significant. But the trust funds I inherited ensure that I will have all the resources I need whether I'm with Giancarlo or not. I'm emotionally vulnerable in a good sense. But I'm not financially vulnerable."

Anna leaned back in her chair, more relaxed. Rita feigned a timid smile. Giancarlo nodded, proud of his companion. Anna then interjected, "On that note, why don't we go to the dining room and have some dinner?"

They got up and gathered at the table. Anna brought out a platter filled with grilled chicken, zucchini, peppers, and asparagus. Rita went into the kitchen and returned with a classic American potato salad - mixed with whole grain mustard, mayonnaise, and dill - resting in a beautiful ceramic bowl.

Oliver poured everyone a glass of wine. They toasted their gathering and began to eat.

"We're still baffled by Oliver's decision to shift majors, to study archaeology," Rita began as she helped herself to a nice slice of the chicken.

"Me, too," Giancarlo noted, everyone now looking at Oliver to explain.

He began, "As I was exploring the sites in Rome, I began to realize that we are in a moment of profound change, a change in paradigms. There have been other moments in history when assumptions were questioned and where new ways of thinking emerged. Think about the transition from a more representational government in Rome to an empire and how that changed life for Rome in the 1st century? Think about the transition to Christian civilization in the 4th century. It is fascinating to examine how new ideas and perspectives were either rejected or incorporated into a new order, and how the new order preserved some traditions and rejected others – like women's roles in early Christianity giving way to Roman patriarchy after Constantine. If you want to understand how new paradigms will emerge within and outside of our institutions, studying ancient history is enlightening."

"Wow!" was all Rita could say.

"I think it was confronting Fr. Henry that helped me see this. He is part of the old paradigm, a world based on assumptions that are no longer supported by research and experience. There's a new paradigm emerging. As in past epochs, new information can be integrated into the established civilization or, if not, a new civilization emerges. We are at that crossroads. Either we embrace environmentalism, racial justice, economic justice, and gender and sexual diversity, or our civilization will recede and a new one will emerge. Henry couldn't make the shift, but his personal struggles showed that the new paradigm is gradually emerging and will take form one way or the other."

"Anna and Rita," Giancarlo began, "this is why I find Oliver so alluring. Yes – he's young, handsome, and fun. But he's thoughtful and insightful and has a passion for justice!"

Anna looked troubled. She took a sip of wine and cleared her throat. "But dear," she said to Oliver. "Don't you think it would be better to finish your degree in finance and then go study archaeology? You'd have something to fall back on if you found it wasn't that appealing or lucrative." Anna was trying to buy time and put some distance between Oliver and Giancarlo.

"I thought about that," he replied. "But I feel inspired to study archaeology now, and I don't feel the same for finance. That might change, but I want to ride the energy I have. Besides, it's not like I have to worry about making a living."

Giancarlo, Anna, and Rita all looked at each other. Rita then interjected, "But you have to find a profession. You could go through the money you inherited quickly. You have to be practical."

"Mom, with the investments Giancarlo is making for me, I would have at least 100,000 euros a year in income even without doing anything."

Giancarlo blanched and evasively picked at his vegetables.

"And what if there is a bad year or two?" Anna noted. "That happens, you know."

"I plan to put money aside to increase the trust, not deplete it," Oliver noted. "Although I haven't finished my degree in finance, I have a lot of practical knowledge and theory. I think I'll be fine."

Anna and Rita looked at each other in frustration. They still weren't comfortable with the changes Oliver was making, but they found it increasingly difficult to find fault with his reasoning. People finished their dinners. Oliver and Giancarlo stood, took the plates, and brought them to the kitchen, rinsing them and placing them in the dishwasher. Anna and Rita could be heard mumbling in the dining room. "They're plotting," Oliver said to Giancarlo.

"They're just concerned – like any good parents would be. Be patient with them. They are good souls, and they will come around."

"I hope so."

Rita slipped into the kitchen. Oliver let go of Giancarlo's hand he had been holding. He wasn't sure why he should be embarrassed with his mothers. She picked up a stack of small plates and said, "Oliver, can you bring the blueberry pie and ice cream to the table?"

He nodded.

They gathered again at the table and enjoyed the homemade pie. "This is incredible," Giancarlo remarked.

"It's an old recipe – a lemony blueberry pie – with lemon zest, lemon juice, nutmeg, and other spices."

"It's refreshing and savory. The ice cream smooths it out, too."

After the pie, Anna said, "Would you all like to go out on the deck for coffee and a liquor?"

Oliver nodded. They all stood up and walked out through the sliding glass doors onto a broad deck overlooking the Charles River and the lights of Cambridge on the other side. Anna began, "When we were looking for places, this deck sold us on this condo. The view is amazing. It's always changing – with ice and snow in the winter, flowering trees in the spring, boats in the summer, and fall foliage in autumn. There are spectacular sunsets all year long."

"It's beautiful," Giancarlo remarked. With Anna mentioning autumn, a thought came to him. "Anna and Rita, why don't you come to Rome in the fall? It's a glorious time of the year, and it would give you a chance to check in on Oliver once he's established."

They looked at each other and then looked to Oliver who nodded. They then turned to Giancarlo, "That's a great idea." They both looked visibly more relaxed and relieved.

"Oliver and I can show you around. By then, he will have become a local."

"Oliver, would you be okay with that?"

"Why not. It would be wonderful to have you visit. That would mean a lot to me."

They smiled warmly and looked approvingly over at Giancarlo who they realized really did have Oliver's and their interests at heart.

"Are there some dates that might work?" Rita inquired of Oliver.

"Ma and mom – *piano piano* – as they say in Rome. Slow down. Let's get through the evening first. We can discuss dates over the next couple of days. There's no need to nail this all down tonight."

"I know, but now you've gotten us excited," Anna said.

"We'll discuss it later during the weekend. Right now, I think we need to get going. Giancarlo's still got jet lag, and we have a busy day tomorrow visiting the MFA and Harvard."

"Rita and Anna," Giancarlo began as they walked back into the living room. "It has been a pleasure meeting you. I look forward to more opportunities while we're here. We'd like to invite you to dinner on Saturday, perhaps to a nice Italian place in the North End?"

"It would be our pleasure."

Everyone gave each other warm embraces. Oliver kissed his mothers on the cheek, and he and Giancarlo left the space, walking down the stairs and out into the nice night air. "How do you think that went?" Oliver asked Giancarlo.

"They seemed to soften as the night progressed. They clearly are concerned, but you seem to have assuaged their biggest worries."

"You were masterful. You showed an awareness of their qualms and addressed them. Thank you." As they walked through the Boston Garden, Oliver interjected, "Do you want to go to a club?"

"Now?"

"Yes, now. There's a nice place on the way home. It should be hopping about now."

"This is where I get to pull the age card. I can't stay out all night like you."

"Just for a quick visit and drink," Oliver implored.

Giancarlo nodded. They walked toward the South End and approached the entrance of the club. There was a short line outside checking IDs, and before long, they were inside. The club was filled. The front of the establishment was a restaurant and a piano bar. Further back was a large bar and then behind that area was a video and dance room where loud music was drifting out the doors. Giancarlo said, "Do you mind if we go to the piano bar? I want to talk with you."

Oliver looked concerned and nodded. They found an intimate table and a waiter came and took their drink orders. Giancarlo looked up at the vocalist who was singing a soft jazzy piece. He then looked over to Oliver and held his hand and said, "Oliver, earlier today you said that we were making a long-term commitment."

"I did?"

"Yes, when you described your moving to Rome and changing careers you mentioned you were making a long-term commitment."

"Oh," Oliver said with an alarmed look on his face.

"Is that not what you meant?" Giancarlo pressed him.

"It just came out of my mouth, but I don't remember being intentional about it."

"So, are we making a commitment?" Giancarlo asked with pensively.

Oliver was quiet and looked deep in thought. He then said, "When I think about it, yes. I think I assumed that is what we were doing."

"We need to talk about this - not make assumptions or just fall into it."

"Okay, let's talk."

"Well, are you ready to make a commitment and, if so, what kind of commitment?" Giancarlo began.

"If we were dating, I would say we're ready to be exclusive. But we're doing more than dating. We're moving in together."

"Yes. And?"

"Well, it feels like it is more of a commitment."

"I don't disagree," Giancarlo said. "But what does that mean?"

"It's a good question. What does it mean to move in with someone you are just beginning to date? Is that a good idea?" Oliver asked, surprised by his own question.

"Are you having second thoughts?"

"No, but you've raised a good question. I feel like I've known you for much longer than the month or so since we met. Our relationship is new, but it doesn't feel novel. It feels familiar," Oliver explained.

Giancarlo nodded.

"But I also feel like there is so much to learn – that this relationship will deepen, that we will grow and develop as persons with each other."

"Let me venture to describe what I'm feeling," Giancarlo interjected. "Chronologically, our relationship is young. Typically, couples require more time to get to know each other and find out if they are a good match."

"Agreed."

"And I did this once, and it turned out bad," Giancarlo remarked, recalling his former partner's infidelity.

"I realize that, and I appreciate what a risk you're taking in welcoming me into your space," Oliver said.

"But I want to. Even though I'm scared, it feels right."

"So, are we willing to make a commitment to ensure that each other's vulnerability is honored in this process?" Oliver asked.

"Yes," Giancarlo said warmly.

"Me, too," Oliver added.

"Is this where I get down on my knees?" Giancarlo said playfully.

Oliver got nervous. Giancarlo noticed. "*Calmati, caro* – be calm, dear. I'm just playing with you."

"So, what are we doing?" Oliver asked.

There was an awkward silence, both wondering what to say next. Giancarlo then said, "Oliver, I would like to embark on this journey with you. You are such a wise and thoughtful soul. I know you will challenge me to grow, and I hope that I can challenge you and support you."

"Giancarlo. You are such a gift to me. Thanks for welcoming me into your life and becoming vulnerable. I look forward to this new adventure with you. I envision growing old with you with a rich circle of family and friends around us. I love you."

"I love you, too."

They kissed. Giancarlo lifted his glass and said, "To love!"

"To love," Oliver said in reply.

They took long sips of their brandies and then looked at each other and began to chuckle. "That was intense," Oliver said.

"*Veramente.*" Giancarlo agreed.

"We need some levity," Oliver suggested. He took Giancarlo's hand and led him back to the video and dance area where they began to push their way into the crowd of young men dancing around them. They stood face to face, pressed closely against each other, and began to move with the music. Oliver stared into Giancarlo's deep brown eyes and then shifted his glance towards his muscular chest, pressing firmly against the soft fabric of his pullover. He wanted to rip it off but was content rubbing his hands over the contours of his torso and squeezing his pecs playfully.

Giancarlo stared at Oliver, crazed by his piercing blue eyes, his tan skin, and shiny blonde air bouncing as he moved his head with the music. He glanced around the room at the sea of hot buff boys undulating with the heavy beat of the music. His eyes kept returning to Oliver – a beacon of light drawing him closer and closer to shore. He smiled contently.

After a while, Oliver whispered into Giancarlo's ear and said, "Are you ready to go home? I found a hottie I want to take to bed."

Giancarlo felt himself get hard and pressed himself up close to Oliver.

"Settle down, sparkie," Oliver said in jest. He grabbed his hand and began to lead him through the club and out onto the street. They wandered back to the inn where they undressed, slipped under the sheets, and held each other tightly as they fell into a sound sleep.

15

Chapter Fifteen

2 Years Later

"Oliver, move over to the left a bit. Anna and Rita, move in closer. Give Oliver a hug. One, two, three –*formaggio*," Giancarlo said as he took several pictures of Oliver and his moms.

"Perfect," Giancarlo added. "I think you'll like these." He looked at his watch and said, "Let's go, our reservation is in just a few minutes."

They walked back into Giancarlo's parlor, headed out the front door and down the stairs to the street level. They began walking down the cobblestone streets, across a busy boulevard, and into the older section of Trastevere to the restaurant Giancarlo had reserved for the reception.

As they walked inside everyone yelled, "*Sorpresa!*"

Oliver's eyes lit up and he looked over at Giancarlo, "*Ma come hai fatto tutto questo* – how did you pull this off?"

"I had some help," he replied as he looked at Anna and Rita. "I'm so proud of you. Who would have thought you could finish your course of studies so quickly and get certified as a local guide. It usually takes people a lot longer."

"I had help from Flavia!" As Oliver said that, Giancarlo looked across the room. Oliver followed his gaze and saw Flavia. He ran over to her and gave her a big hug, "Can you believe it?"

"*Si, tu sei stato bravo!*"

"It wouldn't have been possible without your help and connections."

"I wouldn't have done it if I didn't believe you would be successful and add to the professionalism of our group."

Monsignor Flanagan stood against the wall, adjacent to Flavia and nodded in approval, "You did good boy!" he said.

Oliver reached over and gave Flanagan a hug. "Thanks for your support and inspiration," he said.

Giancarlo walked across the room with two men and introduced them to Oliver, Flavia, and Flanagan. "These are two of the teachers who were to have been removed a couple of years ago."

"My God," Oliver said. "What a privilege to meet you."

"We're excited to meet you. Thanks for all you have done to advance information about our lives and our work. You're making real progress."

They turned to Flanagan and winked, "And, we know you're there, too. Thanks!"

Flanagan blushed, took a long sip of wine, and began to meander through the crowd.

Oliver gave Giancarlo a kiss. "*Grazie, caro.* This is so incredible! I can't believe you kept it a secret."

"It wasn't easy. Your moms helped deflect attention. By the way, how are they doing?"

"*Guarda* - look!" Oliver pointed to his moms who were chatting away with a group of Giancarlo's friends. "Looks like Rita has rediscovered her Italian roots. Look at her hands gesturing!"

"Yes, and her Italian has improved considerably."

"Well, if they're going to have Italian grandchildren, they're going to have to learn the language."

"Every time you say that my heart skips a few beats. I can't believe we are going to be parents."

Giancarlo looked over at his sister, Maria, who was pregnant. She had never wanted to be a mother but, after Giancarlo and Oliver got together, she offered to be a surrogate for them. The idea of being an aunt or godmother appealed to her. She could continue to pursue her career as a lawyer and occasionally visit her brother and the baby. They used Oliver's sperm. The baby would inherit genes from both families.

Oliver smiled warmly and gave Giancarlo a kiss. "He's going to be the luckiest kid alive with you as his father," Oliver said.

Anna approached and gave them both a big hug. "What a wonderful party, boys!"

"It's all Giancarlo's doing, mom."

She grabbed Giancarlo's jaw and squeezed him. "He's so cute!" she said.

"Mom, he's not a little boy."

"I know, but he's my son-in-law, now. I think of him as my boy!"

"There's going to be trouble when the real little boy comes, your grandson."

"Oh, I can't wait," she said excitedly, glancing over at Maria.

Oliver was delighted that his moms had grown more comfortable with Giancarlo, overlooking their age difference. It helped that two years had passed, and that they had vacationed with his moms in Ptown the summer before. Giancarlo was devoted to Oliver, looking after his interests, and being sensitive to the novelties of his coming out, living in Rome, and moving in with someone.

The maître d' of the restaurant tapped his glass with a knife, calling everyone to attention. "In a few minutes, we will begin our dinner. It's buffet style – with everything set up over here," as he pointed to one side of the room. "There's no assigned seating, so take a place wherever you like. I'd like to ask Monsignor Flanagan to lead us in a prayer."

Everyone looked at the heavy Irish man standing near the drink table, pouring himself a glass of wine. He looked up and said, "*Oh, scusi!*"

Everyone laughed.

Flanagan cleared his throat and began to speak. "Two years ago, I had the privilege to meet Oliver over circumstances that were rather sad. I was impressed with him then, and I am even more impressed with him now. He is the product of two outstanding women who raised him with love and principles. He brings great passion to his work in advancing social justice and in his archaeological studies - which we celebrate today. Many of you may be aware of the special seminars he has sponsored to promote dialogue between gay people and the Church. While the Church hasn't made a lot of progress in embracing Oliver's views, the seminars have garnered a lot of attention in Italian society, moving the dial forward in public acceptance and, in the end, this will bear much fruit. I couldn't be happier for him and his husband, Giancarlo. I believe there is a little Russo-Monte-Fitzpatrick on the way. Let us all give thanks to God for Oliver's success, pray for the health of his and Giancarlo's son, and bless this food and wine which we share to celebrate life and love! *Salute!*"

"*Salute,*" everyone said in unison.

Oliver approached the buffet table and began to fill his plate. A couple of men right behind him said, "Congratulations, Oliver. When are you expecting your son?"

Oliver glanced over at Maria and said, "Any day now!"

"You must be so excited."

"We are," Giancarlo interjected, walking up behind them. "There are a lot of legal technicalities we have to work out with Italian and American officials, but we're making progress."

"Where are you going to live?" one of them asked further.

"Our work is here – mine with the bank and Oliver's with guiding. I imagine we will spend most of our time in Rome, although we have thought about dual residency, spending part of the year in Boston and the rest in Rome."

Oliver turned and placed his hand on his friend's shoulder, "I've grown to love it so much here, I can't imagine going back to Boston. But my moms are there, and we'd like our son to spend time with them and get to know American culture."

Rita overhead Oliver and smiled. Oliver glanced back at her, winking.

Oliver milled about the room, thanking people for coming and introducing guests to each other. He had become fluent in Italian, even developing a local Roman accent. Rita approached him with a glass of wine in hand. "Mom, have you met Giulia and Sophia?"

She shook her head no.

"Giulia and Sophia – this is my mom Rita. Rita – Giulia and Sophia."

"*Piacere*," they all said in unison, shaking hands.

"Giulia is a colleague of mine at the university, and Sophia works at the Capitoline Museum."

"We're so proud of Oliver," Sophia said. "He has such a unique insight and perspective into local archaeology. I feel like he will be a pivotal expert in future years."

"I've seen some of his writing," Giulia added. "He's brilliant."

Anna approached and overheard the conversation. "We were nervous when he dropped his studies in finance, but we have come to appreciate this is his passion, and he seems very talented."

They both nodded. "And we hope to see you both here more often in the future. We have a spare room at our place, and you are always welcome."

"*Molto gentile*," Rita said. "And, you'll have to come to the Cape with Giancarlo and Oliver in the summers. We'd love to show you around."

Msgr. Flanagan walked up to them and toasted them with his glass. "Rita and Anna, you must be so proud."

"We are. And thank you for your words today and the welcome you have shown Oliver and Giancarlo. It's giving us hope for the future."

"You are more hopeful than I," he said, winking at them.

"Do you ever get to the States?" Anna inquired.

"Every-once-in-a-while on business. I think I have some trips in the Fall."

"If you're in the Boston area, look us up. We'd love to have you for dinner."

"That would be nice. In fact, I think I have some visits to Boston-area Catholic schools."

Anna raised her eyebrow in alarm.

"Not to worry. They've taken me off the bad cop detail. I'm usually sent to mend bridges."

"You'd be good at that," Rita said warmly.

Giancarlo approached them, beaming happily that the party had gone well, and that people had made new friends. He lamented that his father and mother were not there to witness the cultural changes that were being made in Italy. He reached his arm around Oliver's shoulders and gave him a hug.

One of Giancarlo's friends, Lorenzo, walked up to him. "Giancarlo, thanks for the party. And congratulations!"

"Lorenzo, thanks for coming. It means a lot that you were here."

"I heard you and Oliver are expecting."

Giancarlo nodded.

"If you find yourselves needing more space, let me help you find a new condo. I know your taste, and I could find a good match for the two of you."

"That would be great. I have been thinking that my place might prove to be small once our boy grows – and if we decide to have another child – we'll definitely need more space."

"I'm ready when you are."

The festivities continued, people enjoyed their meals, and then around 9 people began to excuse themselves and make their ways home. Giancarlo paid the owner and staff and then suggested he and Oliver walk his moms back to the Santa Chiara. "It's such a beautiful night. Let's take a walk with you."

They strolled across the Tiber River and into the historic district of town passing a large excavation in the Largo Argentina.

"What are these, Oliver?" Rita inquired. She was standing at the edge of the site holding Anna's hand.

Giancarlo looked at Oliver and glared – a message Oliver had come to know meant 'don't start a lecture now.'

"Well, briefly," he began, looking toward Giancarlo to assure him it would be a short explanation, "these are some of the oldest temples in Rome dating back perhaps to the 4th century before Christ. It's interesting that there are several of them in a row, clearly evidence of religious plurality since they must have coexisted side-by-side."

Oliver pointed to several structures, some with a few small columns, others no more than foundations with marble porches in front of what would have been rather modest shrines. In the evening streetlight, they had a soft mysterious glow to them.

"How did the main religious authorities treat these?" Anna pressed Oliver.

"If you turn around and look that way," Oliver pointed up the hill behind them, "that's where the temple of Jupiter would have been. The Romans didn't see any contradiction in their worship of a more supreme god – like Jupiter – and the presence of other religious groups, cults, or gods. It's probably not a lot different from the Catholic practice of devotion to the saints."

"Hmmm," Rita sighed.

"Think of all the churches in Rome devoted to this and that saint. How different is that from temples scattered about Rome devoted to various gods and goddesses who you could approach for particular needs? If you needed help with an illness or with a troublesome neighbor or with business problems, approaching Jupiter made no sense. You wanted a spirit or god who was closer to you. Many Romans had household spirits they preserved – almost like spirit guides people talk about today?"

"So, they would have still worshiped Jupiter?" Giancarlo inquired, apprehensive that his question would only set Oliver on a longer explanation.

"Yes. There was always the supreme God and then there were the lesser spirits or gods and goddesses that were more approachable and specialized in various affairs."

Oliver looked over at Giancarlo who gave him a nod suggesting something like 'time to draw this to a close.'

Oliver nodded back. "Let's keep walking. I'm sure you're both tired," as he looked over at his mothers whose eyes were getting heavy.

They crossed the busy boulevard and entered the quiet pedestrian zone leading to their hotel, the silence amplifying the soft clacking of their heals on the cobblestone pavement. No one spoke, all savoring memories of the day and offering thanks in their hearts for the love around them. As they approached the front door of the hotel, Anna and Rita turned to Oliver and Giancarlo and gave them both affectionate kisses on their cheeks.

"Sleep tight, ma and mom," Oliver said. "In a few days you're going to be busy with the baby."

"I can't believe it!" Anna said emotionally.

Giancarlo's eyes teared up. He reached his arm around Oliver's waist and gave him a warm hug.

Anna and Rita went inside, and Oliver and Giancarlo began their walk home, both unable to say much as they were choked with emotion. Oliver mused over the vignettes of the day – his graduation as an archaeologist, the celebration with friends and family, the blessing of a priest, and the passing of an ancient religious excavation. He thought about his son coming into the world and the new paradigm they were welcoming with his arrival. He laid his head on Giancarlo's shoulder and sighed deeply, grateful for the journey he had traversed and the one he was about to begin.

Michael Hartwig is a Boston and Provincetown based author specializing in LGBTQ stories set in historic settings around the world. The narratives are remarkable for fast-paced plots, passionate love stories, exploration of sexual identity, and evocative settings. Hartwig's books draw on his having lived in Europe, his professional work in international travel, and his college-level courses in sexual ethics and religion. Plots push boundaries around gender and family and introduce new paradigms of spirituality and magic. His novels are sensual – celebrating sexual desire, food, art, and geography.

For Other Titles and Work Visit: www.michaelhartwig.com

CPSIA information can be obtained
at www.ICGtesting.com
Printed in the USA
LVHW020012211122
733501LV00016B/859

9 780578 955100